The story began in 1866 . . .

Alice stared into the depths of his brown eyes. He brushed a tendril of wet hair off of her forehead with strong, gentle fingers. His face was etched with concern and caring.

Alice managed a weak smile. The young man smiled back, and she couldn't help noticing how handsome he was. She tried to sit up, but she felt drenched to her very core, too heavy to move.

"Shh," the young man whispered. Words followed in a language Alice knew was English, the language of her new home. She didn't recognize most of the words, but she understood the comforting tones of the young man's voice.

She tried to figure out what had happened. There had been a terrible storm. Waves, wind, and—heavens above! There had been the child! The little boy! She sat up and looked around frantically.

There he was, in his mother's arms! He was alive! His mother was smiling warmly at Alice.

The boy's father approached and took Alice's hand gently. He pressed it to his heart in a gesture of thanks. Then he turned to the brown-eyed young man. For the first time, Alice noticed that he was as soaked as she was. As the little boy's father took the young man's hand and repeated his gesture of thanks, Alice suddenly understood. The young man was the one who had saved the little boy's life—and her own! He must have jumped in after her. Alice looked into his e⸻⸻⸻ this handsome man ⸻⸻⸻⸻ dore Wakefield.

The SWEET VALLEY HIGH series, published by Bantam Books. Ask your bookseller for any titles you have missed:

THE WAKEFIELDS
OF SWEET VALLEY

Written by
Kate William

Created by
FRANCINE PASCAL

BANTAM BOOKS
NEW YORK · TORONTO · LONDON · SYDNEY · AUCKLAND

SWEET VALLEY SAGA:
THE WAKEFIELDS OF SWEET VALLEY
A BANTAM BOOK   0 553 29278 1

Originally published in USA by Bantam Books

First publication in Great Britain

PRINTING HISTORY
Bantam edition published 1991
Reprinted 1992, 1994

Sweet Valley High is a registered trademark of Francine Pascal.

Conceived by Francine Pascal.

Produced by Daniel Weiss Associates, Inc, 33 West 17th Street,
New York, NY 10011

Cover art by James Mathewuse

Bantam Books are published by Transworld Publishers Ltd,
61–63 Uxbridge Road, Ealing, London W5 5SA,
in Australia by Transworld Publishers (Australia) Pty Ltd,
15–25 Helles Avenue, Moorebank, NSW 2170,
and in New Zealand by Transworld Publishers (NZ) Ltd,
3 William Pickering Drive, Albany, Auckland.

Printed and bound in Great Britain by
Cox & Wyman Ltd, Reading, Berkshire

Elizabeth and Jessica Wakefield's Family Tree

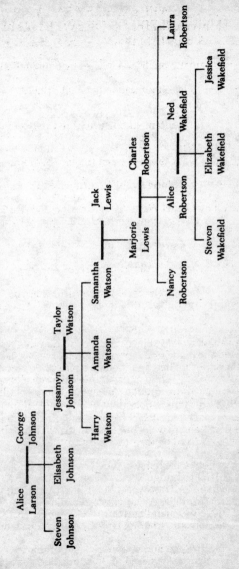

One

1866. Somewhere in the Atlantic Ocean.

The waves pounded against the side of the ship. Alice Larson struggled to keep her balance as the vessel rolled like a toy in the angry ocean. Her dress hung around her in waterlogged folds, the long skirt drenched over the crinolines. Alice shivered. Never in all her sixteen years had she felt so frightened and so alone.

There had been times during the long, hard voyage when she wished she had never set foot on this vessel. There had been nights that seemed to go on forever, nights when she lay seasick in the women's bunkroom in the belly of the ship, wondering why she had ever left her native Sweden. Even after her parents had died and she was on her own, Sweden had still felt like home. Here she truly had no one.

But when the light of dawn would break over the horizon, splitting the sky with rays of rose and fiery orange, painting the ocean with the colors of a new day, Alice would remember that the promise of a new world lay in front of her. She was going to America!

Now, as a giant wave crashed over the deck

and the ship listed dangerously to one side, Alice pressed close to its main mast, fearing that if she strayed too close to the rail, she might never reach the shores of the promised land at all. Up on deck she could breathe more freely than in the bunkroom, but the wind and water seemed to wage a ceaseless attack against her.

Alice glanced at the other passengers on deck. A group of young men were huddled near the stern of the ship, their frock coats and trousers drenched, their heads bare to the storm. No hat could possibly stay on in this gale. Several couples had come up also. One man held his young woman tightly, as if she were his anchor in the howling wind. Another couple tried to take shelter in the stairway leading down inside the ship. With them was a little boy who seemed excited by the power of the storm rather than frightened by it. He strained forward to get a glimpse of the churning water, the waves, and the wind.

Alice could see the worry and fear on the mother's face as she grasped her son's arm tightly. Then a sudden jolt of the ship broke her hold, and the boy darted out onto the deck for a better look at the storm.

Alice could see his mother's mouth forming his name, though the wind carried the sound away from her ears. Another wave washed over the deck. The ship rolled sideways. Suddenly, the little boy was slipping and sliding toward the ship's rail. His mother bolted after him, lunging at him and grabbing his leg. Just then a new wave—a huge wall of water—surged toward their side of the ship. Behind it came an even more monstrous swell.

Alice watched, frozen with cold and terror, as the first wave broke over the boy and his mother, snatching him from her grasp. The ship tilted. Its rail dipped toward the churning sea. Then the second wave hit, pulling the little boy into its curl and sweeping him into the ocean.

Alice felt her scream ripped away from her by the wind. The boy! The little boy! She had to save him! She tore a life preserver free from the ship's rail and threw herself into the black water.

As she thrashed against the heaviness of the ocean, salt water filled her mouth, stung her eyes, blinded her. The powerful currents slammed her one way, then another, then threw her against something solid. The boy! Alice got her arms around him. But as she struggled to pull him toward her, she could feel the sea wrenching her life preserver away from her.

She fought to keep her hold on the boy, but she could feel him slipping out of her arms. The water tugged her down, closing over her head. She wrestled against its pull. She beat at it, desperate to surface for air. But she was no match for the violent sea. *A breath. I must breathe,* she thought.

And then she could resist no longer. Alice inhaled the salty, furious ocean. It was the last memory she had.

She stared into the depths of his brown eyes. He brushed a tendril of wet hair off of her forehead with strong, gentle fingers. His face was etched with concern and caring.

Alice managed a weak smile. The young man smiled back, and she couldn't help noticing how handsome he was—the high cheekbones, the strong, straight line of his nose, the cleft of his chin. She tried to sit up, but she felt drenched to her very core, too heavy with water to move.

"Shh," the young man whispered. Words followed in a language Alice knew was English, the language of her new home. She didn't recognize most of the words, but she understood the tender, comforting tone of the young man's rich voice.

She tried to figure out what had happened. She lay on the deck of the ship, her wet skirts spread around her. The rain was still cold on her face but it came down more lightly now. The ship rocked, but not as wildly.

There had been a terrible storm. Alice remembered that. Waves, wind, and—heavens above! There had been the child! The little boy! She sat up and looked around frantically.

There he was, in his mother's arms! Wet and shivering, the little boy had his face buried in his mother's chest, his body heaving with sobs. He was alive! His mother was smiling warmly at Alice.

The boy's father approached and took Alice's

hand gently. He pressed it to his heart in a gesture of thanks. Then he turned to the brown-eyed young man. For the first time, Alice noticed that the man was as soaked as she was. His dark hair dripped salt water onto his handsome face. His shirt was torn and wet, and his frock coat lay in a puddle beside him. As the little boy's father took the young man's hand and repeated his gesture of thanks, Alice suddenly understood. The young man was the one who had saved the little boy's life—and her own! He must have jumped in after her. Alice looked into his eyes again. She owed her life to this handsome man with the beautiful voice.

Theodore Wakefield came calling like a proper gentleman. No matter that he and Alice were on a ship in the middle of the ocean. No matter that Alice's home, like that of all steerage-class passengers, was a giant, stale-smelling room crowded with hard bunk berths and too many people. No matter that fresh flowers were nowhere to be had. Theodore Wakefield whittled his own beautiful rose from a spare piece of lumber he'd found and presented it to Alice on their first evening together.

Alice could feel herself blushing with pleasure when he handed it to her. "This is the sweetest gift anyone has ever given me," she said in Swedish. In halting English, she added, "Thank you very much, Mr. Wakefield."

"You're very welcome, Miss Larson. A beautiful rose for a beautiful woman."

Alice understood the word *beautiful.* She had learned it earlier that evening from the women in her bunkroom who had helped her get ready for this evening. She felt so special, dressed in her new friends' finery—the few precious items they loved so much that they were bringing them all the way to the New World. As Alice walked down the ship's corridor with Theodore Wakefield, Angelique Stone's favorite kidskin boots from a good shop in London peeked out from under the skirt of Birgitta Svensen's best silk gown. Alice's fine, white-blond hair was plaited and tied with Sarah Thurber's ribbons, and Jane McCarty had helped her powder her face and rouge her lips. On her head Alice wore her own hat, a cherished cream-colored bonnet adorned with little silk flowers, given to her by her mother.

Theodore Wakefield wore a new frock coat, a top hat, and freshly polished boots. He looked so handsome, Alice couldn't keep from blushing every time he caught her eye. As he escorted her into the massive, noisy dining hall, he tipped his hat at everyone they passed.

Alice felt a bit peculiar getting in the usual steerage-class meal line in her fancy clothes. But as she and Theodore approached, the other passengers ushered them to the head of the line, smiling and calling out, "Good evening!"

Theodore took Alice's bowl and ladled out the

gray, watery porridge. "Seafood bisque, specialty of the house, ma'am," he said.

Alice couldn't quite understand what he was saying. A Swedish man near them in the meal line translated. Alice laughed. Theodore Wakefield was as clever and funny as he was handsome.

He put a piece of hard, dry bread on her plate. "Our finest beef filet," he said.

Alice didn't need a translation. She conjured up her own favorite meal—a special kind of meat dumpling her mother used to prepare for her when she was small.

Alice followed Theodore as he carried the trays with their supper through the dining room. She glanced around, hoping there was a spot that was relatively empty and quiet. But Theodore didn't stop at any of the long wooden tables and benches. Instead, he carried their meals right out the dining room doors, up the narrow stairway, and out onto the deck.

The night was as calm and peaceful as it had been stormy and furious on the day they met. The ship glided smoothly through the glassy, flat sea. The sky was bright with stars, and the major constellations stood out like jewels against a curtain of black velvet. A sliver of moon cast a shimmering path out on the water—leading to America, to adventure, to a new life, a new world.

As Theodore Wakefield led her past the sailors on watch that evening, Alice saw that there was a small table set up on the rear deck of the ship—a table just big enough for two, with two chairs. Theodore placed the two trays down on an elegant linen tablecloth. "Courtesy of a woman who got onto the ship in England with me," he said, patiently trying out different words until Alice understood.

He held out a chair for her, and as she sat down Alice felt a shiver of happiness. What a different shiver than the one she had felt the day of the storm. Back then she had been so terrified and so alone. Now, with Theodore Wakefield sitting across from her, his face silhouetted by the moonlight, Alice felt as if she might burst with joy.

Somehow, despite Alice's faulty English, she and Theodore found themselves talking late into the starry night. She told him about how lonely she had been since her parents had died, and how eager she was to be reunited with her uncle and his family when she got to the New World. She told him of her love of art. He told her of his love of horses and riding, the circus, and adventure.

"Certainly, you find much of this—this adventure in America, Mr. Wakefield," said Alice haltingly, trying out the new English word he had just explained to her.

"In America? How about right here on this ship, Miss Larson? We had quite an adventure right here. And I must say, I'm very glad we did. Otherwise we might never have met."

Later, as the night took on a gentle breeze, Theodore wrapped his frock coat around Alice's shoulders. She tingled at his touch. Offering her his arm, he escorted her back to her bunkroom. Outside the door, he shook her hand, holding it for a warm moment.

"I had the loveliest time, Miss Larson," he said.

"I also, Mr. Wakefield."

"I would very much like to call on you again," he said.

Alice took in his serious, hopeful expression. He actually looked as if he thought she might say she never wanted to see him again. She squeezed his hand gently and smiled.

"Yes, I like that," she said. "I like you to call on me again, Mr. Wakefield." *And I like you, Mr. Wakefield*, she thought as she bid him goodnight and walked through the doors of the bunkroom.

Two

"Not long ago, I could not wait to leave this ship," Alice said. "Now I do not want to get off."

On the horizon, the rooftops and chimneys and spires of New York City rose from a haze, materializing against the blue of sky and water.

"Land!" people shouted joyously.

"America! The New World!"

"At last, we've arrived."

The deck was aswarm with passengers. Their faces, haggard and drawn from the long voyage, lit up at the sight of their new home.

But Alice was not smiling. She held tight to Theodore's hand. They had shared nearly every waking moment together since their dinner on deck, and it only served to confirm what Alice already knew. She was in love with Theodore Wakefield. But what would happen when they got off the ship?

"Alice, darling, don't fret," Theodore said. "We have our whole lives to make America our home."

"We?" Alice repeated.

"Well, naturally we," Theodore said. "You

don't think I'd consider getting off this ship and—oh, Alice! You mustn't worry!" He hugged her close, and she could feel the warmth of his arms and chest. "Alice, we could marry right on this ship, you know. The captain could marry us."

Alice felt her spirits soar like the sea birds that swooped above the ship. She glanced at the great city they were approaching. Suddenly, the New World looked every bit as exciting and wonderful as the other passengers on deck seemed to think. Bursts of sunlight glinted off the city windows as if they were precious gems.

"Theodore, it is true? You want—you and me? Together? Always?" Alice threw her arms around Theodore.

"Always and forever," Theodore said.

Alice looked up into his eyes. As Theodore cupped her cheek with a gentle hand, Alice tilted her face toward his. Their lips met. Right in front of all the other passengers, Alice and Theodore kissed each other, long and sweet.

"Theodore," Alice breathed. "Theodore, there is not a thing I would like more than to share my life with you." They kissed again.

"But let us wait," Alice finally said. "Let us marry in the New World, as Americans."

Theodore appeared to think this over. "Yes, you're absolutely right. A beginning together, for our new beginning here. And I shall ask your uncle for your hand in marriage, as a gentleman should."

Alice slipped her arm through Theodore's. Theodore—her husband-to-be! Together, they watched New York City loom larger. Their journey was over. They had arrived.

Alice stood rooted to the bare, hard floor of the Castle Garden immigration station and watched Theodore disappear into a mass of men in dark coats.

Just as the group started squeezing through the door to another room, Theodore turned around. "Alice!" he called. She could see him waving his hat above the crowd.

Alice smiled. There was nothing to fear. Theodore would have his medical exam. She would have hers. They would have their papers inspected. They would sign their names to the immigration registry. And then they would meet outside this place—outside in the New World to begin their new life together.

Alice waited.

Around her, the streets were alive with people—more than Alice had ever seen in one place. There were fancy ladies and gentlemen in fine clothes and elegant hats, entering and exiting the large buildings with their majestic columns. There were other men toting water buckets and carrying sacks or wooden boxes. Their clothing was threadbare, their faces careworn, but they moved steadily and quickly, with a sense of purpose. The air was filled with the constant *clack-ety-clack* of horses' hooves on the cobblestones and the clatter of wheels as the horses pulled carriages and carts behind them.

In the harbor, sailboats crisscrossed paths with tugs and oyster boats. Steamboats, their big side wheels turning, blasted streams of billowing smoke out of their chimneys. Passengers from a ship that had arrived after Alice's were being ferried in barges to the round brick immigration station.

Alice watched her fellow travelers stream in and out of the building. Theodore Wakefield was not among them. Alice held her breath. If she could count to fifty without breathing, maybe he would emerge, waving his hat and running toward her. But when she got up to fifty there was still no Theodore. She turned her back to the building and began studying the swarms of people and traffic around her. Maybe when she turned around again, Theodore would be there. She kept her back turned as long as she could stand it. And then a little longer. Theodore did not appear.

Alice shifted from one foot to the other. Her legs were tired from standing. She felt as if she had been standing in this spot practically forever. She smoothed her skirts beneath her and gingerly sat down on the top of her trunk.

What was taking Theodore so long? Alice had already bid goodbye to Angelique and Birgitta and her other friends from the journey. She didn't recognize any of the passengers coming through the exit of the immigration station now. They must all be from another ship. So why was Theodore still inside? Unless . . .

No! No, Theodore would never have passed through before her and left her sitting here all alone. Theodore loved her. Theodore wanted to marry her.

Alice banished the horrible thought from her head. She waited. The sky began to darken. A young boy made his way down the street with a tall ladder, lighting the street lamps. Alice watched him stop beneath each one, prop the ladder against the lamppost, scale the ladder nimbly, open the glass-and-iron cage on top of the post, and set the lamp flickering with light.

Alice had never seen a street lamp before. Perhaps it was a marvelous invention, but to Alice it made the streets look strange and frightening. Now the passing horses and buggies threw eerie shadows on the ground, and the flickering flames of the street lamps seemed to be doing a weird dance.

Uncle Pär had written that he would be here by nightfall. He had said he would come to the harbor each evening to check whether Alice's ship had arrived. Tonight he would find her there. Would he appear before Theodore did?

Alice felt a chill. The day was giving way to a cool spring night. She wished Theodore were here to wrap his coat around her. She wrapped her own arms around herself and continued to wait.

Theodore caught sight of her for one brief moment. As he was being herded up the gangway from the immigration station to the steamer that would take him to the hospital at a place called Ward's Island, he saw the small, faraway figure of Alice being helped into a hansom cab. Theodore yelled her name, his cry echoing across the pier, but it was no use.

Alice! How would he ever find her again? He didn't even know her uncle's name, and Alice herself had had no idea where her uncle and their family were headed. She had said something about traveling west. But where?

Just as he boarded the steamer, Theodore watched Alice disappear into the horse-drawn cab. Not even the dreaded typhus that the doctors thought he might be carrying frightened him as much as losing the girl he loved.

They had told him that if he was extraordinarily lucky, he might not become ill, but would suffer only a long and dreary quarantine, with the hospital ward as his first home in the New World. He also knew that the disease might take his life, that he might die after icy chills and fiery fevers and unimaginable aches. But what difference would it make? What joy could there be in his life if Alice was gone from it?

15

From the very first moment he had pulled her from the raging ocean, Theodore had known there could never be anyone more brave—or more beautiful. He watched the cab carrying Alice move off down the street.

"No!" he cried. "Alice, no!" But the carriage moved away from the harbor until it disappeared behind the buildings.

"We can't go!" Alice sobbed.

Inside the railway station, bundles of tools and household goods and clothing lay at Alice's feet. Trunks and suitcases were stacked next to her. Uncle Pär was at the ticket window purchasing the train tickets, and Alice's little cousins, Helga and Anika, were already squirming restlessly.

"Child," her Aunt Elisabeth said, "we returned to the port every day for a week. And every day it was the same." She spoke gently but firmly. "Perhaps it is best if you forget your young man. Forget him and start anew, in a new place."

Forget Theodore? Impossible. Alice felt her eyes well up with tears. There had to be some explanation for Theodore's absence. But what?

"My darling Alice, you will be happy in Minnesota. You will see," Aunt Elisabeth said. "Our friends from the old country have sent word of a decent life there, with plentiful land, fresh air, and a good harvest. We have been planning this trip for a long time, and now that you are here, we are ready to go."

"But Aunt Elisabeth, I can't leave Theodore behind," said Alice. "I can't, and I won't."

"My dear," replied her aunt, "it would seem to me that perhaps your Theodore has been the one to leave you behind."

Alice's tears began to flow. She tried to blink them back, but they rolled down her face, as salty as the ocean in which she had almost drowned. *Why did he pull me out?* Alice thought miserably, her tears coming faster than she could wipe them away. *Why didn't he just let me drown?*

Aunt Elisabeth put her arms around Alice. "There, there, dear. I didn't mean to make you cry. I only want you to see that you must be realistic. Life must go on. There will be other Theodores, I promise. Shh, now, shh. It's all right. You'll be all right."

Alice felt herself melting into her aunt's embrace. Not since before her mother's death had she been babied this way. She buried her face in her aunt's shoulder and cried, hard and long.

But she knew Aunt Elisabeth was wrong. There would never be another man like Theodore Wakefield in her life again.

"Elisabeth, Alice!" said Uncle Pär.

Alice tried to be brave as she climbed into the railroad car behind her cousins, but her heart was too tender with the memory of Theodore. The journey ahead could hold nothing but loneliness.

* * *

The sound of the train's wheels on the rails was musical and soothing as they left behind the closely packed houses of New York City and began to pass country homes and tree-lined lanes.

And then the trees turned to forest, and the small farms to the hills and mountains of Pennsylvania, a place whose name Alice couldn't get her tongue to master. She thought of Theodore and how he had helped her so patiently with her English. How could someone who had seemed so wonderful and kind disappear as soon as he'd stepped off the ship? What if something horrible had happened to him? What if he'd been turned back at the shores of the New World? One terrible possibility after another followed Alice on her journey.

Along the way the train stopped at stations big and small. While Alice's relatives got out to stretch their legs briefly, Alice stood outside the train and searched the crowds for Theodore, hoping against hope that somehow he had found out where she was headed and had come to be with her.

The hills of Pennsylvania flattened out, and endless fields took the place of forest. Many of the fields were filled with a strange plant. Its leaves and stalk were a light green and bore huge, swollen, cocoonlike pods of the same color. Her uncle explained that the pods were corn, and before the trip to Minnesota was over, Alice came to know it in many forms. In the train's dining car, she and her relatives were served corn bread and fried corn kernels with butter. As they pushed further west, Alice would stand on the platform of the observation car at night and watch the gently waving fields of corn gleaming under the bright stars and moon. As she stood gazing at the silvery gray landscape rushing by, the night air still warm from the tail end of summer, Alice could not keep herself from thinking of Theodore and the night they had dined on the ship's deck under the starlit sky.

Finally, Alice and her relatives reached the great Mississippi River and transferred all their belongings to a steamboat bound for their new home. The paddle wheels churned through the water. Twin chimneys blew smoke high into the air, and the river danced with fleeting shadows from small clouds and puffs of steam. Alice's cousins raced around the boat, giddy with excitement.

"Alice, Alice!" shouted Helga. "Come look! We're swimming through the water like a great big fish!"

Helga and Anika were too young to remember the long voyage to America. For them, a boat ride was a new adventure. But for Alice, being out on the water was laden with memories—her first glimpse of Theodore's wet, handsome face, their romantic dinner on the deck, their conversations long into the night, the sunrises they had shared, their struggle to find common words, Theodore's sense of humor. . . .

As the steamboat cut through the water toward the port of St. Paul, Minnesota, Alice thought about the new life she would be starting in her new home. No matter what happened, she knew she would be waiting for Theodore Wakefield forever.

Three

1877. Prairie Lakes, Minnesota.

"The new, sweet, sparkling brew, for our new, sweet, sparkling twins!" George Johnson announced. He brought a glass of foamy root beer to Alice's lips. Alice's hands were full.

On one arm, little Elisabeth slept contentedly, the sweetest smile on her lips. On the other, baby Jessamyn kicked her tiny arms and legs in her blanket, gurgling noisily and happily, as if celebrating her own birth along with all the friends and neighbors in the small cabin.

"But how are we to tell them apart?" Uncle Pär asked, drawing a sip of root beer from his own glass.

Aunt Elisabeth shook her head. "They say no two snowflakes are ever alike, but these two, well, I know one is named after me, but I have no idea which one!" There was laughter all around the cabin.

Alice joined in as she pulled the edge of Elisabeth's blanket down gently to reveal her tiny shoulder. Aunt Elisabeth had spun the softest wool for both the twins' blankets. "Elisabeth has a tiny mole on her shoulder," Alice said. "And a lucky thing, too, or even I might not be able to say who was who!"

"Lot of good that one little mole will do when they're grown and clothed," said Jim Wilkens, who owned the neighboring farm. "Mark my words, those two are going to give you quite a time of it, Alice!"

"Well, we'll show them," George said. "We'll paint a mark on little Jessamyn's shoulder, and then *they* won't know who's who, either!"

Everybody roared at George's joke, but Alice saw the pride in his face as he gazed at his new baby daughters. He had barely taken his eyes off them all day.

No, there had not been another Theodore Wakefield in Alice's life, but there was George. He loved her with every sturdy bone in his body. He worked hard every day of his life, milking the cows, tending the crops, and making their farm one of the best in this part of the state. Somehow, he always found time to help Jim Wilkens with his own farm or help Alice churn the butter when her arms grew tired. Best of all, George made Alice laugh.

Not too long before, Alice had thought she might never laugh again. Her little son, Steven, had lain sick with scarlet fever, his throat so sore he couldn't even cry, his head aching so that he would bang it against his bedpost in pain and frustration.

It had been nearly impossible for Alice to believe that her son was dying. With his chubby face rosy from the raging fever, he had looked so pink and healthy. But he had died after less than a week of illness, his misery finally ended.

Alice's sorrow and grief had lasted for months. The pain of losing Theodore Wakefield was dull compared to the pain of losing a child—something Alice would never have thought possible.

But now Alice held joy and new life in her arms. Her home once again rang with laughter. Her neighbors had filled her table with good food —chicken and dumplings, luscious ham, apple cobbler, and fresh buttermilk. Her husband had filled her life with love.

Alice kissed Jessamyn on her wide-eyed little face. Then she kissed Elisabeth on her sleeping one. The twins would make up for all her losses. Alice felt doubly blessed. And she hoped that wherever he was, Theodore Wakefield was equally happy.

Four

1884. Prairie Lakes.

The smells of hay and sawdust and animals mixed with the smell of fresh popcorn.

"Come on! Hurry up! You're so slow!" seven-year-old Jessamyn said impatiently. She grabbed hold of Elisabeth's arm and pulled her forward. Elisabeth stumbled on the hem of her long dress as she tried to keep up. She didn't know how Jessamyn did it, but she managed to run around in her Sunday best as if she were in a pair of boys' trousers. The girls looked identical, from their long spun-gold hair and the dimple on one cheek to their high, lace-up black boots. But their personalities were as different as town and country. Jessamyn sought out adventure while her sister sought out quieter pleasures.

"Whoa, cowgirl!" Jessamyn's father said. "We're going to see it all, I promise. Every last elephant, tightrope walker, and strong man. But it doesn't have to be a race, does it?"

Jessamyn ignored his question. "You left out the horses and the bareback rider, Papa."

"Well, we certainly wouldn't miss those," he said with a wink.

"Horses, horses, horses," said Elisabeth.

"Well, I suppose *you* want to see the tiniest ballerina in the world in her silly pink costume," Jessamyn said.

"It's not silly. It's beautiful," Elisabeth said.

Jessamyn gave her a cross look. "That's what you say about those boring samplers we're supposed to be learning to stitch, too," she said.

"Girls, girls," the twins' mother said, her words softened by her Swedish accent. "No fighting today. Not on such a special day."

Elisabeth was instantly sorry. Her mother was right. When the circus was in town, it was a holiday. "I didn't mean we shouldn't see the horses," she said to Jessamyn. "We can even go see them first, if you want."

"How about if we visit some of the sideshows first?" their father suggested. "We saw the horses in the parade this morning, and we'll be seeing them again in the main show later."

The corners of Jessamyn's mouth turned way down. Elisabeth wasn't sure if she was going to yell or cry. But then her frown turned into a big smile. "I know! We can go look at the snakes!"

"Ugh, snakes," said Elisabeth, but she felt a secret thrill at seeing something so horrible.

Their father paid their admission and bought each twin some roasted nuts. Then they headed for the snake house. Three big, fat snakes slithered slowly and lazily in their cage.

"My, they're as thick as small tree trunks,"

their mother said, taking a step forward for a closer look.

Elisabeth hid her face against her father, but she peeked out of one eye. Jessamyn went right up to the cage and stared, calmly popping nuts into her mouth.

A young woman in a glittery dress approached the back of the cage. Elisabeth gasped as she opened it, sliding her hand toward the hugest snake of all and taking it out. Then, as if she were adorning herself with a fancy necklace, she wrapped it around herself.

Jessamyn stared in awe as the snake slithered around the woman's neck.

"She must be terrified," Elisabeth said.

"No, she looks like she's not afraid of anything," Jessamyn said. Elisabeth could hear how impressed her twin was.

"I guess if she were our schoolmistress, she wouldn't even be afraid of Billy Tyrus, huh?" Elisabeth said. Billy was the oldest boy in school and the biggest bully in Prairie Lakes. Even the teacher did what Billy told her.

Jessamyn giggled. "Right. If this lady came to school with that snake, I bet Billy would listen to her."

Next they went to see the strong man, the tattooed lady, and the baby elephant that had just been born that summer. Then they went to see the hog with the skin of a leopard.

"Jess, how can you tell they don't just paint

26

those leopard spots on the hog's skin?" Elisabeth said, turning around to ask her sister. But Jessamyn wasn't behind her. Her parents strolled over, arm in arm. "Where's Jess?" Elisabeth asked.

"Jessamyn?" Her mother instantly sounded worried. Elisabeth had heard about how when her mother was young, she had plunged into a stormy ocean to rescue a little boy. She was still the bravest woman Elisabeth knew, except when it came to her and Jessamyn. Then she always imagined the worst. Her father said the death of the twins' brother, Steven, had made their mother afraid for them.

"Don't fret, Alice," Elisabeth's father said. "She's around here somewhere."

They retraced their steps all the way back to the strong man, but they didn't find Jessamyn.

"Oh, George, what if something has happened to her?" Elisabeth's mother said.

Elisabeth was beginning to worry, too. She thought about the snake slithering around the lady in the glittery dress. What if it had gotten loose? Or worse, what if one of the tigers had broken out of its cage? Suddenly, the circus seemed full of mysterious people and scary beasts.

The beat of hooves distracted Elisabeth for a moment. She turned around to see three golden stallions being led from the stables toward the main tent. The horses! Instantly, she wondered why she had worried at all. Of course! They had passed the stables right before they had gotten to the leopard-skinned hog. Jessamyn must have wandered away then.

"Jess must have gone to see the horses being groomed for the show!" she said to her parents.

"Why, naturally," her father said. "We should have realized that right off." They hurried over toward the makeshift stables that had been set up for the few days that the circus was in town.

"Excuse me, sir," Elisabeth's mother said to a clown. He was dressed up as a horse trainer, but his britches were covered with patches and his big toe stuck out of one of his riding boots. Before she could get another word out, the clown turned his attention to Elisabeth. He snapped the tip of his riding crop on the ground near her feet. Elisabeth gave a startled cry and jumped back.

"Little miss, I told you once and I'll tell you again. No one's allowed in here when we're getting ready for the show!" the clown said.

"But it wasn't me!" Elisabeth protested. "It must have been Jessamyn, my twin sister."

"Yes, we're looking for our other little girl. We think she may have come to see the horses," Alice said.

"She did indeed," the clown said. "But I sent her away."

"Please, sir," Elisabeth said. "My sister sometimes doesn't understand when people say no.

She might have sneaked in anyway, when you weren't watching."

"Don't you think you should let us have a look around?" her mother asked.

The clown shook his head, his oversized hat flopping all over. "Circus master's orders. No outsiders back here right before the show," he said.

"But you have to let us in!" Elisabeth struggled to hold back her tears. She didn't want to act like a baby. "You must be the meanest clown in the whole world," she sniffled.

The clown let out a big sigh. "All right, all right. Believe me, I don't like to make little girls cry. Go ahead."

"Thank you," Elisabeth's father said, leading her and her mother into the stables.

They walked up and down the rows of stalls. Grooms brushed the horses' coats and slipped jeweled bridles over their heads, getting them ready for the show. In a field behind the stables, more horses were being walked.

And then Elisabeth saw her twin. Atop the largest, whitest horse in the field sat Jessamyn, her petticoats sticking up all around her, her legs dangling down the horse's side. A lady with long jet-black hair in a beautiful white dress, sashes of every color of the rainbow tied around her slender waist, led Jessamyn around the field in a wide, gentle circle.

* * *

Jessamyn couldn't stop talking about Laura the Lovely and how she was going to grow up to be a bareback rider like she. She had proudly tied the yellow silk scarf Laura had given her around her waist. Laura had given Elisabeth a scarf, too—a deep rose one. "Now we both have costumes like hers!" Jessamyn said as she and Elisabeth and their parents approached the main tent. "And isn't Arctic Prince the most wonderful horse you've ever seen?" Jessamyn went on. "I got to help brush and groom him, and the Magnificent Theo W. showed me how to put on his bridle."

Suddenly their mother stopped walking. "The magnificent *who*, Jessamyn?"

"Theo W. He takes care of the horses. They call him magnificent because they say he can talk to animals, and the animals understand him."

"That does sound rather magnificent," her father said. "Wish I could do the same. It sure would be helpful around the farm. Betsy, why aren't you giving any milk today? Gerty, your new calf doesn't look well. Do you know what the matter is?"

Elisabeth giggled, but she noticed that her mother was barely listening. She had turned around to look back toward the stables, and she'd even taken a step or two in that direction. Her father had noticed, too.

"Alice," he said, "are you all right?"

"Excuse me? Ah . . . yes. Yes, I'm fine," she

answered, but she had a funny expression on her face.

"Well, come on, everyone. We want to get good seats for the show, don't we?"

The twins nodded and started to follow their father. Their mother didn't move. Why was she acting so strangely? Elisabeth wondered. After a moment, she followed them into the big tent. As the music announced the beginning of the show Elisabeth sneaked a glance at her mother. She looked as if she were far, far away.

Alice Johnson hurried past Otto's General Store, the post office, and the barber shop. Everything was closed. The main street of Prairie Lakes was deserted. In Dr. Good's house, a candle burned in the window near the door, but Alice knew it was in case someone came by for an emergency in the middle of the night. The doctor was probably asleep. Even the saloon had shut for the night.

This is the silliest thing you have ever done, Alice told herself, reaching the edge of town and walking toward the great field where the circus was camped. *Yes, Theodore Wakefield loved horses and adventure and the circus. He told you so. But you have absolutely no proof that he is the Magnificent Theo W. And what if he is? What will you say to him? You are happily married. You love George. You have two wonderful daughters.*

Still, Alice kept walking. Her boots sank into

the soft dirt with each step. She had often thought of Theodore Wakefield over the years. But since marrying George, the memories had come less often. They had become soft around the edges, faded. Now they rushed back, sharp and strong. As she pictured her first meeting with Theodore Wakefield back on the boat, Alice could almost smell the salt air, feel the ocean wind on her face.

She was so lost in thoughts of Theodore that she didn't realize she had reached the field. She was halfway across it before she realized there were no longer any tents or coaches or makeshift stables there.

Alice stood stock still. No! It couldn't be. She had thought the circus was leaving the next day, not that evening. But all that was left in the field were the marks in the mud where tent stakes had been pulled out and wagon wheels had rolled across. The evening wind swept across the empty field and Alice shivered. The circus was gone! And with it, the Magnificent Theo W. Now she would never find out.

Alice didn't know which was more powerful, her disappointment or her relief. She stood under the starless sky pulling her cloak tightly around her and clutching a carved wooden rose.

Five

"And then they were both pedaling along right next to each other, those huge front wheels almost touching," Jessamyn recounted.

Elisabeth stripped the husk off another ear of corn, listening to her twin describe the bicycle race she had gone to see in St. Paul. She brushed the strands of corn silk away from the yellow-white kernels. Around her, all her neighbors in Prairie Lakes had gathered in the Johnsons' barn for a corn-husking bee to shuck the late summer's crop.

Jessamyn had a piece of corn in her hand, too. She moved it through the air as if it were a bicycle racing toward the finish line. "Then one of them pulled ahead," she said. "Then the other one caught up and passed the first one. But only for a moment. They both finished at the exact same time. Oh! It was so exciting! I'd like to learn to bicycle and enter a race myself!"

"On one of those three-wheelers the ladies ride?" Bobby Tyrus asked. "You wouldn't have half a chance of winning. You should just stick to

33

horses." Bobby was getting to be just as big a bully as his older brother, Billy.

"Who said anything about a three-wheeled bicycle?" Jessamyn shot back. "I'd ride a real bicycle."

"With your dress over your head?" Bobby said. He laughed as if he had said the funniest thing in the world. "No, I know, in those ridiculous bloomers invented by that crazy suffragist."

"You bet," Jessamyn said, yanking the husk off her corn.

"That's my girl," the twins' father said, the pile of shucked corn next to him growing at a rapid rate. The entire floor of the barn was thick with husks and corn silk.

"You mean that's my *boy*," Bobby Tyrus said meanly. "Pretty soon she'll be rallying right along with those suffragists for the women's vote, wanting the men to stay home and have the babies!"

Elisabeth felt herself getting angrier and angrier. It was true that her father sometimes treated Jessamyn like the son he'd never had the chance to see grow up, but Bobby had no right to make fun of that. Elisabeth noticed her mother blushing at Bobby's words. She knew her mother worried about Jessamyn's daring. She was always saying how she hoped Jessamyn would settle down and become a lady now that she had turned sixteen. Elisabeth couldn't imagine her twin ever really settling down. But she didn't need Bobby Tyrus reminding her.

"Bobby, maybe you're sore because Jessamyn scored more runs than you at the Prairie Lakes baseball game," Elisabeth said sweetly. Jessamyn was almost as good at baseball as she was at riding.

The twins exchanged identical, dimpled grins. With their long blond braids and blue-green eyes, it was impossible for people to tell them apart—until they got to know how different the girls could be.

"Baseball," muttered Bobby. "It's a stupid fad. It won't last." Everyone else in the room was laughing.

"You twins tell him," Tom Wilkens said enthusiastically.

Elisabeth felt her face grow warm. Tom was the nicest, most handsome, and smartest boy in Prairie Lakes. Then Elisabeth noticed Jessamyn flashing Tom her brightest smile. She felt her heart sink like a pebble in one of the town lakes. *Forget about him, Elisabeth Johnson,* she told herself. Jessamyn was funny, fascinating, brave . . . any boy would be crazy about her.

Elisabeth went back to her work, shucking corn as fast as she could. Jessamyn worked more slowly, talking and laughing not just with Tom, but also with Carl Bergman and Tad Schmidt. Alycia Germond shot Jessamyn a nasty look and moved closer to Tad.

They all sipped hot, spiced apple cider while they worked, and Jim Wilkens, Tom's father, picked up his banjo and everyone joined in singing.

A chorus of "O, Susanna" was interrupted by Tom's cry. "The red ear!" He held it up high, a big grin on his fine-featured face, his brown eyes sparkling.

The singing stopped. "Hooray, Wilkens!" Carl Bergman said.

"Lucky Tom," others said, for the red ear meant that Tom had won the privilege of kissing the lady of his choice.

Elisabeth caught her breath and held it. Then she saw Jessamyn, already shifting toward Tom. She let her breath out.

But Tom stood up. Then he walked right over to her! Elisabeth could barely believe it. In front of half of Prairie Lakes, Tom Wilkens leaned down and kissed her softly!

Elisabeth blushed furiously with shyness and joy.

"Good choice!" Carl called out.

There was a sprinkling of applause.

Elisabeth turned to sneak a look at her twin. Jessamyn was scowling. Elisabeth felt her pleasure beginning to evaporate. But Jessamyn's scowl vanished so quickly, Elisabeth thought she might have imagined it. Her body tingled with happiness once more.

Soon everyone returned to shucking corn. Jim Wilkens began picking his banjo again. Jessamyn went back to Carl and Tad, showering them with her silvery peals of laughter.

It was as if nothing had happened. But when Tom sat down beside Elisabeth and gave her a tender, private smile, she looked into his warm brown eyes and knew something *had* happened. Something very special.

"Jess, I hope you didn't mind terribly," Elisabeth said. "It would be so horrible if you hated me for it." She turned a wooden crank to bring up a cool bucket of water from the well.

"Hate you? For what? Mind what?" Jessamyn asked. She passed Elisabeth an empty pail.

"Mind that, uh, well, that Tom and I . . . I mean that Tom—"

"Tom what?" Jessamyn asked, a note of impatience in her voice.

"Well, that perhaps you . . . you know, you might like Tom just a bit yourself," Elisabeth managed, turning her flushed face from her sister.

"Me? And Tom?" Jessamyn gave a laugh. "You think I'd like someone who's going to stick around this one-horse town and be a farmer like his father? Someone who's going to have the same boring old life we have now? No, thank you. I mean, it's OK for you. . . ."

Elisabeth began filling the empty pail from the well bucket, pausing to drink a cool dipperful of water. "Gee, that's very big of you, Jessamyn," she said. Her twin *was* angry about Tom. She knew it! Even though they were twins and best friends, Jessamyn was always competing with Elisabeth. She wanted Elisabeth's friends to be her friends, and now she wanted the boy Elisabeth liked. And if she couldn't have him, she would have to criticize Elisabeth instead. Elisabeth frowned.

Jessamyn waved her hand. "Oh, Elisabeth, I didn't mean to make you feel bad," she said hastily.

"You just think I don't mind it here." Elisabeth handed the newly filled bucket to her sister.

"Well, you don't mind it, do you?" Jessamyn said, handing over another empty pail. Elisabeth set to work filling this one as well. "You love Prairie Lakes."

"Lots of things here are fun," Elisabeth said. "Like the husking bee." Her cheeks grew warm with the memory of Tom's kiss.

"Husking bees. How dull," Jessamyn said. "We must be the last town in the entire world to still have them."

"You didn't look like you were having such a terrible time," Elisabeth said. She finished filling the second pail, dropped the dipper into the well bucket, and lowered the bucket back into the depths of the well. She heard the bucket splash into the water way down in the ground.

"I suppose a husking bee is all right if you have nothing better to amuse yourself with," Jessamyn said. "And in Prairie Lakes, we have nothing better. But did you know that in New York City and San Francisco they have horseless carriages and buildings that stretch way up into the sky, and there's always a million things to do . . . a million adventures, new people every day? Not to mention that if we lived there, we'd have running water in our home. They're up to the moment on everything."

Elisabeth picked up one of the pails of water. Jessamyn picked up the other, and they started back to the house. "Well, I'll wager it isn't half this beautiful in New York City," Elisabeth said.

Their lake sparkled blue against a backdrop of lush green trees. Soon some of the trees would be a blaze of red and yellow and orange, their colors set off by the deep forest green of the pines, which would keep their coats against the heavy winter snows. Sometimes Elisabeth thought that Minnesota must be the most beautiful place in the world. She couldn't imagine a city such as New York, where instead of trees the landscape was made up of granite and brick.

Jessamyn shrugged, causing some water to spill from her pail.

"And the circus is coming to town soon," Elisabeth added. "Even *you* like the circus."

It was the magic word. Jessamyn's face lit up like a crackling fire on a cold night. "I know! The other day I spent nearly a half-hour just standing in front of the circus posters and staring at them.

39

People in town must have thought it was awfully odd. But for me those posters are like doors opening onto exciting new adventures. I can't wait to go this year."

Jessamyn's eyes sparkled, and Elisabeth smiled. Her twin might have dreams of big-city life, but when the circus was in town, Elisabeth knew there was nowhere else in the world Jessamyn would rather be.

"I wonder what new acts they're going to have this year?" Jessamyn went on. "Remember the Pirelli Brothers and their fabulous hand-to-hand balancing act? And that clown you thought was so mean when we were little!"

Elisabeth giggled. "I loved it last year when he pretended to be an old man from the audience who wanted to try to ride bareback."

"Yeah, the way he was getting bumped all over that poor horse!" Jessamyn laughed. "It's too bad Laura the Lovely isn't with them anymore."

"Too bad," agreed Elisabeth. She listened to Jessamyn go over the previous year's show. From the first clown skit to the grand finale, Jessamyn knew the entire spectacle by heart.

Elisabeth smiled again. It was good to see her twin so genuinely enthusiastic. And if Jessamyn harbored any secret disappointment about Tom Wilkens, even the teensiest, tiniest one, Elisabeth was certain it would vanish with the first blast of the circus train's whistle as the troupe rolled into town.

"Elisabeth, dear, isn't it Jessamyn's turn to help put up the peaches?" her mother asked. She dropped a peach into boiling water for a few seconds, then fished it out and removed the skin. "You've been doing all her chores this week."

Elisabeth cut the skinned peach into slices, discarding the pit and dropping the rest of it into a glass jar. "It's all right, Mama. We made an agreement. Jess will do all my chores for a week when it gets too cold and snowy to go riding."

Her mother raised an eyebrow. "As long as you don't end up doing everything for both of you," she said. "Somehow I seem to remember that last year you and I put up all the fruits and vegetables ourselves."

Elisabeth laughed. "And Jess went to work on them when it was time to eat them!" Last winter she had been furious. She'd vowed not to let Jessamyn get away with it again. But Jessamyn had been so happy recently that when she had begged and cajoled and promised by the tail of her favorite horse that she'd do her part this year, she really would, only please, please could she trade a week now for a week later, Elisabeth just couldn't find the heart to refuse her twin.

Her mother poured a bit of sugar syrup into each of the jars of peaches. "Jessamyn might do well to thank your Tom for your big-hearted mood," she commented.

"Oh, Mama." Elisabeth busied herself closing up all the jars.

"You might not believe it, but I was sixteen years old once myself," her mother went on. "I know what it's like." Her voice sounded far away.

Elisabeth sneaked a look at her mother. She wore a funny, glazed expression. Then she seemed to catch Elisabeth looking at her. She gave her head a hard shake and laughed. "But boys or no boys, we have work to do." She put the jars to soak in a bath of boiling water. Elisabeth helped her.

Later, as they cooled, the jars made a familiar *pop, pop, pop* as the airtight seal was formed. Now the fruit would stay good for the entire long, cold winter ahead.

Elisabeth had a feeling that it was going to seem a lot less long and a lot less cold now that Tom was coming to call.

Jessamyn rode across the grassy plain. The wind rushed past her. The sound of her heart beat in her ears with the sound of her horse's hooves. Blue sky and green grass danced crazily as Jessamyn posted up and down, bouncing rhythmically against her horse's flank. "Good, Smoke Signal, good boy."

She rode out to where the plain was cut by a wooded glade, then gently tugged on the reins, steering Smoke Signal around and riding back to where she had begun. She pulled to a stop in front of an old, old man with deep lines in his weathered red-brown skin, his long white hair in a braid down his back.

"How did I do, Blue Cloud?" Jessamyn asked, her words coming between breaths.

"Very good, Jessamyn. Very good indeed. You are getting to be a better rider every time you come to visit." Peter Blue Cloud helped her dismount. Jessamyn landed in a patch of delicate pink flowers.

"Look, Blue Cloud," she said. "Lady's-slippers."

"Lady's-slippers?" Blue Cloud chuckled. "I know these flowers as moccasins. There is a legend about them." He took hold of Smoke Signal's bridle and began leading him toward a tiny cabin nestled in a grove of trees. "My people tell of a beautiful young girl who went off seeking adventure. She must have been much like you, Jessamyn. But this poor young lady met an unfortunate end when a forest fire broke out as she walked through the woods. Her mother never got over her death."

Jessamyn nodded, thinking about how her mother would often get a sad, faraway expression in her eyes as she thought about Steven, the brother Jessamyn had never known.

"It is said that the mother wandered over the plains and through the forest, searching for the spot where her daughter's spirit had passed on to the eternal resting grounds," Blue Cloud

43

continued. "One day, the mother found two perfect pink-and-white blossoms growing together. They were the very same shape as her daughter's moccasins. She dropped to the earth and pressed herself into the ground, sure she had found her daughter at last.

"Since that time," Blue Cloud concluded, "her daughter's moccasins have been growing all over this land."

Jessamyn patted Smoke Signal's neck as they walked. "That's a sad story," she said.

Blue Cloud nodded. "The history of my people is often sad." He was quiet for a long time. When he spoke again, his voice wavered. "Once there were many of us in this land, hunting and fishing, dancing, and teaching our sons and daughters our ways for generations and generations.

"Then came the wars with the white man, when many of my people died. Most of the rest of my people were forced from this home, marched to barren lands that other men could not till, lands where nothing grew and water rarely flowed.

"Sometimes I take comfort in looking at the pink moccasins and thinking that they are the spirits of people I knew and loved," Blue Cloud said.

Jessamyn felt her eyes getting moist. She blinked hard against the tears. She very rarely cried, and she didn't intend to do it now. Instead, she slipped her hand into Blue Cloud's free one.

She thought of him as something like a special grandfather. "Blue Cloud, I am here. You have me."

Blue Cloud smiled. "Yes, it is true, and I am deeply grateful. It is good to have someone to tell my stories to, someone to teach to ride, as a parent teaches his child, someone who will roam the plains with Smoke Signal when I am gone."

Jessamyn looked up at her friend. His back was as straight as a boy's, and he led Smoke Signal with a sure step. True, the deep lines in his face made it quite impossible to imagine him as ever having been young. But Jessamyn thought he was like a great, ancient tree that had been growing almost forever—and would always be there for her.

Six

"Here it comes!" Jessamyn announced.

Elisabeth could hear a distant *clop, clop, clop,* then a faint call of trumpets. "Jess!" She reached out and tugged at Jessamyn's skirt. "Jess, don't stand in the middle of the street, for heaven's sake. You might get trampled by the horses!"

"More likely she'll wind up leading the parade," Tom Wilkens said with a laugh.

Jessamyn stepped back into the row of townspeople lining the street, many in their Sunday best. It was a big occasion when the circus train rolled into Prairie Lakes and the performers put on a parade to greet the townspeople. Jessamyn and Elisabeth wore new leg-of-mutton-sleeved dresses that they had sewn themselves. Actually, Elisabeth had sewn hers and about half of Jessamyn's, too. Jessamyn's dress was a deep royal blue, and Elisabeth's was a lighter sky blue, setting off their blue-green eyes and their long blond hair. Elisabeth felt very grown-up, especially with Tom by her side, but Jessamyn jumped up and down like a child.

The crowd buzzed excitedly as four ladies on

horseback trotted into view, trumpets to their lips. Their feathered costumes and plumed hats danced to the horses' movements. Behind them came a band of musicians in smart red uniforms trimmed with silver braid. They played from their perch on a bandwagon pulled by row upon row of horses.

Two, four, six . . . Elisabeth counted the horses, the numbers in her head taking on the rhythm of the brassy music. Cymbals punctuated the trumpet calls, throwing glints of sunlight into the crowd. A huge bass drum marked time.

"There are at least twenty horses!" Elisabeth shouted to Tom over the music.

Following the musicians, two rows of elephants held one another trunk to tail. Around the huge beasts skirted a tiny clown, his hand above his eyes, looking up, up, up, as if he couldn't see high enough to take in the enormousness of all the elephants at once.

Tom's little nephew put his hands to his mouth and laughed. Elisabeth felt herself chuckling, too.

Then came the lions and tigers, pacing nervously in their cages. As the lion cage rumbled past Elisabeth, one of the lions pressed close to the bars and let out a ferocious roar.

Elisabeth jumped toward Tom, grabbing his arm. Tom gave her arm a squeeze and laughed loudly.

Elisabeth joined in as the snake wagon passed. For most of the crowd, just the picture painted on the side of the wagon of the monstrous, scaly reptiles was enough to draw loud oohs and ahhs. But the snake wagon reminded Elisabeth of her imaginary picture of the lady snake charmer standing up at the front of the school, putting fear into Billy Tyrus. It had been a running joke for Elisabeth and Jessamyn for many years now, since back in the days when the circus had come to town packed into horse-drawn coaches.

Elisabeth leaned past Tom to give Jessamyn a tap on the arm and share their joke. But Jessamyn wasn't standing there anymore. Elisabeth slowly rotated full circle. She didn't see her sister anywhere.

Oh, well, she thought, going back to watching the parade. *That seems to be a circus tradition, too.* As soon as the circus rolled into town, Jessamyn wandered off after it. By now, Elisabeth knew not to worry. When the circus train whistled out of town, Jessamyn would come home looking like the world was about to end. For weeks, she would mope around the house and sigh loudly at the supper table.

But little by little, the sparkle would return. Jessamyn would start making deals at school for the contents of her dinner bucket, somehow convincing Carl Bergman to trade her a piece of chicken *and* a large slice of his mother's blueberry cobbler for an apple. She would start flirting with the boys again. Everything would return to normal.

And then the same thing would happen again the next year.

"How long do we lose you for this time?" Jessamyn's mother asked. She brought a plate of fried potatoes and sausage to the table.

"This year the circus is in town for three days," Jessamyn said. "Yesterday being the first." She bolted down a biscuit and gravy and managed a few quick forkfuls of potatoes, just to satisfy her mother. "Might I be excused now?" she asked.

"Child, you'd think the circus couldn't start without you," her father said. He had already milked all the cows and done a morning's work, turning the soil of the newly harvested fields. He was eating his second helping of breakfast.

"Papa, it's only a few days a year," Jessamyn said. "Pretty please let me go." She showered him with her brightest smile. It never failed.

"All right, Jessamyn, but be home before nightfall," he said.

"And don't forget your hat," her mother added.

"OK. Bye!" Jessamyn said. She kissed Elisabeth on the cheek. "Look for me at the show."

"I will."

Jessamyn stuffed her hat on her head and was out the door. She took a few steps down the front path, going just far enough so she could look into the kitchen window. Her parents and Elisabeth were sitting at the table. No one was looking out

49

at her. Quickly, she doubled back around the house and slipped into the woodshed.

She breathed in the smell of logs and mildew as she wedged her arm behind a stack of logs and pulled out a pair of men's trousers. Then she dislodged a shirt, a jacket, and a cap, all smelling of the wood in the shed.

The trousers were an old pair of her father's that Jessamyn had shrunk as best she could by repeatedly bathing them in boiling water. She had had to feign illness when the rest of the family went to a barn dance to manage the time alone at home. The trousers were still way too large for her, so she had also helped herself to one of her father's old belts—one she convinced herself she hardly ever saw him wearing anymore.

The other items had been acquired slyly, one by one. Jessamyn knew Elisabeth would be horrified if she knew why Tom had never recovered his cap after forgetting it at the house one day. The jacket, the biggest and most difficult article to come by, had once belonged to Carl Bergman. Jessamyn had convinced Carl that she desperately wanted something warm to wrap around herself to remind her of him. It had cost her a kiss behind the school, too.

The shirt had been the most daring acquisition —and the sneakiest. Jessamyn even felt a trifle guilty about it. One day she had offered to help Alycia Germond bring a kettle of her special soup over to Tad Schmidt's when he was sick. Jessamyn wasn't sure Alycia really loved the idea of letting her help, but that kettle was awfully heavy, and Alycia was too polite to turn down Jessamyn's offer. Jessamyn had borrowed Tad's shirt right off the line where it was drying—almost under Alycia's pretty little nose. She told herself she would return the shirt one day, but it was getting rather worn after its second circus season.

Jessamyn shed her own clothes and made a pile in the farthest, dimmest corner of the woodshed. She climbed into the large trousers, tucking in the shirt and securing everything with the belt. She had punched an extra hole in it with an ice pick. It wasn't the neatest package, but she could cover some of it up with the jacket. She hoped no one would look too hard at her boots. Not even she could manage to get her hands on a pair of boys' shoes—especially ones that were small enough for her. Finally Jessamyn tucked her long blond braid under Tom's cap.

She peeked out of the woodshed to make sure the coast was clear. Now she was ready—ready to give the elephants water in return for a free admission pass, or sneak under a tent like some of the boys did, or otherwise get to see every possible bit of the greatest show on earth.

Alice Johnson stared blankly out the window, her hands floating in a basin of soapy dishwater.

"Mama? Mama, what is it?" Elisabeth asked, a dishtowel in her hands.

The sound of her daughter's voice brought Alice back to Prairie Lakes and her cozy little home. She rinsed a soapy plate in the basin of clear water and handed it to Elisabeth. "Oh, it's nothing, dear."

"You're not worrying about Jessamyn, are you, Mama? She's having a time and a half at her favorite place in the world right now."

"Yes, yes, of course she is." Alice tried to clear her head of the memories playing on center stage there, but she couldn't. It was always like this when the circus was in town. It had been like this ever since Alice had gone looking for the Magnificent Theo W. in an empty, muddy field.

Theo W. had never returned in the years that followed. But that was not true of Alice's recollections. For the few brief days that the horses, clowns, wild beasts, and brave acrobats delighted the people of Prairie Lakes, Alice found herself slipping in and out of thoughts of a girlhood long past. At moments, it was as if she really were sixteen again, walking on the deck of a great ship with a handsome young man.

Perhaps that was why, at about this time every year, Alice surprised herself. She managed to keep the questions, worries, and reproaches of a mother in check. She swallowed the fears about her children that she had fought ever since the death of her baby, Steven. And she let her daughter run off to the circus disguised as a boy.

"Elisabeth! Elisabeth, the most amazing, incredible, marvelous thing happened to me today," Jessamyn said.

Elisabeth looked up from the book she was reading under a tree. Her father said it was too cold to be reading outside, but Elisabeth was bundled up in heavy woolen clothing and thick gloves that she had to remove each time she wanted to turn a page. This was her favorite spot. It was so peaceful by the lake, the first few fallen leaves floating on the water, a light, crisp breeze blowing through the trees.

Old Matthew, one of the farm hands who helped her father, had come by earlier, smiling his missing-tooth smile, to say that if he could read, he would surely do it in a beautiful spot like this. Elisabeth knew Matthew had been a slave, and that he'd gained his freedom after the Civil War, right around the time her mother came to America. When Matthew was a boy, no one had thought he was important enough to teach him to read.

"Perhaps you'd like me to teach you," Elisabeth had volunteered shyly. It wasn't the first time the thought had occurred to her. It had warmed Elisabeth to see Matthew's lined face light up like a child's as he nodded his head eagerly.

53

"Would you, Miss Elisabeth? Would you really?"

"Of course!" Elisabeth had said. She couldn't imagine not being able to sit quietly with a book. It was one of the most pleasurable things she could think of. She had told him they would have their first lesson the following day.

Now she put down her book as Jessamyn plopped down under the tree with her. She noticed that her sister smelled vaguely of wood and must.

"Did they put you to work chopping wood at the circus, Jess?"

Jessamyn's brow furrowed. "Chopping wood? Why would you think—oh. No. No, of course not. That hardly falls under the category of amazing, incredible, and marvelous, does it?" Jessamyn went right on to the second question without waiting for an answer to the first. "So, don't you want to know what happened?"

"Hmm, amazing, incredible, and marvelous, let's see," said Elisabeth. "It sounds like you spent a day at the circus. Just like yesterday and the day before."

"Well, yes, of course I did." There was a note of impatience in Jessamyn's voice. "But something happened today. Something different."

"OK, what?" Elisabeth asked. She could see that Jessamyn couldn't stand to hold back her news a second longer.

"I met the new bareback rider, Suzanne Silver."

"Really? The one with the long, curly hair?" Elisabeth asked. "She was awfully good, wasn't she? Every time she jumped through one of those dangling hoops, I held my breath for fear she might not land back on the horse again. So you met her. Did you actually talk to her, too?"

Jessamyn nodded excitedly. "And that's not all. Elisabeth, this is the most fantastic. You won't believe it. I got to ride for her. Suzanne watched me ride bareback, the way Blue Cloud's been teaching me. And guess what? She says I have talent. She says I could learn to ride the way she does. She really said that!" Jessamyn's eyes were as shiny as the blue lake.

"Jess, that's wonderful," Elisabeth exclaimed. "Imagine it. My twin, riding for a circus star."

"Imagine it, your twin *being* a circus star," Jessamyn said. "Oh, Elisabeth, I think it might be possible—the biggest dream in my whole life come true."

Seven

Rain beat on the roof. Elisabeth turned over on her straw mattress. She opened one eye. Slowly, sleepily, the wooden ceiling beams came into view. Weak gray light filtered in through the bedroom window.

Poor Jessamyn, Elisabeth thought. *What nasty weather on a day when she will already be so sad.* The circus had pulled out of town that morning. Elisabeth dimly remembered the train whistle punctuating her dreams. Now she turned her head to see if her twin was awake. Jessamyn was not in her bed.

Elisabeth pushed off the evening-star-pattern quilt she had spent all summer sewing and sat up in bed. Jessamyn had probably been awakened by the circus train whistle also and been too upset to go back to sleep. Elisabeth slid into her slippers and woolly robe. She would try to cheer her twin up.

She looked for Jessamyn on the parlor sofa, and then in the kitchen. She was about to go peek her head out the front door when a leaf of paper on the kitchen table caught her eye. It was covered in Jessamyn's bold hand, the black ink splotchy, as if she had been in a hurry.

Dearest Elisabeth, Mama, and Papa, it read. *Please do not be unhappy. I have joined up with the circus as a bareback rider.*

Elisabeth's cry echoed through the house. The note fluttered to the ground before she had even finished reading it.

"Gone!" Elisabeth's mother wept. Her eyes were red. Her nose was raw. Elisabeth knew she looked the same way.

"There, there, Alice, it was bound to happen sooner or later," Mr. Johnson said. "Children grow to adulthood and move on to their own lives." His voice trembled as he spoke.

"Adulthood?" Alice Johnson shook her head over and over again. "Jessamyn is only sixteen."

"At sixteen, my darling, you made a long ocean voyage all by yourself, did you not?" Mr. Johnson reminded her.

She nodded, but her tears continued to flow faster than her husband could wipe them away. "Perhaps I did," she managed between sobs. "But I had no choice. Jessamyn—well, this is all my fault. I saw her sneaking off each day in her boy's costume. I knew she had a wild streak. Why did I not stop her?"

Elisabeth swallowed back her own tears. "Mama, Jess must be so happy right now. You know, yesterday she told me that this was what she wanted most in the whole world, that joining up with the circus was her most precious dream."

Elisabeth knew the truth of her words. She tried to feel she was sharing Jessamyn's joy. But all she really felt was that she and Jessamyn might never share anything again. Never plait each other's hair in the morning. Never fight over a favorite dress. Never stick up for each other against Bobby Tyrus. Never pick apples together at fall harvest. Never tell each other their biggest secrets in the middle of the night. Her twin, her very own identical twin, the closest person in the world to her, was gone.

I'll miss you, Jessamyn had written. *Especially you, Elisabeth. Take care of Peter Blue Cloud for me. He is a very old man.*

How could Jessamyn have done this? Elisabeth couldn't keep herself from wondering. Worse, how could she have done this to their parents? And Peter Blue Cloud? Just as she had tried to feel joy a moment earlier, now Elisabeth tried to get angry. Anything was better than this hollow ache, as if something inside of her was missing, some part of her that she'd never been without.

She ran her fingers over her twin's note, the writing streaked by tears. Elisabeth just couldn't be angry at Jessamyn for following her dream. But she didn't know how she could bear to live her life without her.

* * *

"I win," Elisabeth said, without much enthusiasm. She laid out her cards, a seven, eight, nine, ten, and jack. The jack, sword in hand, was perched on a horse. Elisabeth hated drawing this card. It reminded her too much of Jessamyn. Her twin had been gone for four long months. The winter seemed to be stretching on endlessly.

"Goodness," her father said. "I don't know what your secret is, but you just can't be beat."

Elisabeth could tell he was trying hard to be cheery. But it felt as if they had repeated this exact same scene night after night, a million and one times in a row. Elisabeth yawned. Maybe Jessamyn was right about Prairie Lakes. Of course, it had never been this boring when she was around.

Somehow, even in the dead of winter, Jessamyn had managed to keep things lively. Right now, if she were still here, they might be out for an icy nighttime snowball fight. It would last until their fingers and toes were frozen. Then they'd stomp into the kitchen and rub their hands and feet until they came back to life. Jessamyn would grimace and make all kinds of noises, as if her feet were frozen ten times worse than Elisabeth's. Over steaming hot cocoa, they'd plan to sneak something really awful into Bobby Tyrus's dinner bucket—a frozen worm, perhaps. They'd talk about the skating party coming up this weekend, and even if they played cards afterward, somehow it would wind up being exciting. Things

59

just turned out that way when Jessamyn was there.

Of course, Tom would be taking Elisabeth to the skating party, but there would be no one to get ready with, no one to style her long blond hair, no one to talk to after it was all over. Whom would she tell about Ingrid Palme's new skating outfit, or how Carl Bergman had skated after two different girls all afternoon, or how Jacob Pauling had gotten too close to a patch of thin ice?

Elisabeth sighed. Her mother put down her own cards and patted her arm. "Yes, dear, we miss her, too. It hurts. I know."

Elisabeth swallowed hard and thought about what old Matthew had said to her earlier that week. He had been looking for her, the beginning reader she'd lent him in his hand, to ask what a word meant. He had found her in the barn burying herself in hay, the way she and Jessamyn used to do when they were little. Elisabeth had been horribly embarrassed. There she was, her dress covered with straw, her hat slipping down over one ear, behaving like a child.

But Matthew understood. "I remember how you and Miss Jessamyn always loved that game when you were babies," he said. He didn't seem to think there was a thing wrong with forgetting to be ladylike for a few moments.

"Did I ever tell you about how it felt the day I got my freedom, Miss Elisabeth?"

Elisabeth had shaken her head.

"It was scary. About the most scary thing that ever happened to me, suddenly not knowing what the next day was going to be like. But then I got to thinking about how it used to be. When I was a slave, my day was either bad or worse. That's it. Always the same. Bad or worse. Then I thought how it didn't have to be that way anymore. I didn't know how the next day was going to be, but I just knew it could be better than bad or worse. You see what I'm saying, Miss Elisabeth? Getting my freedom was like getting a future. For the first time in my life, the next day could be different from the one before it."

Elisabeth had nodded slowly. "I think I understand."

"Well, maybe this is Miss Jessamyn's time of freedom," Matthew had said. "A chance for tomorrow to be different from today. Everybody who wants that chance should have it."

Elisabeth knew Matthew was right. She was sure Jessamyn was happy with her new freedom. And she was grateful for Matthew's kindness and understanding.

Everybody had been so nice to her since Jessamyn had left. Alycia Germond had invited her over to bake butter cookies. Carl and Tad had come calling on the whole family one evening. And of course Tom had been wonderful. He had showered Elisabeth with fall flowers as long as they'd been in bloom, then brought her fiery bright bouquets of autumn leaves. In the winter he had switched to armfuls of freshly cut pine boughs and branches of red-berried holly.

But not even Elisabeth's growing love for Tom could fill the emptiness inside.

"Jessamyn!" Peter Blue Cloud's leathery face creased with joy. "Don't you want to step in where it's warm? Come, this is your home. There is no need for an invitation."

Elisabeth stood outside the door of the one-room cabin. But before she had a chance to say a word, Blue Cloud seemed to sense that in fact she *did* need a formal invitation.

"Ah, but you are Elisabeth."

Elisabeth nodded. "I—I'm sorry to disappoint you."

"No, no, child," Blue Cloud said. "Why would I be disappointed by a visit from Jessamyn's lovely sister? Come in, child, come in."

Timidly, Elisabeth crossed the threshold. She had met Peter Blue Cloud when she was with Jessamyn, but she had never come to his house before. There was almost no furniture but it was cozy, a crackling fire throwing soft, orange shadows on the bare wood walls. On the floor, in front of the hearth, was a large, furry animal-skin rug.

"Would you like to sit?" Blue Cloud asked.

Elisabeth looked around for a chair, but there was none. Peter Blue Cloud seated himself on the skin in front of the fire. Elisabeth hesitated before removing her coat and gloves and lowering herself gingerly onto the floor. She sat stiffly at first, but the skin was warm and soft, and it made Elisabeth feel warm, too. She took a deep breath; the fire smelled deliciously of pine and Minnesota winter.

"It's so comfortable here in front of the fire," she said.

"Yes, Jessamyn loved to sit here on cold nights, too." Blue Cloud smiled. In the fire's glow, Elisabeth noticed his face looked tired.

"Are you—I mean, how are you?" Elisabeth inquired. She didn't add "without Jessamyn." She didn't have to.

"I would like to tell you I am not lonely," Blue Cloud said. "But it would not be true."

Elisabeth sighed. "I'm lonely, too. So lonely. It is as if . . ."

"As if the sun is just a bit farther away this year?" Blue Cloud suggested.

"I hadn't thought of it quite that way," Elisabeth said, "but you are right. Yes, the winter seems so cold—and so terribly long."

"But we must think of Jessamyn and her happiness," Blue Cloud said. "She always wanted to go off and seek adventure, and now she has her chance."

"I know," Elisabeth said. "Still, I can't help but wonder what Jessamyn would be doing if she were here at this very moment."

Blue Cloud laughed softly. "I know the answer to that," he said.

"You do?"

He nodded. "Smoke Signal. She'd be out riding Smoke Signal."

"In the winter? In the snow?"

"Oh, I would have tried to tell her she had to wait until the thaw, but Jessamyn doesn't much like to wait."

Elisabeth thought about all the peaches she'd put up, and all the tomatoes and peas and berries, so that Jessamyn could ride before it got too cold. Well, now it seemed that for Jessamyn it would never get too cold. Her twin had probably never intended to do her share of the chores that winter at all.

Elisabeth burst out laughing. "Well, I should have known! Just wait until the circus rolls into town next year! I'm going to haul her right off that train and put her straight to work in the kitchen!" She told Blue Cloud the whole story.

Blue Cloud's face folded into a thousand creases as he laughed. "Jessamyn knows how to get her way," he said. "That's why I know that if she were here, I'd end up letting her take Smoke Signal for a ride. Even in the snow."

"Do you think I might see Smoke Signal?" Elisabeth asked. "I know Jess would want me to look in on him."

"Yes, of course. I'm sure Smoke Signal will be just as delighted as I am to get a visit from Jessamyn's sister."

* * *

Elisabeth couldn't believe she was doing this. She had been on a horse before, but always with a saddle, and always on a traveled road. And never, never in an open field blanketed with snow.

"Are you ready?" Blue Cloud asked. From astride another horse, he held Smoke Signal by the bridle.

"Yes, I think so," Elisabeth said. In the chilly afternoon, her words came out in puffs of steam. She patted Smoke Signal's charcoal-gray neck.

Blue Cloud gave his horse a gentle nudge, and they set off across the field at a walk. The snow squeaked under the horses' hooves. The field sparkled. Elisabeth rocked gently with Smoke Signal's stride.

Next to her, Blue Cloud tapped his horse again and went into a trot. Elisabeth felt Smoke Signal pick up speed. She swiveled one foot under her and stretched the other leg out to the side for balance, the way Blue Cloud had shown her. Up, down, up, down. She posted with Smoke Signal's movement.

"Excellent!" Blue Cloud called across to her.

Elisabeth saw the snow-dusted trees surrounding the fields begin to dance as she rode. She breathed in the icy, crisp afternoon air and felt her body fall into Smoke Signal's rhythm, as Jessamyn's had done so many times before.

Here she was, the timid twin, riding through a snowy field with Peter Blue Cloud. Bareback. Not long before, Elisabeth would never have believed it. Not long before, Elisabeth would have let Jessamyn be daring enough for both of them. But with Jessamyn so far away, Elisabeth was going to have to try to be a little more adventurous on her own. She knew Smoke Signal's gentle trot wouldn't have been as slow and tame for her twin. But she was proud of herself nonetheless.

Up, down, up, down. Elisabeth felt the caress of cold air on her face, the power of Smoke Signal's hooves lifting through the snow, the pure, crisp quietness of winter. Her happy laughter rode the wind. She wished Jessamyn could see her now.

Eight

"You miss her dreadfully, don't you?" Tom said.

"Does it still show?" Elisabeth asked. She closed her eyes and concentrated on the lulling, rocking motion of the porch swing. A hint of sweet warmth rode the fresh breeze toward spring. It was a perfect afternoon. Except that there would be no one to tell about it when it was over.

"It's just that sometimes you have a faraway expression on your face," Tom said. "I worry that I can't make you happy."

Elisabeth's eyes flew open. "Oh, Tom! Don't say that!" She studied his handsome, strong-boned face, and held him in her gaze. Even after all the time they had spent together over the past eight months, she felt her heart pick up speed. "I don't know what I would have done without you this winter. You cheered me up when I was sad, and made me laugh when I started out crying."

"But it's not enough," Tom said. "Nothing besides Jessamyn's return would be enough."

Elisabeth let out a quiet sigh. "Tom, you have to understand. All our lives it had been Jessamyn and Elisabeth, Elisabeth and Jessamyn. The girls. The twins. Now it's just me. Alone. Elisabeth. It has such a different sound, such a different rhythm. It's as if someone had changed the tune of an old, familiar song, and I don't know how to sing it anymore."

Tom listened attentively, giving the swing a gentle push with his toe.

"Sometimes I think of going and finding her. Telling her she has to come home. Not just for me, but for Mama, too. She's so sad without Jessamyn. Now it's as if she's lost two children. But then I remember how Jess always made up her own rules. I can't tell her what she must or mustn't do."

They sat swinging quietly for a few moments, listening to the songs of the first birds that had returned north after the winter. Then Elisabeth continued. "You know, sometimes I find myself doing things just a teeny bit more the way Jessamyn might have. Maybe to feel she's still somehow around."

Tom nodded. "Like your visits with Blue Cloud?"

"Yes. That and other things," Elisabeth replied.

"Other things." Elisabeth saw Tom's serious expression melting into laughter. "You mean like the time you sabotaged Bobby Tyrus's dinner bucket?"

Elisabeth blushed furiously. "Tom! How did you know that I was the one? I didn't tell a soul!"

68

She hadn't been quite brave enough to go hunting for frozen worms, and even if she had found one, she knew she would never have been able to pick it up. Instead, Elisabeth had settled for a moldy, smelly chunk of cheese. She had slipped it into Bobby's dinner bucket when she thought no one was watching.

"I know because I saw you do it," Tom said. "You might have thought no one was looking that day at school, but you don't realize that there is one boy in that classroom who can't take his eyes off you!"

Elisabeth felt her face coloring. "Oh, Tom!"

"It was a very daring thing to do, Elisabeth." He chuckled.

"Why didn't you say something to me about it?" Elisabeth asked.

"Well, I thought it might have something to do with your sister," Tom said seriously. "A time for you to be with her, even though she wasn't actually there. Does that sound strange?"

"No." Elisabeth shook her head. "In fact, you're quite right." Tom understood her so well. She shifted ever so slightly closer to him. The swing moved in response.

"And that. That's perhaps your sister's influence also," Tom said lightly.

"What do you mean? What is Jessamyn's influence?"

"Perhaps you're a bit, well, bolder than you

69

once were," Tom suggested. "Remember the hayride?"

Elisabeth thought her face must be turning the color of the town's new steam-pump fire engine. "Tom," she said, her voice a whisper of embarrassment, "after the husking bee, I waited and waited. I started to think you might never kiss me again. Finally, well, finally, I . . ."

"Yes, and I'm glad you did," Tom said softly. "I must remember to thank your sister when the circus comes to town."

This time he didn't make Elisabeth wait. All thoughts of Jessamyn were temporarily swept away as Tom's lips met hers.

Elisabeth watched Dr. Good climb out of his buggy and tether his horses to a fence post in front of the Johnsons' house. His face looked grim as he hurried up the walk. It could not be pleasant news. Elisabeth steeled herself as she opened the door to greet him.

"Hello, Dr. Good."

"Miss Elisabeth." The doctor wasted no time getting to the point. "It's Peter Blue Cloud. He is very sick."

Elisabeth felt her chest go tight. It was a sensation she had often had right after Jessamyn had left. "Blue Cloud? Oh, no, Doctor. Is he—what's wrong with him?"

Dr. Good shook his head. "He is very, very old. I could give you one fancy diagnosis or another, but I think the truth is that it is his time to leave us."

Elisabeth knew she shouldn't be surprised, but she felt numb at the news. She stood frozen in the doorway, her mind filled with a picture of the old man who had so recently become her friend. Then she realized with a start that she hadn't even invited the doctor in.

"I'm sorry, Dr. Good. You must think I left my manners in the other room. Why don't you come in? I can make you a cup of fruit tea."

The doctor shook his head again. "No, I must go right back and attend to Blue Cloud. But he has been asking for you. And for your twin sister."

Elisabeth nodded. "I'll be there right away."

"But, Mama, he is dying! Surely Jessamyn would want to see him one last time!" Elisabeth pleaded. "And his greatest wish is to be able to see her."

Her mother pushed away her half-eaten breakfast. "Elisabeth, dear, what will you do? Ride the trains from one destination to another, asking whether the circus has been in town? And not just any circus, but Jessamyn's troupe? If I thought it would be possible to find her, I would have done it myself six months ago."

"I know what direction they were headed in," Elisabeth said stubbornly. She heard her words come out sounding like Jessamyn's. Well, fine. She would need every ounce of her sister's

71

stubbornness to convince her parents. "And news of the circus travels so quickly. Surely it wouldn't be so hard to locate her." Her mother and father thought it would be impossible, but they didn't have a twin's intuition to guide them. Elisabeth felt certain she could find Jessamyn no matter where she was.

"And what about your train fare?" her father asked.

"I'll pay you back, Papa. I promise."

Her mother sighed. "Really, Elisabeth. This whole idea is so crazy, so unlike you."

"Mama, wouldn't you like to have Jessamyn home again?" Elisabeth asked. "Even for a little while?"

She nodded. "Of course I would. More than anything in the world. But I can't permit you to start riding one train after another when you don't even know where you are going. Think how dangerous it might be. And my goodness, having both of you gone . . ." She shuddered.

"Mama, you made a long and dangerous voyage when you were my age, too," Elisabeth reminded her.

"The answer is no," her father butted in. "I will not have my daughter going off like a vagabond. Is that clear?"

Elisabeth's voice came out quiet and tense. "Yes, Papa." But for the first time in her life, Elisabeth was not telling the truth. She hadn't any intention of taking no for an answer. What's more, her father had unwittingly given her an idea.

The gray, flat light of the cloudy new day was just pushing up over the horizon. Elisabeth's heart beat so loudly, she was sure every farmer pulling his horse and wagon up to the station could hear it. Including her father.

Behind a row of scraggly bushes alongside the train tracks, Elisabeth tried to make herself as small as possible. The beat of her heart was accompanied by a word that ran through her head over and over. *Vagabond. Vagabond. Vagabond.* With shaking hands, Elisabeth clutched the bundle that contained a change of clothing, a few precious books to keep her company on her trip, some beef jerky and some fruit and nuts, and the handful of coins that were all her savings in the world, everything wrapped up in her evening-star quilt.

She watched the farmers dragging their milk and cream cans toward the depot. A railroad agent prepared to load them as soon as the train arrived. There was Alycia's father, and there was Tom's. And heavens! There was Tom, helping his father! Elisabeth's pulse, fast enough already, took off like a locomotive that was out of control. Tom! She wanted to call his name, to rush up to him and throw herself into his arms.

Instead, she willed herself to stay put in an undignified squat, her skirts brushing the dirt.

73

Scared and alone, she touched her lips and thought of Tom's kiss out on the porch swing. Not even he knew of her plans. Elisabeth hadn't dared tell a soul.

Tom and his father hauled their final milk can onto the platform. Then they helped her father with his. Elisabeth could hear laughter exchanged as they walked back to their wagons. She could only imagine how different they would feel when they found her note saying she was gone.

Shame heated her cheeks. How could she do this? She began to rise from her hiding place. She could still race across the tracks to her father and confess the whole wild scheme. She felt far too frightened to go through with it, anyhow.

The round, rich whistle of the train filled the air, and Elisabeth stopped still. Behind that sound was another one, the metallic *chug* and *clang* of the train itself, rolling down the tracks toward the station. Elisabeth ducked behind the bushes again, peeking her head up just enough to see the huge black engine, breathing gleaming sparks and charcoal cinders and great clouds of smoke into the air.

The locomotive squealed to a stop. Elisabeth could hear the milk cans being loaded onto it. This was it. It was now or never. The train cut off her view of the station, but she could picture her father—and Tom and his father—getting into their wagons. She imagined her mother waking to find she was gone. Then she thought about

Peter Blue Cloud, his sun-burnished face so lined and motionless against the stark white cover of the straw pillow Dr. Good had slipped under his head. She thought about the faint smile that had formed on Blue Cloud's lips when he'd opened his eyes and seen her. He had mouthed her name, barely strong enough to make a sound. *Elisabeth.* And then he mouthed another name. *Jessamyn.*

Elisabeth thought about the joy her twin's visit would bring him—if she could find Jessamyn in time. She thought about what it would be like to have her sister back in Prairie Lakes, back in the bedroom they had shared all their lives, back as one of a set of two. The twins.

Elisabeth left her hiding place and quickly moved along the length of the train until she found a wooden boxcar with the door partway open. She flung her bundle into the depths of the car. Then she pulled herself up after it.

Nine

Jessamyn peered into the mirror in the tiny compartment of the circus train that was her home. The door was open, and out in the hall she could hear the chatter and laughter of her circus family as they wound down after the night's show.

Jessamyn checked to see if she had removed all her stage makeup. She dabbed at a dark smear under one eye, wiping it away. Suddenly, she saw her reflection split into two. She blinked hard. The second image was still there, just to the side of the first. Two heart-shaped faces with blue-green eyes and silky blond hair that—wait! Jessamyn had tied her hair back with a shiny ribbon. Her double had hers in a bun that stuck out from under a dark green bonnet.

She whirled around. "Elisabeth!"

Elisabeth laughed. "You look like you've seen a ghost."

Jessamyn worked her mouth, but no words came out. For once in her life, she found herself speechless.

"Well, they seem to have everything else in the

circus," Elisabeth said. "Perhaps they might hire me as the bareback rider's phantom."

"Elisabeth, I don't believe it!" Jessamyn finally managed. In her six months with the circus she hadn't regretted her decision for a second. But she couldn't help missing Elisabeth terribly. Time and again she'd imagined being with her. Time and again she'd pictured hugging her sister in happy reunion. She flung her arms around her twin.

"Elisabeth, I've missed you so!"

"Me, too," Elisabeth said. "Jess, it's so wonderful to see you!"

"Same goes double for me," Jessamyn said. "Oh, I can't believe it! What are you doing here? How did you get here?" Her questions rushed out like a blare of circus trumpets. "I thought I was seeing my reflection! You look exactly like me!"

Elisabeth laughed. "Identical twins who look exactly alike? How novel. Now I'm *really* sure the circus will hire me!"

"No, Elisabeth, I'm serious," Jessamyn said. "There's something different about you. Something in your eyes, in your expression . . ." She stepped back and took in the rest of the picture. Elisabeth was wearing a long, prim forest-green dress with a small bustle in the back, one which Jessamyn had seen on her many times before. The bonnet matched the dress, and Elisabeth's hands were covered by a pair of white gloves. But the gloves looked a bit worn, and the dress was

77

somehow not as neat and proper around the edges as it should have been. Then she noticed Elisabeth's quilt bundled under her arm.

"Are you going to tell me how you got here, or not?" she demanded.

"I hopped a boxcar," Elisabeth said simply. "Well, several, to be more precise."

"What?" Jessamyn heard her cry of surprise echo down the passageway of the train. "Elisabeth, you've never fibbed to me before in your life."

"And I'm not fibbing now," Elisabeth said. "In Sioux Falls they told me the circus had moved on to Rapid City, and in Rapid City they said you were here. Oh, I'm awfully glad you are, because I had only enough food for another day or so. And that was only because the first train was a milk train, so I was able to have a snack on board."

Jessamyn stared at her twin as if she'd grown a second head—and not the fake kind that Terrence Two Brain removed after the sideshow was over. "You, Elisabeth Johnson, stole milk from the milk train?"

Elisabeth looked offended. "Stole? No, of course not. I left a few coins by the milk can."

"Oh, Elisabeth, it *is* the real you!" Jessamyn laughed. She gave her twin another big hug. "But I just can't believe you hopped boxcars to find me. Whatever got into you?"

"You know, Jess, I think perhaps you left a few

drops of daring behind in our bedroom, and I found them," Elisabeth said.

Jessamyn studied her twin. There really *was* a new expression in her eyes—one that had made Jessamyn think she was looking at her own reflection. "Wait, don't tell me! You've decided to join the circus, just like I did!"

"Jess, I said a *few* drops of daring. Just enough to get me here. No, I have my schoolwork in Prairie Lakes . . . and Tom."

"You're blushing," Jessamyn teased. "How is Tom?"

"Tom is the most wonderful boy. . . ." Elisabeth's face turned an even deeper shade of red. "And you, Jess? Is there someone special you've met in the circus?"

"Oh, Elisabeth, almost everyone here is special," Jessamyn said. "I mean, not just because they're the fattest or the tallest or because they get shot out of a cannon, either. I've made so many wonderful friends—it's like we're one big, wild family, sometimes."

Elisabeth smiled. "It's good to see you so happy, Jess. But I meant special in the way Tom is special to me, you know?"

"To tell you the truth," said Jessamyn, lowering her voice, "Mario Morelli is awfully handsome and awfully attentive to me. But sometimes I think his brother, Dario, is even more good-looking. And when you watch them doing their flying trapeze act and they're so brave and graceful and

79

skillful, well, it's impossible to choose between the Morelli brothers."

Elisabeth giggled. "Jess, the circus hasn't changed you at all, has it?"

Jessamyn thought seriously about her sister's question. "Well, I'm happier than I've ever been. I mean, I miss you dreadfully, but now you're here," she added quickly. "I'm getting to see all kinds of new places, and I love everyone here, and the best part of everything is that I get to ride every day and do my act for hundreds and hundreds of people. Oh, Elisabeth, I can't wait for you to see me! It's so great that you came to visit."

A shadow flitted across Elisabeth's face. "Well, actually, Jess, it's not really a visit. I mean, it is, because I wanted to see you so badly, and I can't wait to meet all your new friends and watch you perform, but—well, there's another reason I came."

Jessamyn took in Elisabeth's expression and heard the dark note in her sister's words. She felt her stomach drop, as if she were falling from her horse. "Oh, no! What is it? Mama, Papa—"

"They're fine," Elisabeth assured her. "They miss you very much, but it's not either of them. Jessamyn, it's Peter Blue Cloud. He's sick. He's going to die."

"Blue Cloud?" Jessamyn pictured him as she had last seen him: strong and tall despite his age, leading Smoke Signal across the grassy plain. "Blue Cloud." She repeated his name more softly. "But he was supposed to live forever." Her words came out sounding choked, and she felt the sting of tears gathering in the corners of her eyes. Then she felt Elisabeth's arms around her.

"I'm sorry, Jess. I know how important Blue Cloud is to you. He has become my friend, too, now. Maybe it was wrong of me to come at all. You're so happy here, and now I arrive with such sad news. . . ."

Jessamyn looked up at her sister and wiped her tears away with the back of her hand. "No, it wasn't the wrong thing to do, Elisabeth. I can't stop Blue Cloud from coming to his natural end, but I'm glad you told me. Tomorrow, after the show, we move on to Montana. Well, the rest of the circus does. But I'll come home with you." It was hard to add the next part. "I'll come home and say goodbye to Blue Cloud."

"Ladies and gentlemen! The most stupendous show this side of the Mississippi—and the other side, too!" the ringmaster announced.

Elisabeth leaned forward in her ringside seat. She felt as eager as the little children all around her, who were barely able to stay in their seats for all their excitement. The circus band struck up a tune, filling the big tent with music.

Elisabeth caught sight of Geronimo the Clown winding his way through the audience, peering at his ticket stub, checking seat numbers, and looking lost. Then he sat down right in the lap of a finely dressed gentleman, looked straight ahead at the circus ring, and waited for the show to begin as if there were nothing at all out of the ordinary. Suddenly he swiveled around, his nose inches away from the man's nose. He jumped up, his painted face contorted in surprise. Next to Elisabeth, an angel-faced little girl laughed with delight.

Elisabeth laughed, too, just as she had when she'd met Geronimo the night before. He had looked her right in the eyes, then turned to Jessamyn and done the same. Then he looked back at Elisabeth. Then at Jessamyn. He had bowed low to Jessamyn. "Pleased to meet you," he'd said formally. "No, that's not right, is it?" He'd bowed low to Elisabeth. "Pleased to meet you," he'd said again. He had looked quickly from one to the other again, then made a huge show of scratching his head and shrugging his shoulders, as if in a state of confusion.

Geronimo's theatrics were followed by the impressive might and control of the dancing elephants, led by the Greek husband-and-wife team of Taso and Ariadne, whom Elisabeth had also met the night before.

Then came a drumroll, and two young men in sequined costumes bounded into the ring. One was tall, blond, and very handsome, the other shorter and just as good-looking, with a shock of jet-black hair. Their muscles bulged as they grabbed hold of the trapezes that were lowered down to them. Then they rose up, up, up through the air as the trapezes were pulled toward the top of the tent. Mario and Dario, the Morelli brothers, had been thrilled to meet Jessamyn's twin sister, thinking it might be a solution to their biggest rivalry, until Jessamyn told them Elisabeth had a young man back home. Elisabeth was sure Jessamyn rather liked the way they competed over her.

Elisabeth held her breath as Dario and Mario flew through the air, their bodies furling and unfurling, sculpting perfectly controlled shapes in space, diving like dolphins and soaring like birds.

Elisabeth felt the magic of the circus racing through her like a locomotive moving at top speed. It seemed more wondrous, more spectacular than ever before. Maybe it was because she had met the performers, and because they were Jessamyn's friends. Maybe it was because they'd told her so many wonderful circus stories—such as about the time the circus train had derailed and the elephants had pushed the cars back onto the track, or about the days when the Magnificent Theo W. had been with them, and how he could talk to the animals. Maybe it was because Elisabeth was now old enough to appreciate fully the art and skill behind each show. Maybe it was her train ride, all by herself, all the way from Prairie Lakes, that had given Elisabeth a taste for adventure. She felt a thrill of pride that she had gotten up the courage to find her sister. And a tickle of impatience to see Jessamyn ride out into the ring.

A tiny, delicate woman named Marie Pierre was the next act, gliding along the high wire in a satiny white dress. She held a matching white parasol for balance as she danced up near the peaked top of the tent.

As Marie Pierre finished her act, the band went from slow, romantic ballet music into a faster number. Elisabeth's pulse picked up, too. Jessamyn was riding into the ring on a golden horse. Elisabeth slid to the edge of her seat. This was the moment she had been waiting for.

Her twin, dressed in a shimmering pink gown, waved to the audience, her best smile on her face. That smile had always gotten Jessamyn exactly what she wanted. Now was no exception. The audience cheered wildly. Jessamyn drank in the enthusiasm of her fans. She walked her horse around the ring slowly, posting in the half-cross-legged position. Elisabeth clapped so hard she could feel her hands stinging.

The music picked up speed. Jessamyn tapped her horse and picked up speed, too. Gracefully, like a ballerina, she rose to her feet, making even, little jumps as her horse's back rose and fell. Then she jumped higher. And higher. In one swift move, she spun in the air, doing an about-face. She rode backward, standing. She spun forward again. Then she headed her horse for a series of hoops suspended from the tent top. The first one hung just about level with the horse's honey-colored ears. As the horse passed under the hoop, Jessamyn jumped right through it and landed back on her horse. The second ring was higher, the third still higher.

After the last hoop, Jessamyn circled around and headed for the first one again, but not before hopping around in a half-circle so her back was to it. Elisabeth caught her breath. Jessamyn couldn't even see the hoops. How could she possibly—

The crowd roared as she jumped backward through the first one, the next one, and the next. And then, as she and her horse thundered around the ring, Jessamyn executed a perfect front flip. Then a back flip. The audience was on its feet, stamping and applauding. Little children laughed with delight and amazement.

Elisabeth felt a surge of pride. No matter how much she missed her twin, it was clear that Jessamyn was where she belonged.

Ten

"I'll tell you a secret," Jessamyn said. She and Elisabeth stood in the ring, the final bow over, the audience gone. "That last back flip is easier than the front flip I do before it."

"It is?" Elisabeth asked.

"Sure. With the back flip, halfway around you can see the horse's back, where you're going to land. With the front flip you can't. You have to do it all by feel. I do the back flip second because it looks harder, more impressive." She reached into the pocket of her cover-up robe and pulled out a sugar cube. Goldilocks nudged her warm and wet nose into Jessamyn's palm as she licked up the cube.

"And that trick Geronimo did with the tablecloth," Elisabeth said. "When he pulled it out from under that huge stack of dishes, and then he asked the man from the audience to do it, and the dishes went all over the floor, and then he set them up again and asked that girl to do it, and she did. How did that work?"

"Easy. One edge of the tablecloth has a hem; it's not smooth, so it's impossible to pull it out from under the dishes without upsetting them. The other edge is smooth. Makes the trick easy. It all depends on how Geronimo sets up the table-cloth."

Elisabeth laughed. "Even finding out the secrets doesn't make the show any less wonderful. I think I'm starting to understand the spell this place has over you." She stroked Goldilocks's mane. "Could I ride her around the ring? Just to pretend there's a cheering crowd, and to imagine what it must be like for you. Would that be all right?"

Jessamyn saw that expression in her sister's eyes again. "Elisabeth, you surprise me. I thought you didn't even like riding. But if you really want to . . ."

Elisabeth nodded. "I do."

"Well, all right, then," Jessamyn said warily. She helped Elisabeth onto Goldilocks. "Now, just swing one leg under you and keep the other one out for balance. And don't be scared."

Elisabeth made a motion so graceful it caught Jessamyn by surprise. But she was even more astounded when her twin reached down, took the riding crop right out of her hand, and touched Goldilocks's flank lightly.

"Elisabeth, what are you doing?" Alarm rang in Jessamyn's voice.

Goldilocks took off around the ring. Jessamyn expected to see utter panic on her sister's face. Instead, Elisabeth posted easily, raising her hand in a wave. "Can't you see me greeting the crowd?" she giggled. "Don't look so nervous, Jess! I told you I'd been visiting with Blue Cloud since you left."

"I don't believe this!" Jessamyn watched her twin coax Goldilocks into a faster stride. "You got Blue Cloud to teach you to ride!" She had to admit that Elisabeth was a natural. "You always were a fast learner!"

"I *am* your identical twin, Jess!" Elisabeth called back. "Boy, this is fun!"

Jessamyn watched Elisabeth circle the ring on Goldilocks. Once again, she had the curious sensation of seeing her own reflection. "You know, you *could* join the circus. We could be the beautiful bareback twins," she yelled to Elisabeth.

This seemed to encourage Elisabeth to put on even more speed. "I feel like I'm flying!" Elisabeth shouted, her words trailing behind her. Faster she circled. Faster, faster. And then Jessamyn saw her slipping.

"Elisabeth! Slow down!" But Goldilocks's hooves beat the dirt floor of the circus ring at a furious pace. Elisabeth's arm flailed out, groping for something to grab on to. Jessamyn bolted out into the ring.

It must have been her sudden movement. Goldilocks whipped around toward Jessamyn in an abrupt and lethal change of direction. Jessamyn screamed as Elisabeth was flung from the horse's back.

The inescapable end took shape in her mind before it actually happened. Jessamyn watched in terror as her sister was hurled through the air. Elisabeth hit the ground with a dull thud and lay absolutely motionless.

Jessamyn's anguished cries filled the tent as she rushed over and flung herself on top of her twin. "Elisabeth!"

There was no response.

"Elisabeth! Speak to me! Say something! Elisabeth! Get up! Wake up!"

Elisabeth was like a limp, silent rag doll.

"Elisabeth! Please! Stop playing! You can get up now! Elisabeth! I'll never leave your side again. Elisabeth! Elisabeth! Oh, God, please!" Jessamyn's screams gave way to a chilling, mournful wail.

Elisabeth did not move. The life was gone from her body.

"Ashes to ashes, dust to dust."

A fine rain misted Jessamyn's face and mingled with her tears. She was sure her tears would never stop, sure they flowed from a bottomless well of grief. She was so wet, so cold. No summer sun would ever warm her enough again, no joy would ever fill the chilling emptiness she felt.

Her mother and father looked so old, so frail and bent under their load of sorrow. They stood at the head of the fresh grave as the minister intoned words that gave Jessamyn such little comfort. Next to them was another, smaller grave, long covered over with earth and grass, and marked with a tiny, child-sized headstone.

"She's gone to be with Steven," her mother sobbed quietly. "They'll take care of each other now."

Across the raw hole in the earth where Elisabeth's coffin lay, Tom Wilkens stood hollow-eyed and drawn. He looked like he hadn't slept since he'd gotten the news. His parents bolstered him, one on either side, as if on his own he might slump to the dirt.

"Rest in peace, amen," the minister said.

"Amen," echoed Jessamyn.

The minister took several steps back from the grave. Tom's parents turned and led him away. Was this all, Jessamyn wondered? Was this the end? She was numb, looking down at the wooden box sunk into the deep, dark rip in the ground.

Soon this grave, too, would be covered over with earth and grass and the pink lady's-slippers that pushed up from the damp soil. Blue Cloud had called these flowers "the spirits of people I knew and loved." Now he, too, lay beneath the ground. He had died before Jessamyn returned— on that same chilling day that Elisabeth died, as if all the light and happiness had been extinguished from Jessamyn's life in one dark moment.

Jessamyn stooped down and picked one of the lady's-slippers. Pretending for a brief moment that it was Elisabeth's spirit, she brought the flower to her lips, feeling the silky petals moist with rain and tears. Then she flung it into Elisabeth's grave and bid her twin the most final of goodbyes.

Eleven

1900. San Francisco, California.

"Five! Four! Three! Two! One! Happy new year! Happy new century!" Jessamyn shouted out.

Tin horns blared, corks popped, glasses chimed as toasts were made. The ballroom of the hotel Jessamyn had been managing for several years now was filled with elegant ladies and gentlemen, the women's sweeping gowns trimmed with lace and ribbons and beads, their perfume scenting the air. Confetti rained down—the first shower of the twentieth century.

A tall blond man in a smart bow tie and a long, well-tailored frock coat, a flower in his buttonhole, held his glass up to Jessamyn. "Wonderful party," he said.

"Thank you." Jessamyn tried to remember the man's name. Hudson, or Hodgson. Something like that. A young railroad baron here on business. Staying in suite 203.

"Beautiful hostess," he added. "Might I have the first dance of the nineteen-hundreds with her?" He offered Jessamyn his arm.

She took it, her fingers light on his sleeve, noting the glint of candlelight on what looked to be diamond-studded cuff links. "My pleasure. Mr. Hudson, is it?" Jessamyn asked.

"Hodgeson," the man responded. He whirled Jessamyn around the polished oak dance floor.

Jessamyn fell into the rhythm of his step, following the music of the orchestra she had hired for the party. Mr. Hodgeson was a good dancer. He was handsome. He was obviously fabulously wealthy. But when the orchestra went into a slower song and he moved to hold her closer, Jessamyn thanked him for the dance and excused herself. She threaded her way around the happy couples dancing, the party guests noisily cheering and toasting, and let herself out onto the balcony of the hotel.

It wasn't Mr. Hodgeson who was the problem. Or Mr. Rhodes, or Mr. Gladstone, or any of the other gentlemen who came to the hotel for a night's lodging and left with a broken heart. Oh, sometimes Jessamyn would let them court her, take her to the theater and the best restaurants, buy her flowers, walk with her by the ocean. Sometimes it was lots of fun.

But it was never love. Not for Jessamyn. She leaned over the balcony, breathing in the mild, never-ending spring of San Francisco. The streets were noisy with revelers, the horses and carriages all caught in a hopeless snarl of traffic. It was like one huge party down there. But Jessamyn felt distanced from it all. She wondered if she could ever feel passion for anything again, if she could ever feel love. She often thought those emotions had died with Elisabeth.

She closed her eyes and allowed herself to imagine, just for a moment, that her twin was with her, celebrating the dawn of a new century, spinning on the dance floor, throwing confetti, watching the throng in the street with the amazement of a farm girl.

Jessamyn's eyes flew open. No. The picture wasn't right. The girl dancing and celebrating with her was sixteen years old, just as she always would be in Jessamyn's mind. Jessamyn was twenty-two. It had been almost six years. Six long years. Yet sometimes the pain was as fresh as if it were six days.

At first, Jessamyn had thought that city life would be the medicine she needed for her pain. Going back to the circus was out of the question. Oh, she still thought it was the most wonderful place in the world, but Jessamyn couldn't imagine getting back on a horse in that ring. Not after what had happened to Elisabeth.

So she packed her bags and followed her dreams of tall buildings and boulevards that never slept, of cafés filled with sophisticated people, of adventures calling just outside every window. She hadn't been disappointed. But the emptiness inside her had never entirely gone away.

Up in her room, in her night table drawer, Jessamyn kept a carved wooden rose that her mother had given her after Elisabeth had died. It had been made for her by a special friend she had met on her journey to America. She had never seen him again after she'd gotten off the ship, but she had told Jessamyn she would always have her beautiful memories—memories that would never die, just as the petals on the wooden flower would never wither. She wanted Jessamyn to have the flower now, to keep her memories of her sister alive.

Jessamyn sighed. She was happy to keep the flower. But she didn't agree with her mother. What good was a flower with no scent, one whose petals weren't soft and dewy with life?

Down below her, the crowd swelled and the buzz of excitement rose to an even more feverish pitch, distracting Jessamyn from her sad thoughts. Horses reared skittishly at the far end of the street. Then it rolled into view—an automobile! There were quite a number of automobiles in the streets of San Francisco these days, but Jessamyn still couldn't get over the sight of that carriage with nothing in front to pull it, moving as if by magic.

The automobile rumbled down the crowded street. People parted and carriages steered to the side to let it through. Looking down at the strange, open-top vehicle, Jessamyn could see that the man driving it sported an elegant suit and a shiny top hat. He steered it toward the hotel, the engine coughing and sputtering importantly. As he neared the balcony, the driver looked up. His deep-set eyes met Jessamyn's. He tipped his top hat, uncovering a head of wavy dark hair, and called out to her, "Happy new year, pretty twentieth-century woman!"

It seemed every face in the crowded street turned to see who he was calling to. "Happy new year!" someone else yelled to her.

"Happy 1900!"

"Happy twentieth century!"

Suddenly, Jessamyn felt like a modern Juliet, with dozens and dozens of modern Romeos beneath her balcony. "Happy new year," she called back. She waved at the man in the automobile. "Happy new century!"

The automobile driver held Jessamyn in his gaze for a beat longer. Jessamyn felt a little thrill go through her. Then he tooted his horn and continued down the street. The crowd followed him. Jessamyn was alone again. Alone. As she had been ever since Elisabeth had died.

Twelve

"Don't say no right away. Please, my darling. Think about it while I'm gone."

Jessamyn tilted the velvet-lined jewelry box from side to side. The large, perfect diamond in the ring glinted more brightly than the light from the new electric lamps recently installed in the hotel. "I will, Taylor. I'll think about it," she promised.

"I'll make you so happy. We'll have such a good life," he said. "I'll give you everything you could possibly want."

"I know you will, Taylor," Jessamyn said. She was awfully fond of Taylor Watson. When he was home in Michigan, running the Watson Motor Company, she missed him. She daydreamed of his deep-set green eyes, his wavy dark hair, his strong-boned, oval face, his gentle smile. When he visited her in San Francisco, she spent happy days strolling down Market Street with him, going to the new and wonderful moving pictures, or rumbling down the boulevards in Watson Motors' latest automobile. Perhaps Jessamyn even loved Taylor Watson. But she wasn't sure.

Back in her circus days, she had always imagined love as something that would make her pulse race, that would make her head dizzy, that would take her breath away—something that felt like getting on a horse for the first time, or like riding into the circus ring and hearing the thundering applause of the audience. With Taylor, love felt more like a hearty Sunday dinner back in Minnesota, or hearing someone sing her favorite song—a solid pleasure she could count on, but nothing to set her head spinning.

Taylor had once said he thought Jessamyn was afraid to love after what had happened to her twin, afraid of losing someone else she cared about.

"Me? Afraid?" Jessamyn had scoffed. "I'm not the type to be afraid." But sometimes, secretly, she wondered if Taylor was right.

Now he leaned closer. Jessamyn could smell the clean scent of shaving soap on his skin. "Won't you put it on your finger, Jessamyn? Just so we can see how it looks? You don't have to make a decision right now, but it would make me happy if you would wear the ring while you think about it."

"Oh, Taylor, of course I will." Jessamyn let Taylor take the ring out of its box and slip it on her finger. The diamond shone like an icy rainbow. "It's beautiful," she said.

"*You're* beautiful," Taylor breathed. "I thought so the first time I saw you, standing on the balcony welcoming in the century. You know, Jessamyn, it was fate. Fate that I drove down your street and you were the first person I tipped my hat to in the new century, fate that brought me to stay at the hotel that next year. It is fate's wish that we share the century we began together."

Jessamyn studied the ring on her finger and said nothing. Fate was something that hit a person over the head, something beyond anyone's power to control, wasn't it? Or was that just some romantic idea she had never outgrown? Was fate really as simple as a yes or a no? Yes, and she packed up her life in San Francisco and made her home with Taylor in Michigan. No, and—what?

"Jessamyn, do you really want to spend your years ministering to the needs of travelers who come and go and leave no real trace in your life?" Taylor whispered, as if answering her wordless question with a question of his own.

Jessamyn shook her head. She touched the shimmering stone in her ring. "I just need time," she said.

Taylor kissed her softly, and Jessamyn felt a tingle of warmth. "You'll have time," Taylor said. His serious tone melted into a chuckle. "I'm betting that Bruce Farber will turn out to be one of the fastest auto racers in the world, but it will take even him some time to get us to the East Coast and back."

"I'll miss you," Jessamyn said. "I'll be reading

the newspapers carefully every day to follow your progress."

"Well, I hope there will be lots of articles about us," Taylor said. "The more publicity for the Watson Motor Company, the better. That's the whole idea. I hate to be away from you for so long, but when this race is finished I expect Watson Motors to be a household name, even bigger than Ford. Of course, you may be reading about how we had to get pulled out of a ditch by a team of horses, or how many tires we had to change." He laughed and waved a hand. "But if anyone can win us this race, it's Bruce. The man was the most daring, best bicycle racer before he met me, and now he's going to be the most daring, best race car driver."

"Well, when you win we'll have a big celebration here at the hotel," Jessamyn said.

She watched Taylor's face grow serious again. "And perhaps we'll have something else to celebrate as well." He took her hand and covered it with his.

Jessamyn felt the gentle strength of his touch, read the tenderness and caring in his eyes. She would have a good life with Taylor if she married him. She knew he would love her forever. What was it that was stopping her from accepting his proposal right away? Was it foolish to hold out for a tidal wave of passion that might not exist for her? What would Elisabeth have said if she had known Taylor? Probably that he was caring, kind, and intelligent—and handsome. And that Jessamyn should have said yes to him long before.

Down in the street, a horn sounded.

"That must be Bruce," Taylor said, not taking his hand from Jessamyn's. "Just think about it. Think about me, Jessamyn. Me and you. Think about us."

"I will, Taylor. Come on, I'll see you down."

"Yes, do," Taylor said, letting go of her hand. "I'd like you to meet Bruce."

Jessamyn followed Taylor down the hotel staircase, the diamond heavy on her finger. She knew how happy it would make him to have her "yes" to keep him company on his trip. But she couldn't say it. She had never even told Taylor she loved him. She stepped out into the gray San Francisco afternoon. Not yet. Maybe when the race was over . . .

"Jessamyn, I'd like you to meet my best racer, Mr. Bruce Farber. Bruce, my best lady, Miss Jessamyn Johnson."

Jessamyn felt her breath catch. The man who hopped out of the Model E Watson was one of the most handsome men she had ever seen. His blue eyes twinkled as if he knew some juicy secret, his dark mustache rode the most charming smile, and beneath his suit she could make out his athletic frame. But there was more to him than just good looks. There was a sureness to the way he held himself, a smoothness to the sweep of his arm as he dipped his derby hat toward her.

"Ah, Miss Johnson." He held her gaze as he spoke her name. "Taylor has told me so much about you. And you are every bit as lovely as he says."

Jessamyn was sure she was blushing—and she didn't blush easily. "Thank you, Mr. Farber. Taylor has spoken highly of you, too. He says you were the best racer on a bicycle."

"The fastest man on two wheels," Bruce said with a boyish grin. "Soon to be the fastest man on four wheels."

Jessamyn knew someone else might be put off by Bruce's lack of modesty. But it only made her heart beat faster. She was used to those words from her circus days—*fastest, best, most daring, most wonderful.* And when she had watched Mario and Dario soar through the air, or Marie Pierre dance on a high wire, she knew the words were nothing less than the truth.

Bruce took Jessamyn's hand and kissed the back of it. She felt a shiver of excitement that started right where Bruce's lips touched her and raced through her arm up into her whole body. "I'm so glad to know you," Bruce said. His eyes never left Jessamyn's.

"Glad to know you, too," Jessamyn echoed.

"Well, I guess we'd better be off," Taylor said.

Jessamyn turned toward the sound of his voice, reminded with a jolt of surprise that he was by her side. Was his gentle voice just a little louder than usual? He put his arms around her. She let him pull her toward him.

"Goodbye, my darling," he said. In a whisper he added, "Think about us."

"I will," Jessamyn said. She felt good in Taylor's arms. But over his shoulder, she was watching Bruce position himself in front of the automobile as he cranked it to life.

Taylor kissed Jessamyn softly and sweetly. "I'll miss you, Jessamyn."

"I'll miss you, too." As she whispered in Taylor's ear her eyes followed Bruce getting into the driver's seat.

Taylor released her and got into the automobile next to Bruce. "Root for us, my dear!" he said. "Goodbye!"

"Goodbye!" Jessamyn said. She looked from Taylor to Bruce, from Bruce to Taylor. "Goodbye and good luck!"

"Goodbye, Miss Johnson," Bruce said. There was something in the way he said it—the easy way her name rolled off his tongue, the jaunty wave that went with it. To Jessamyn, it felt as if Bruce Farber was really saying hello.

Thirteen

1906. San Francisco.

"You have to make up your mind," Bruce said. "Taylor or me, Jessamyn. You've got to choose one of us."

"And your lady friend back in Michigan?" Jessamyn asked pointedly.

"Well, you can't expect me to say goodbye to her when you still wear Taylor Watson's ring," Bruce said.

Jessamyn sighed and gazed at the twinkling nighttime lights of San Francisco spread out below them. Now that electric lights had come into so many homes and establishments, it was like looking down at an earthbound sky filled with stars. If only she could find the brightest one—the brightest light in all of San Francisco—and wish on it the way one could wish on the North Star. She would wish for someone as exciting and daring as Bruce and as loving and caring as Taylor, all wrapped up in one handsome package.

Bruce lay back on the blanket they had spread out for their supper picnic. "You know I'm the one you want," he said huskily. "Why don't you take off that ring and admit it?"

Jessamyn touched her finger to the diamond's hard, shiny surface. "Taylor loves me so much," she said. She didn't add, *and he doesn't break dates or go for long drives with other women.* She didn't add, *Taylor Watson is one hundred percent there for me. I never doubt his love.* But she knew that sometimes the strength of Taylor's love frightened her. She hadn't felt any emotion that strong since Elisabeth had died. But Bruce had other ideas about why she didn't marry Taylor.

"Taylor is a fool," he said. "He has been waiting for you year after year. Men like him spend their whole lives waiting."

Jessamyn put the remains of their dinner back in the wicker picnic basket. "Bruce, how can you be so cold about Taylor? You've spent weeks at a time driving with him; together you've basked in the glory when you win a race; he's made you a name people know from coast to coast."

"You mean I've made *him* a name known coast to coast," Bruce said. "Jessamyn, that may all be true, but it doesn't change the fact that I want you and I'm not going to let Taylor have you."

Jessamyn stretched out on one elbow, smoothing her bodice over her corset. It was uncomfortable and she wished she had tied it less tightly. "Bruce, what if I said I would give Taylor's ring back if you told your other lady friend goodbye for good?" she asked. "Or should I say lady *friends*?"

"What if you give the ring back first?" Bruce

said. "Then I'm yours." He pulled Jessamyn close to him. "Say it. Say you'll tell Taylor it's over between you."

Jessamyn felt the thrill of Bruce's strong arms around her. "Oh, Bruce, I want to, but—"

"But what?" Bruce let go of Jessamyn immediately.

"But—well, Taylor would never love anyone besides me," Jessamyn said. "He's the proper choice."

"Proper? For whom?" Bruce asked. "For someone who plays one man off another?"

Jessamyn could hear the anger creeping into his words. She put her arms around him and tried to snuggle back into his embrace. But Bruce wasn't giving in. "Proper for whom?" he repeated.

"Elisabeth," Jessamyn heard herself saying. It just slipped out. "Proper for Elisabeth." She let out a long, sad sigh. "Sometimes I miss her so much. . . ."

Bruce softened. "Oh, Jess," he whispered, pulling her close. "I know. I know you do. But honey, you can't bring her back. Marrying Taylor won't do it." He kissed her eyelid. Then her cheek. Then his lips met hers.

Jessamyn felt herself falling into the power of his nearness. Her body tingled. She was heady and dizzy. "Jessamyn, be with me," Bruce whispered in her ear. "You know we belong together."

"Oh, Bruce," she murmured, drinking in one kiss after another. Bruce was right. She *did* want him. Jessamyn abandoned herself to his spell.

It was thundering in the ground under her head. Jessamyn sat up in terror, blinking the sleep out of her eyes. She and Bruce must have fallen asleep up on the hill, but what the devil was going on? The land was rolling like waves on the ocean, and trees were moving up and down with the ground swells. The earth under their blanket trembled like a bowl of pudding. Below the hill they sat on, the lights of the city blurred like fireflies shaken in a jar, then began to go out.

Next to Jessamyn, Bruce sat bolt upright, suddenly awake, suddenly alert. "Jess!" he breathed, his voice filled with horror. He extended a finger at the ground a few feet away. By the pale moonlight, Jessamyn watched as the earth split open in a crack that was wide enough to swallow her whole body.

Then, as she stared in frozen terror, it closed back up. The underground thunder stopped. The ground was still. The trees were still. Somewhere, a dog let out a frightened howl. Only then did Bruce pronounce the word that was in Jessamyn's head.

"Earthquake," he said.

"My God!" Jessamyn was still trembling all over. She tried to breathe deeply. *You're alive,* she told herself over and over. *You're fine.* But her panic surged up even more strongly as she looked back down toward the city. Fountains of fire had erupted in many places, and crimson and orange and blue flames lapped up whole blocks of buildings. Thick clouds of black smoke rose from the destruction.

"All of San Francisco's on fire!" Jessamyn screamed. Along with her, a wail seemed to rise from the city itself—the clanging of bells, the crackle of fires, the collective screams of the people below, crying out at nature's cruelty.

Jessamyn searched the nightmare valley for her own neighborhood. No flames consumed the buildings there. But not far away, geysers of fire and sparks were spraying out in the direction of the hotel. Jessamyn jumped to her feet, her legs weak with terror.

"Jessamyn, where are you going?" Bruce asked.

Jessamyn pointed toward the city. The blaze near the hotel grew even as they spoke.

"But you can't," Bruce said. "Don't you know the safest place is up here? Outside, where no buildings can collapse on us and no fire will reach us?"

"But Bruce, the hotel! I have to see what's happened! What if any of the guests are hurt?" Jessamyn's fear pounded in her chest.

"Are you mad?" Bruce said. "You're alive. Don't you want to stay that way? Can't you see what's going on down in that city?" He caught hold of the hem of Jessamyn's skirt, trying to anchor her to the spot. "Jessamyn, I don't see you as the type to play Florence Nightingale. Be happy you're all right."

"But, Bruce, people could be dying down there. We have to help." A picture of Elisabeth lying motionless in the circus ring formed in Jessamyn's mind. Suddenly, the motionless figure in her head took on a different face. "Taylor! Bruce, what if something has happened to Taylor?"

"Jessamyn, I thought you were finished with Taylor," Bruce said. "I thought we'd decided that tonight."

"Oh, Bruce, I am, but still . . . can you really stay right here, not knowing how he is?"

Bruce didn't move a muscle. His silence was Jessamyn's answer.

"But what if he's trapped? What if he's injured?" Her heart felt tight with fear. She could barely breathe.

"Jessamyn, Taylor Watson is my rival."

Jessamyn looked out at the burning city. "Bruce, please," she begged. "You must drive me back down there." She kneeled down and threw her arms around him. "If not for Taylor, for me. Show me that you love me. Then, I promise, I'll be yours forever."

"Forever? Your one and only man?"

"The only one," Jessamyn said.

Bruce got to his feet. "All right, then. For you."

He helped Jessamyn into the Model E, and they began their descent into the inferno below.

One side wall of the hotel had been ripped right off the building by the quake. In the early morning light, Jessamyn could see inside the hotel rooms, as if she were looking into some life-size, nightmare doll house. The familiar furniture had been tossed all over the place, some of it lying smashed in a heap on the ground outside. The painting over the mantelpiece in the hotel sitting room hung at a sharp tilt.

Around Jessamyn, the streets were a theater of confusion and despair. Two men, their hands raw and bloody, clawed at the rubble of a collapsed house across from the hotel, trying to free a young woman whom Jessamyn had often seen in the neighborhood. A family stood dazed and hollow-eyed in the middle of the street. A man and a woman pushed a cart loaded with everything they owned. A boy roamed up and down calling for his mother.

Jessamyn recognized some of the hotel guests standing in front of the building, their faces numb with shock. The thin, pale-faced newspaper man from New York who had checked in a few days before came rushing over to her and Bruce. "Someone is still inside the building!" he said. There was a bloody gash across his forehead.

Jessamyn felt sick with fear. She imagined Taylor trapped like the woman across the street. Jessamyn looked behind her to see the woman being lifted out of the rubble of her home. Her eyes were closed and her body was limp. What if Taylor was hurt like that, too?

"It's the old woman up on the second floor," the newspaper man said. "The one who was visiting her granddaughter."

"Mrs. Burnham." Jessamyn felt a twinge of relief. It was quickly followed by a stab of guilt. "Mrs. Burnham. Poor thing. Why, her room is right—" Jessamyn finished her sentence by pointing her finger at one of the exposed rooms. A chest of drawers had slid across the floor, and the brass four-poster bed was turned on its side and wedged into one of the remaining corners. Jessamyn looked closely and saw one stockinged leg sticking out from behind the bed.

"She's pinned back there, against the wall," the newspaper man explained. "Earlier she was calling out, but her voice grew weaker. . . ."

Jessamyn turned to Bruce. "You've got to do something."

"Me? Jessamyn, that whole building could come down at any moment. You can't expect anyone to go in there."

"You mean you'd just leave Mrs. Burnham there? Frightened, hurt, maybe dying? Bruce, you've got to help her. You're not a coward, are you?"

Bruce gave a start, as if the word were a slap in the face. He looked toward the sheared-open

111

building, then back at Jessamyn. He squared his shoulders, marched toward the hotel entrance, and disappeared inside.

Jessamyn held her breath and fixed her eye on the bed that held the poor old woman captive. To the right of the bed was the door Bruce would be coming through at any moment.

"Jessamyn! Oh, Jess, thank heavens!" All of a sudden, Taylor came up from behind her and wrapped her in a hug. "Where have you been? I've been looking everywhere for you! I was so frightened. . . . Oh, but we have to hurry! Everyone in this area has to hurry. The fire is spreading this way!" He gestured frantically at the purple-blue flames blazing over the tops of the buildings several blocks away. "We have to move!"

Jessamyn circled her arms around Taylor and gave him a hard squeeze, as if to convince herself of his solid presence, of the fact that he was very much alive. She took immediate comfort in his loving arms, but full relief was impossible. "Taylor, we can't go!" Jessamyn said, her words toppling out in a frenzy. "Bruce—he's gone into the hotel to rescue Mrs. Burnham."

Taylor let his arms drop to his sides. Sadly, softly, he said, "Ah, you were with Bruce." But he didn't waste another second. "He may need my help." Jessamyn pointed out Mrs. Burnham's room, and without a moment's hesitation, Taylor rushed into the devastated hotel.

Upstairs, Bruce burst through Mrs. Burnham's door. Jessamyn saw him talking to Mrs. Burnham behind the upturned bed. He pulled on one of the bedposts with all his might. The bed didn't budge.

"Bruce!" Jessamyn yelled.

Bruce looked down toward where she stood in the street. "Mrs. Burnham says she's all right," he yelled back, "but part of the bed has fallen into a crack in the floor. I can't move it—"

The end of his sentence was swallowed by a roaring gust of hot wind, billowing with clouds of dark smoke. The fire! Jessamyn could see it engulfing building after building—and it was headed right toward them!

When she looked back toward Bruce, Taylor had entered the room. The two men struggled with the overturned bed. But the flames grew nearer and nearer to the hotel. At last they reached it and began licking the side of the building.

"Hurry!" Jessamyn yelled. "Please! Hurry!" She watched Bruce and Taylor straining against the bedframe. The flames lapped upward. The fire was climbing toward them.

The two men pulled with all their might. Suddenly, the bed gave way. They pulled it into the center of the room. Near the wall, Jessamyn could see Mrs. Burnham lying next to the huge crack in the floor where the bed had been wedged.

As Taylor and Bruce rushed back to help the old woman, Jessamyn watched the fire spreading to a wooden beam over their heads. It raced along the ceiling like a flaming chariot. "Quick!" she cried. "Oh, hurry!"

Bruce helped Mrs. Burnham to her feet. Her step looked shaky, but he supported her with a firm arm as he led her toward the door. Taylor followed, a few steps behind them. Suddenly, Jessamyn saw a huge chunk of the burning ceiling beam break off and plummet to the floor directly in front of him. Her own terrified scream rang in her ears. Taylor was trapped behind the flaming wood!

Bruce looked toward the barrier of flame. "Go!" Jessamyn could hear Taylor yelling to him, his voice fighting the roar of the fire. "Save yourselves! And Jessamyn—take her to a safe place!"

"Taylor, no! Taylor!" Jessamyn screamed. "Bruce, help him!" But as she watched in horror Bruce disappeared out the door, leaving Taylor in his fiery prison.

And then, her terror raging like the flames, Jessamyn heard the underground thunder again. Around her, the cobblestones began dancing like popping corn. The ground rolled toward her like a wave. Again! A second quake! No! It couldn't be! But Jessamyn felt herself being lifted on the swell of earth, then dropped so that she fell in a heap. The ground shook under her body, then after a moment grew still. Jessamyn's heart pounded out of control. She was afraid to lift her head.

"Jess."

No. She didn't hear that. Impossible. She didn't hear Taylor saying her name. He was a prisoner in that fiery room. But when she looked up, he was coming toward her, his face blackened with soot. "Good heavens, how?" she whispered.

"The second quake widened the crack in the floor that the bed had been stuck in. I was able to drop down to the room below and walk right out where the side wall used to be," Taylor said. He glanced around. The whole neighborhood was going up in flames. "Mrs. Burnham and Bruce— where are they?"

Through a haze of smoke, Jessamyn saw the door of the hotel open. Mrs. Burnham emerged, her wrinkled face shriveled even further with terror. Jessamyn got to her feet. She and Taylor raced over to the old woman.

"That young man," Mrs. Burnham said. Her voice was a wavering whisper of fear. "Part of the ceiling fell in during the second tremor. He's trapped. Just like I was."

"The whole building is going up in flames!" Taylor said. "I've got to get Bruce out now!"

"You're going back in there?" Jessamyn cried. But her words were lost on Taylor. He was already running toward the plumes of fire, the cracking walls and falling timber.

It was like seeing Elisabeth hurled through the air all over again. Time stood still. Jessamyn was frozen in a moment of helpless, horrified waiting that felt like an eternity. But this moment was filled with Taylor, not Elisabeth.

And then the moment was broken. Taylor was coming out of the burning building with Bruce right behind him. Jessamyn raced toward them. The air was thick with smoke. But there was one thing that was suddenly crystal clear.

Jessamyn threw herself into Taylor's arms. "He left you to die, and you saved him," she said. She felt as if she never wanted to let Taylor go.

But he eased himself from her arms and moved away from her. "I would do the same for anyone who needed help," Taylor said. "But especially for the man you love." His quiet words almost disappeared in the roar of the flames.

Bruce took a step toward Jessamyn's side. "Jess," he said, reaching a hand to her.

Jessamyn studied Bruce's handsome face, streaked with ashes and sweat. Was this the man she loved, the man who once had made her pulse race with his bravery and daring? He was nothing more than a coward. Taylor was the man who had risked his life. Taylor was the one who knew what it meant to care. Bruce cared for no one except himself. She realized that now, and saw all the broken plans, Bruce's other lady friends, and the unthinkingly cold way Bruce had treated Taylor in a new light. Bruce Farber believed in taking whatever he could get from people—and giving nothing back. He didn't know what love was.

Taylor had turned his back on both of them. He was walking away. Jessamyn called his name.

He stopped and turned around slowly. "Jessamyn, I know you love Bruce, and I want you to be happy," he said.

"Taylor, please! Listen to me! It was you I was thinking about when you were inside that burning building."

Taylor began walking again.

"Jess!" Bruce called to her. "Jess, remember how it was up on the hill!"

She did. She thought about lying in Bruce's arms, and wondered how she could ever have let herself been fooled. She caught up with Taylor and grabbed his singed sleeve. "Taylor, it's you I want to be with. You." Her cheeks were wet with tears. "Taylor, don't leave me. You said it was fate. Remember? You drove by this very spot, right here, and tipped your hat to me. . . . Taylor, I love you."

Taylor stopped. "Tell me again," he said softly.

Jessamyn looked into Taylor's deep green eyes. "I love you, Taylor Watson, I love you." In all the years since he had tipped his hat to her, this was the first time she'd said those words. "I love you. I love you. I love you. I want to become Mrs. Watson."

Her words were silenced by Taylor's long, sweet kiss. In the ruin and misery of the burning, devastated city, Jessamyn gave in to the purest happiness she had known since before Elisabeth's death. Out of the ashes of sorrow, she could feel the flames of love burning.

Fourteen

1908. Detroit, Michigan.

It was like being in a circus parade again. The Watsons' automobile rolled down their normally quiet street outside Detroit, and the neighbors raced outside to greet them.

"They're home!" yelled Mrs. Donovan, the gossip of the neighborhood. "All of them in one automobile! Frank," she called to her husband, "come see!"

Jessamyn laughed. "Taylor, you and Harry wave to Mrs. Donovan for me. The twins are about all I can manage right now." She snuggled her new babies to her, her heart filled with pride and joy. Amanda sucked contentedly on Jessamyn's pinky while Samantha flailed her tiny arms and legs about, adding to the commotion. Baby comforters and fragrant, colorful bouquets of flowers decorated the auto like a parade float.

"Harry, can you wave like Daddy at Mr. and Mrs. Donovan?" Taylor asked, making an exaggerated motion over his head. "See? This is how we wave." He repeated the gesture and the word until one-year-old Harry gurgled happily and imitated his father.

"Very good, Harry!" Jessamyn encouraged her son.

Taylor honked the horn, and Harry's puppy, Gidget, accompanied him with her barking. They stopped the car in front of the Donovans' house, and Mr. and Mrs. Donovan peeked their heads into the auto, cooing at the twins and patting Harry on the head.

Across the street, little Jaimie Franklin came running out of his house to look, too. Jessamyn let him touch Amanda and Samantha's tiny fingers.

"They look exactly the same," Jaimie observed.

Jessamyn smiled. "Yes, isn't it wonderful?" It seemed to be wild odds, a twin having twins, but perhaps she was the luckiest person in the whole world. She hugged her babies to her, feeling them warm in her arms. It was as if somehow the entwined spirits of her and Elisabeth were back in her beautiful twin daughters.

Fifteen

1920. Detroit.

"Amanda, let's play the motion picture game," twelve-year-old Samantha said.

Amanda looked up from her book. "Again, Samantha? Do we have to play it every day?"

Samantha struck a pose she'd been trying out in the mirror all morning. Amanda recognized it from her twin's favorite photo of Theda Bara, one of the brightest stars of the screen. "We have to practice so we can grow up to be in motion pictures," Samantha said.

"You mean so *you* can be in them," Amanda corrected her. "You're the one chopping off your hair and pinching Mother's makeup and dreaming about how you're going to get discovered." Amanda put her hand to her own long flax-colored braid, as if to protect it. Ever since Sam had cut her hair, she'd been after Amanda to do the same.

For most of their lives, the twins had worn their hair long. They'd been a matched set from their hair to their blue-green eyes to their perfect heart-shaped faces. It had been impossible for people to tell them apart, until they got to know them better. Then they would see how different the girls' personalities were. But now, with Samantha's new bob, the twins were no longer identical.

"It's really no fun if people can tell the difference between us," Samantha said. "Besides, if you want to look like a vamp, like Theda Bara, you've got to cut it." Samantha sure had a one-track mind. Now Amanda watched her assume one of Theda Bara's sultry, vampy poses.

"You know, Sam," she said, "motion pictures and motion picture stars are just fine, but I still like plays better. When you go to a play, you can actually hear what the actors are saying. And that's important, don't you think?"

Samantha gave an exasperated sigh. "Well, they print the words on the screen when they need to," she said. "But I really don't want to have this conversation for the hundred and thirty-seventh time. Are you going to play star of the screen with me or not?"

"Oh, all right," Amanda said. She put her book down. "On one condition: we have to pretend we're making a motion picture about a story I've written. Famous actress Samantha Watson starring in a new picture based on a novel by famous writer Amanda Watson." Amanda could almost see their names on the marquee. What if it really happened? What if she grew up to be a real writer? And Samantha grew up to be an actress?

Samantha liked the idea, too. "That's perfect,

Amanda. I don't like making up the story, anyway. The thing people really remember is the face on the screen, right?"

Amanda laughed. "Well, in that case, people might not know if it's you or me."

"Except for the hair," Samantha reminded her. "You really ought to do something about it, Amanda."

Amanda changed the subject quickly. "This picture is going to be about a lady who is waiting for her boyfriend to come back from the war."

"You mean like Elsie DeCecco was doing before the Great War ended?"

"Right," Amanda said. Elsie was their next-door neighbor, and just about all she had done while her boyfriend was overseas was to sit by the window and look outside, a tragic expression on her face.

"Great! I'll go get into my costume." Samantha disappeared up the staircase.

Amanda looked out their own window toward the house where Elsie lived with her parents. Since the war had ended, and Jimmy McTeague had come home to a hero's welcome, Elsie no longer sat by the window. But Amanda still wondered what it would be like to love somebody so much that she would wait for him day after day, week after week, nothing mattering except his return.

"Ta-da!" Samantha announced, breaking into Amanda's thoughts. She glided down the

123

staircase as if she were making an entrance at a ball. Her mother's feather boa was wrapped around her neck, one end trailing behind her on the stairs. Her lips were smeared with bright lipstick. In one hand she held an unlit cigarette in a long carved-ivory holder, and in the other she carried one of the good champagne glasses that their mother kept packed away.

"Sam, what are you doing with that glass and Mother's best boa?" Amanda asked.

"Amanda, Mother is only the most stylish, up-to-date mother in the whole neighborhood. Why shouldn't I look like her?"

"But you're supposed to be pining away for your boyfriend," Amanda protested.

Samantha fluffed the boa around her neck. "Not me," she retorted. "I'd have some fun while I was waiting. Go out dancing, meet new people. You wouldn't catch me sitting at the window every day."

Amanda felt a flicker of annoyance. "Sam, I'm the writer, remember? Not you. And I think it's very romantic to wait like Elsie for the boy you love. Besides, you can't have that champagne glass in your hand. Not with that new constitutional amendment. You saw them dumping all that liquor into Lake Erie a few months ago."

Samantha giggled. "Yeah, there must have been some mighty drunken fish in there."

Amanda frowned. "Sam, Prohibition is serious. People aren't supposed to drink. Especially not when they're worrying over whether their boy-friends are going to come home from the war or not."

Samantha came into the living room, still holding the champagne glass. "Well, they didn't have Prohibition yet when the war was on. Besides, I heard Mother say that Elsie drank an awful lot while she was waiting. If her boyfriend hadn't come back soon, she would have floated away."

Amanda didn't like hearing those kinds of things about Elsie. Not when Elsie had waited so loyally for so long. "Look, Samantha, you said I could be the writer, so now you have to let me make up the story. Do you want to play or not?"

Samantha pouted. "Spoilsport."

Amanda crossed her arms. "Is that what you're going to say to them in Hollywood?"

Samantha stroked her boa. "For your information, I'm going to be so famous that nobody's going to tell me what to do. Besides, what's wrong with a stylish pining-away girlfriend, anyway? Do you want the star of your picture to be so dull that nobody cares about her?"

Amanda bit her lip. Perhaps Samantha had a point.

"See?" Samantha said. "You know I'm right."

Amanda sighed and agreed to let Samantha stay dressed the way she was. Sometimes she wondered why she even bothered to argue with her in the first place. Samantha always seemed to get what she wanted.

Sixteen

1925. Detroit.

"Girls! Girls, come on downstairs," the twins' father called from the dining room. "There's a letter from Harry! Samantha, Amanda!"

Amanda pulled her favorite cloche hat on over her new bob and made sure both her dangling pendant earrings were clipped in place. The long string of matching beads around her neck swung back and forth as she walked into the dining room.

"Don't you look terrific," her mother said.

"So where are you going all dressed up like a grown-up lady?" her father asked.

"Oh, Father," Amanda said. Sometimes he treated her and Samantha as though they were still his baby girls. "We're invited to a party at Geoffrey Aiken's house."

"Ah, yes, your young man. The football player, I believe."

Amanda could feel her face turning pink. "Yes, he's a first-string running back at school."

"Well, perhaps your sister will meet a nice young man at the party, too," he said.

Amanda laughed. "If I know Sam, she'll meet

lots of nice young men. Sam!" she called upstairs. "Come on! Don't you want to hear what Harry has to say?" She picked up her brother's letter from the dining room table. She had missed him terribly since he'd gone away to college.

Samantha made her entrance in a cloud of perfume, her buckle-toed pumps clicking against the polished wood floor. Where Amanda wore one string of beads, her twin had on several. The girls' father raised an eyebrow at her.

"Samantha, did you bathe in perfume?"

Samantha twirled one of her necklaces. "Well, Clara Bow does it," she said. Clara Bow was now Samantha's favorite actress.

"I see," her father said. "Does Clara Bow also wear her dresses so short? Goodness, when I was courting your mother that dress wouldn't have been decent even as underclothes. Surely you're not going out in public like that."

"Oh, Father," Samantha replied, "Amanda's wearing the same dress in a different color, in case you hadn't noticed."

Amanda felt her father's eyes on her. "Hmm. Well, that's true, but Amanda's dress isn't nearly as short, and her heels aren't as high. And she's not wearing lipstick that could stop auto traffic."

Jessamyn Watson came to Samantha's defense. "Taylor, darling, that's how girls dress these days. Samantha looks very fashionable. Don't forget that things are different now. Women can even vote."

127

Her own skirt wasn't much longer than the twins', Amanda noticed. In fact, the best things from the twins' wardrobe had often started out in their mother's drawer.

"Let's see what Harry has to say," Mrs. Watson said, closing the discussion of Samantha's outfit. Samantha shot her a grateful look.

Amanda opened the envelope, and unfolded Harry's letter. " 'Dear Mother and Father, Amanda and Samantha,' " she read.

"He always puts me last," Samantha said.

"That's because you're the youngest," Amanda said.

"Yeah, by four lousy minutes," Samantha said. "What a lot of hokum."

"Sam, do you want me to read this or not? 'Dear everybody,' " she started again. " 'School is wonderful. I'm at the top of my class in Latin, and I made the tennis team. But here's the real reason this year's so swell: a new jazz club opened up in the next town over, and every weekend musicians come from all over the state (and even farther) to get together on the club's little stage and play. Often the musicians have never played together before. There are different combinations of instruments every time, and people play without music. They improvise and you never hear the same thing twice,' " Amanda read.

"Cat's pajamas!" said Samantha.

The girls' parents looked at each other. "Cat's pajamas?"

128

"It means great," Samantha explained with a note of impatience in her voice. "What else, Amanda?"

Amanda continued reading. " 'I usually go to the club with my roommate, Ted Wakefield, who knows all about jazz and the latest dances and motion pictures.' "

"Motion pictures?" Samantha said. "Sounds like my kind of guy. Keep reading, Amanda."

" 'Ted says he has to keep up with the times so he can write about them,' Harry writes. 'Sometimes he sells stories or articles to some of the local newspapers to help put himself through school. But in my opinion, this may all be an excuse for Ted to go out and Charleston all night.' "

"Oo, this Ted guy sounds better and better," Samantha said.

"Yeah, and he's a professional writer," Amanda added. "Published and everything!" She was impressed. Her own brother's roommate! "Hey, look, Harry sent a photo of the two of them."

Samantha grabbed the picture out of her hand before Amanda got a solid look. "Oh, Amanda, he looks as good as he sounds," Samantha breathed.

"Well, you could let me see," Amanda said.

"Hey, don't we know him or something?" Samantha asked. She held the picture out to Amanda. "There's something familiar about him. I feel like I met him somewhere a long time ago. Or maybe he's famous! That could be it."

"Come on, Sam. Harry would say so if his

roommate was famous." Amanda took Ted's picture and studied it. He was definitely handsome, with high cheekbones, a strong, straight nose, and a slight cleft in his chin. And it was true—he did look like someone she knew. But she couldn't figure out why. Was it something in his dark eyes?

"See what I mean?" Samantha said. She took back the picture, looking at it with the same expression she wore after a particularly good motion picture.

"Maybe you've seen him in your dreams and you're destined for each other," Amanda teased. "Maybe that's why he looks so familiar. It's fate, you know."

Samantha sighed. "Yes. Maybe you're right. It must be fate. I'm in love."

The sound of a brass band filled the air. Samantha closed her eyes. In her mind she saw a dark, smoke-filled room, beautiful people dressed to the nines, a tiny stage crowded with musicians, and a saxophone player, his shiny brass instrument pointed high in the air, wailing out the melody. In her mind Samantha sat at a table in the corner, a table just for two, a candle lighting the impossibly handsome face of her date—Ted Wakefield.

She opened her eyes. Amanda stood talking to Geoffrey Aiken, their gazes intent on each other, their smiles bright. The dancers moving to the saxophone music pouring out of the Victrola were all boys and girls Samantha recognized from school. She sighed. This party wasn't bad, but she knew it would be kid stuff for someone like Ted Wakefield. Samantha shut her eyes and went back to her daydream.

"Want to dance?"

She opened her eyes again and found herself staring at Scott Turner from her English class. "Oh, hi, Scott. OK, sure." She moved into the middle of the room with him. Scott was tall, with wavy brown hair and brown eyes. If she squinted and angled her head a certain way, he even looked a little like Ted Wakefield. Samantha moved her body to the music, trying to pretend she was doing the Charleston with her brother's roommate. But the daydream just wasn't possible with her eyes open.

All of a sudden, Scott stopped dancing. "Well, will you look who the cat just dragged in," he said, looking over Samantha's shoulder.

Samantha whirled around to see a boy in a long raccoon coat and baggy white pants, his hair perfectly parted in the center and slicked to a patent-leather shine. He held a long cigarette holder. It took Samantha a second to recognize him.

"Omigosh, it's Kevin Hughes!" Samantha had never seen him so spiffed up. "Since when did he get to be such a lounge lizard?" she asked Scott.

Scott raised an eyebrow. "Haven't you heard? I

131

thought you and Kevin were sort of . . . friends."

Samantha rolled her eyes. Was she never going to live down a few dates with Kevin? At first she had thought he was intriguing, dangerous. It didn't take long to discover he was just dangerously boring. He had one topic of conversation: himself—how he had sold fake jewelry as the real thing, how he had been picked up for truancy, how he had siphoned gasoline from cars. He told these stories as if showing off medals for bravery. The truth was, Kevin Hughes was just a punky minor hoodlum, not the kind of glamorous, elegant guy who was right for a future Hollywood star. Kevin was still totally stuck on her, but Samantha had avoided him for quite some time. She didn't want Scott feeding the rumor mill.

"Scott, if Kevin Hughes were my friend, I wouldn't be asking you how come he's suddenly turned into Mr. Spiffy, now, would I?" Samantha asked.

Scott shrugged. "They say Kevin's moved from pinching candy bars to bigger things."

"What things?"

"The way I hear it, he's running hooch," Scott said.

"You mean delivering bathtub gin and stuff?"

Scott nodded. "I guess he decided to drop in and show off all the things money can buy."

Kevin swaggered toward the center of the room. "Well," he said, loudly enough to be heard over the music, "how's the malted-milk set doing?"

Geoff Aiken made his way toward Kevin. "Kevin, I don't recall extending a party invitation to you," he said tightly.

"Loosen up, pal," Kevin said. "Ain't you heard of gatecrashing? It's the latest thing. You don't invite me? I come anyway."

Samantha stifled a giggle. Kevin might be a common thug, but at least it looked like the party was going to get more interesting.

"Hey! Samantha Watson!" Kevin said. He sauntered over to her. "The dame I was too low-class for." Suddenly Samantha was sorry Kevin had walked in the door.

"I, ah—"

"Hey, everyone makes mistakes," Kevin said. "How do you like the coat? Real raccoon." He leaned in close and his breath came out in a puff of tobacco smoke laced with the smell of liquor. "Get a load of the cigarette holder. Solid gold inlay. Bet you're sorry you didn't stick with me, huh?"

Samantha took a step away from Kevin. He looked pathetically hopeful but he was the same old low-down, big-headed bore in a new, fancy package.

Kevin closed the distance between them. "I wouldn't mind giving you another chance," he said. He put a hand on her arm.

Samantha yanked her arm away from him. "Kevin, grow up," she said.

Kevin reached for her again and gave a drunken laugh. "Me grow up? You're the one drinking—what is that?—fruit punch? Golly gee, how exciting. Geoff, don't you got anything better in this joint?"

"Kevin," said Geoff, "if you don't like it here, you're welcome to leave. In fact, I wish you would."

Kevin took a long drag of his cigarette. "Hey, maybe I will. Come on, Sam, how about we go over to the Cellar Door?"

"How about we don't," Samantha said. The Cellar Door had the reputation for being the dingiest, dirtiest speakeasy in Detroit. The authorities kept closing it down, and it kept opening up again in one location or another.

Kevin looked crestfallen. Then he seemed to remember his big-guy act. He stuck his chest out and ran a hand over his raccoon coat. "Suit yourself, kiddo. When you get tired of these stiffs, you know where to find me." He strutted off as if he were the king of Detroit—but not without sneaking a backward glance at Samantha.

Boy, is he all wet, Samantha thought as she watched him go. *Imagine some glamorous star like Clara Bow going to a place like the Cellar Door with a cheap hood like Kevin.* Now, Ted Wakefield—there was a fellow who was classy through and through.

Samantha danced another dance with Scott, and then a few more with some of the other boys from school. None of them were half as exciting in real life as Ted Wakefield was in a photo.

She wound her way through the party crowd and helped herself to some punch from the refreshment table. Well, at least Amanda seemed to be having a good time. She watched her twin whisper something in Geoff's ear. Geoff nodded and raised a glass of punch.

"Excuse me!" he shouted above the music. "May I have your attention?" Someone near the Victrola lifted the stylus off the record. "I'd like to make a toast," Geoff announced. He looked at Amanda. "Of course, I'm not as good with words as Amanda is, so I think I'll let her do it for me."

Amanda seemed to think for a moment. Then she raised her glass. "To airplanes and a new generation and a new world." Her eyes searched the room until they met Samantha's. "And to motion pictures."

Samantha raised her glass, and added her own silent toast. *And to Ted Wakefield.*

Dear Harry, Samantha wrote. *Ted Wakefield sounds so dreamy. Have you told him all about your fabulous twin sisters—especially me? I'm enclosing a photo so you can show it to him and tell him all about your baby sister, who is going to be a Hollywood star. Love, Samantha. P.S. Have you heard Bessie Smith's new record? I'm so wild about it I'm afraid I'm going to wear it down to nothing playing it over and over. There's some great trumpet playing on it by a guy named Louis Armstrong, too.*

Samantha folded the letter over her favorite picture of herself, in which she thought she looked just a little like Clara Bow. She dotted a drop of perfume on the envelope. Then she sealed it, addressed it, and kissed it for good luck.

Samantha raced up the stairs waving an envelope over her head. "Amanda, Amanda!" She burst into the room they shared and found her sister sitting at her roll-top desk, writing in her notebook. "It's the best news," Samantha announced.

Amanda blotted her pen on a piece of blotting paper. "Let me guess. It's Hollywood. They've heard all about you from some mysterious source, and they want you to get on the next train to the West Coast."

"Almost as good," Samantha said. "I'll give you a clue. Who's about six feet tall, dark and handsome, loves jazz and motion pictures, and is coming to visit?"

Amanda grinned. "Did you forget to say that he's a writer?"

"Oh, yeah. Plus he's a real, live writer."

"And he's coming here?" Amanda wiped the tip of her pen and capped it. "The famous Ted Wakefield is coming to Detroit?"

Samantha sighed happily. "Uh-huh! Harry showed him my picture and told him all about me, and he wants to meet me. He's stopping here on his way home to Chicago for vacation. Can you believe it?"

"Of course I can, silly. You're interested in all the same things, and you sound perfect for each other," Amanda said.

"You really think so?" Samantha asked.

"Sure. It's fate, remember?" Amanda said.

Samantha nodded. "Yeah, fate. Me and Ted Wakefield." She reached over and picked up the photo on her night table—the one of Harry and Ted. In her mind, she replaced the image of Harry with one of herself. Fate. Now all she had to do was wait until Christmas.

Seventeen

"Get hot, get hot!" Harry called out to the couple letting loose on the dance floor.

"They don't have to *get* hot; they *are* hot," Amanda said as she watched her twin and Ted Wakefield, their legs and arms a blur of motion, their faces flushed and happy. Samantha crossed and uncrossed her hands on her knees, and Ted followed suit.

Amanda took a sip of her soda pop to cool her off after dancing song after song with Geoff. She needed a rest, but it looked as if Samantha and Ted could keep going all night. Amanda could see why her twin was so smitten. Ted was even more handsome in person than in the photo, and he was every bit as terrific as Harry had described. At dinner, he had talked cars to her parents, motion pictures to Samantha, and new writers to her. They had discovered that they both loved F. Scott Fitzgerald and Ernest Hemingway.

"Ted is the bee's knees, huh?" Harry said. "Figures it'd take my roommate to show me a spot in my own hometown that I never even knew about."

"Yeah, this place sure is swell," said Geoff.

Amanda thought so, too. She had never been in a real roadhouse with a jazz band before, and she was feeling awfully sophisticated and grown-up. Around her, men and women who were the height of fashion danced, listened to the music, and sipped cocktails that Amanda had a feeling were a lot less innocent than the soda pop Ted had ordered for their table.

"That's Ted for you," Harry said with a laugh. "Polite, well-mannered, smart—and then you find out he knows every nightspot in every town. And every musician, too."

As the musicians blew the last notes of the song and announced a short break, Ted escorted Samantha from the dance floor and led her toward the stage. The trumpet player, a tall dark-skinned man with thick glasses, came forward and clapped Ted on the back. Amanda could see Ted introducing him to Samantha and then pointing across the room to where she and Harry and Geoff sat. Her brother waved to them, and they came over to the table.

Ted made the introductions. "This is C. C. Earl, King of the Trumpet. Earl, Samantha's brother Harry, her sister Amanda, and Amanda's friend, Geoff."

"Nice to meet you all," he said.

"Nice to meet *you*, Mr. Earl," Amanda said. "I loved hearing your music."

"My pleasure to play for such a beautiful

matched set. And please call me Earl—all my friends do," he said. Amanda felt herself blushing. Samantha gave Earl her brightest Hollywood smile.

"Would you like to sit down with us for a few minutes?" Harry offered.

"Don't mind if I do," Earl said. He eased his big frame into the chair next to Amanda, and Ted sat down in the empty seat across from her. Amanda noticed some of the people at the other tables looking at them, and a thrill ran through her. It was a little like all of them were famous, just by having Earl sit down with them.

Ted held up a hand for the waitress. "Something to drink, Earl?" Then he turned to the rest of them. "Least I can do for the guy who's responsible for me still being in school."

"You don't owe me a thing," Earl said.

"Don't listen to him," Ted kidded. "Earl gave me my first big interview, the first article I ever got published. Really helped me earn some extra money to get through this semester."

Earl ordered himself a near beer. "Well, what else could I do? This little pipsqueak comes up to me after the show telling me I have to give him an exclusive interview—exclusive, mind you, I wasn't supposed to talk to anyone but him—and he's telling me it has something to do with digging for gold and his dear mother and getting a higher education. Well, I have to admit, I was curious. Frankly, I thought he was spinning some fantastic tale."

Harry punched Ted lightly on the arm. "He's pretty good at those."

Ted laughed in protest. "I beg your pardon, but it wasn't a fantastic tale at all. Every word I told Earl was true."

Amanda felt her own curiosity bubbling like her soda pop. "What did you say to him?" she asked.

"Started out with some cat with a broken heart, didn't it?" Earl remembered.

"Yes, that's right," Ted said. "With my grandfather, Theodore Wakefield. It was right after he came over to this country from England. It seems my grandfather's first experience on American soil was a tremendous case of heartbreak. Some girl he'd met on the ship, I think."

"Sounds exciting," Samantha said. "Heartbreak on the high seas."

"Your poor grandfather," Amanda said.

"Yes, poor Granddad," Ted agreed. "He went looking high and low for this girl, even though he had absolutely no idea where she might be. For a while, he took a job with a circus. I think he secretly hoped they'd travel to wherever it was she'd ended up, and somehow their paths would cross again."

"The circus? What a coincidence!" Samantha said. "Mother was a bareback rider in the circus when she was young!" She took her gaze off Ted

141

just long enough to catch Amanda's eye and silently mouth the word *fate*.

Amanda winked at her. Then she turned to Ted. "So did your grandfather ever find his lady?"

"I'm afraid not," Ted said. "Granddad got discouraged and finally left the circus. He wandered for a long time, working a variety of odd jobs. Eventually he wound up in Colorado, a place called Cripple Creek. Well, my grandfather may not have found his true love there, but he found something else."

"What was that?" Samantha asked. Amanda noticed that her twin's eyes never left Ted's face.

"Gold. My grandfather struck gold."

Amanda gasped. "Really?"

Earl chuckled. "I had the same reaction. You can imagine me wondering what this had to do with my giving some young upstart an exclusive interview. Finding gold. Sounded like a fairy tale to me."

"But it actually happened?" Geoff asked.

Ted nodded. "My grandfather hit it rich. So rich that there was enough for my mother and me to live on rather well after my father died."

"Instant wealth," Samantha said. "Sounds like a plot for a motion picture."

"You're right," Ted said. "Except that in a Hollywood picture we would have lived happily ever after. Instead, last year, during my first year of college, the money began to run out. My mother didn't know it because I was managing the fi-

142

nances and didn't intend to let her find out. I was sure that she would pawn her jewelry or sell our home, or make any other sacrifices she had to, in order to keep me in school. Luckily, I was able to make a few prudent investments, and now she has a modest income from the interest. As for me—"

"You decided to write newspaper articles to supplement your own income," Amanda said.

"Not at first, though that's what eventually happened." Ted smiled. "What happened first was that one night I went out to try to forget my troubles. I'd heard about a new place that had opened up near school where you could go and listen to the latest jazz."

"I wrote you about it," Harry said to his sisters.

"We remember," Samantha answered for both her and Amanda. Amanda shot her twin a private smile. It would be hard not to remember Harry's letter and the picture he'd enclosed of himself and Ted. It still sat on Samantha's night table so she could look at it and moon over it anytime she wanted. *It's awfully swell to finally have the real McCoy here tonight, and not just his photograph*, Amanda thought as Ted continued his story.

"Well, I did forget my troubles that evening," he said, "thanks to the C. C. Earl Band."

Earl gave a laugh that sounded like his trumpet call. "You flatter me, my friend."

"Not at all," Ted said. "I heard your sound and I fell in love with it. And apparently I wasn't the

143

only one. When I went backstage to congratulate the band, I couldn't get past the crowd of journalists, each one trying to beat out the next one for a story about the hot new music of the modern generation. Well, I thought, I'm part of that generation, why shouldn't I be the one to tell our story?"

"Sort of like F. Scott Fitzgerald did in *This Side of Paradise*," Amanda said.

Ted smiled warmly at her. "Why, yes! That's exactly right."

"And so you convinced Earl to give the band's story to you and only you," Samantha said. "That's just so clever." Ted turned toward her, and she showered him with her most dazzling smile.

Harry clapped Ted on the back. "What a hep cat," he teased. "My own roommate."

Ted grinned. "More like a desperate cat," he said, as if being a published writer was no big deal. "But that desperation led me to a part-time career!"

Amanda was as impressed by his modesty as by his cleverness. Ted really was terrific. She leaned back and took a sip of her drink. A whole evening of music and dancing and fun lay ahead. She hoped there would be many more nights like this —maybe with her and Geoff double-dating with Samantha and Ted. She was happy that her brother had brought Ted Wakefield to town. And even happier that her sister had met such a wonderful guy.

"My darling, I know we belong together," Samantha said in her throatiest, sexiest, voice. Later that night, Amanda watched her twin dancing around their bedroom with her pillow clasped tightly in her arms. "You're the most handsome, charming sheik I've ever met." She switched voices, imitating a man's low register. "And you, my dear, are as beautiful as Cleopatra. I will love you forever, and we will never stop dancing. . . ."

Amanda stretched out on her bed and laughed. "Sam, are you sure you didn't sneak any sips of giggle water tonight?"

"Giggle water?" Samantha continued to twirl her pillow around the room. "Who needs it? I'm drunk enough already."

Amanda's laugh died on her lips. "You are?" She sat up and stared at Samantha.

Samantha whirled her pillow around and stopped right in front of Amanda. "Of course, silly! I'm drunk on love!"

Amanda flopped back down on her bed. "Oh, that!"

"Yes, that! Oh, Amanda, isn't Ted just darb, the berries, the bee's knees?"

"Yes, yes, and yes," Amanda answered with a laugh.

145

Samantha took one last spin and collapsed onto her own bed. "Amanda, I'm so stuck on him."

"And I'm sure he's just as stuck on you," Amanda said. Ted Wakefield was a special guy. He and Samantha would make a wonderful couple.

Amanda couldn't sleep. Images of the evening kept going around in her head: dancing until all hours; C. C. Earl's smooth trumpet sound; a rail-thin, raven-haired woman sipping from a champagne glass; Harry tinkling the piano keys between sets; Ted telling stories, wonderful stories. . . .

Amanda rolled over and tried a different position. No luck. She was wide awake. She tried counting backward from one hundred, but the numbers came out to a jazz beat. The excitement of the night was too powerful for sleep.

She threw off her bedclothes and slipped into her robe and slippers. Quietly, so she wouldn't wake Samantha, she got her notebook and writing supplies out of her desk and crept downstairs.

It was a perfect winter night. The moon shone brightly on a satiny blanket of snow in the yard. Its light came through the living room window, casting a silver river of light on the rug. There was a stillness in the air against which the memories of Amanda's evening beat clearly. She curled up on the sofa and opened her notebook. On the

146

table next to her, she put down the cap to her pen and set out a piece of blotting paper. She wrote:

> *A moonbeam,*
> *as perfect as the sweetest*
> *note of a trumpet.*

She let the moonlight bathe her, giving in to the night's images so she could capture them on paper. Ted Wakefield's face appeared in her mind without her meaning it to. And then there he was, standing in the doorway.

Amanda gave a start, almost dropping her pen.

"Excuse me," Ted said softly.

"Ted! You startled me." Ted's face was highlighted by the moon, and he looked even more handsome than he had in Amanda's mind.

"I'm sorry," Ted said. "I couldn't sleep."

"Me, either," Amanda said. "I keep thinking about everything I saw and heard tonight. I thought I'd try to write a poem about it."

Ted nodded from the doorway. "Then maybe you'd prefer that I didn't disturb you."

"Oh, you're not disturbing me," Amanda said. "You can come in and sit down if you'd like." She blew on her poem to make sure the ink was dry, and closed her notebook.

Ted came over and seated himself on the other end of the sofa. "Please don't close it," he said. "I was hoping you might read me one of your poems."

"Oh, I couldn't!" Amanda exclaimed. Shyness washed over.

"Sure you could," Ted said.

"But you're a real writer—published and everything," Amanda protested.

"That's exactly it," Ted said. "I'm a writer, and so are you. Writers should share their words, don't you agree?"

Amanda raised her shoulders. She was sure her face was bright red. "I guess I do, and, well, I do write for our school paper, but I'm not a real writer. Not like you."

Ted smiled. "Anyone who sneaks downstairs in the middle of the night to put her feelings into a poem is a writer, Amanda. A real one." Amanda felt a funny, warm tingle as Ted said her name. There was something about him, something about the whole wonderful evening, that made her feel open to new experiences. She could hardly believe it herself as she opened her notebook to her favorite poem and held it out to him.

"I—I'd be too shy to read this out loud to you, but here. I wrote it last summer, after I got caught in a thunderstorm." Ted moved closer and took the notebook. Amanda's heart pounded as she watched him read the poem she had worked so hard on.

Sheets of rain
shimmering, slicing through the sky,

splashing in silver streams
at my feet,
exploding
in thunder,
I soak
in nature's embrace.

He looked up from the last line and held her gaze for a long, silent moment. "That's beautiful. I love the way you use all the *s* and *sh* sounds so you can really hear the rain." As he handed Amanda's notebook back his hand grazed hers. She felt an electric tingle go through her. "I knew it," Ted said. "I could just tell by being with you tonight that you have a poet's soul."

"Thank you," Amanda whispered. She lowered her eyes, feeling bashful at Ted's praise and even more bashful at his nearness. Bashful . . . and something else as well. She could feel her blood racing through her veins, making her warm and dizzy.

"Amanda." The way Ted said her name was like a poem itself. "Your words are beautiful, and so are you."

Amanda felt short of breath. Her pulse raced. No! She couldn't let herself feel this way. Not when Sam—not when Geoff—no! She giggled nervously. "You're just saying that because I look like Sam," she managed.

"No," Ted said. "I'm saying that because *you* are beautiful. At first, from all that Harry had told me, I thought that maybe Samantha was the one for me. But after tonight, I know I was wrong."

"But *Sam* has always been the fascinating one," Amanda protested in a whisper.

"Well, now it's your turn," Ted continued earnestly. "You're fascinating to me. You have an inner beauty . . ."

Amanda didn't know how it happened, but suddenly her hand was in Ted's. She looked up into his face again. It was only inches from hers. *No!* she told herself. *Think of Samantha. Think of Geoff.* She felt as if she were drowning in Ted's caring brown eyes. He reached out and cupped her face in his warm hand. He was so close, so close.

Maybe it was the excitement of the evening. Maybe it was the irresistible magic of the moonlight. Amanda felt herself giving in to the longest, sweetest kiss in the world.

Eighteen

"Goodbye, Watsons!" Ted called with a wave. Amanda watched him crank his automobile to a start and jump in behind the wheel.

"Goodbye, Ted! I'm sorry you couldn't stay for breakfast," Mrs. Watson said above the sound of the motor.

"I wish I could, but my mother's expecting me. With all the snow, I need to get an early start back to Chicago," Ted replied through his open window.

"Come again whenever you like," Mr. Watson invited.

"Thank you," Ted said. "And thanks again for everything. I had the most swell time." His eyes moved to Amanda and held hers.

Remember, Amanda told herself. *Last night is over. You have Geoff, and Samantha loves Ted.* But she couldn't pull herself away from Ted's gaze. She felt his eyes moving over her face in a gentle caress, and she found herself responding, memorizing the expression in his eyes, the curve of his eyebrows, the shape of his mouth, the angle of his jaw, the sweep of brown hair under his hat . . .

Out of the corner of her eye, Amanda saw Samantha sprinting to the car. The spell was broken. Amanda felt her breath catch as she watched Samantha lean her head into Ted's window and give him a big kiss on the cheek. A jolt of jealousy went through her.

And then she remembered what she had been telling herself since she woke up that morning. *Samantha and Ted belong together. Stick with Geoff. Forget about last night.* She tried to breathe slowly and evenly as her twin skipped back toward her with a big smile on her face. Amanda looked down at the tips of her shoes, which were disappearing into the snow. All of a sudden, she was aware of the morning chill. She pulled her coat around her more tightly, exhaling puffs of steam.

"Samantha!" she heard her father say. "Young women these days are awfully forward."

Her mother laughed. "Oh, Taylor, I'll bet you just wish some beautiful young woman had done that to you when you were young. And anyway, I wasn't particularly shy myself, remember?" She leaned close and gave him a kiss.

"See you back at school!" Harry said to Ted.

"Right!" Ted answered.

Amanda kept her eyes on the ground until she heard the car begin to move.

"What a nice young man," the twins' mother said as Ted's coupe grew smaller and smaller.

"The nicest!" Samantha agreed. "And the most fun! Isn't he, Amanda?"

Amanda gave a silent nod, not trusting her voice.

"Sweetheart, you're awfully quiet this morning," her father observed as the family turned to go inside.

"Oh, Amanda's not used to wild nights like last night," Samantha said.

"Listen to her," Harry teased. "My little sister, the picture of sophistication!"

"Well, she's not, are you, Amanda?" Samantha prodded.

Amanda hoped her twin would think her cheeks were red from the cold. "No, I'm not," she said. If that wasn't the biggest understatement, she didn't know what was.

"Hmm, hope you kids behaved yourselves," Mr. Watson said, a touch of amusement in his voice.

"Hope you had a good time," Mrs. Watson added.

"The best!" Samantha exclaimed. She took off her coat and Charlestoned her way into the kitchen for breakfast, humming one of C. C. Earl's tunes.

Amanda stamped the dusting of snow off her shoes and followed her twin. In time to Samantha's humming, a tiny voice in Amanda's head

153

chanted *guilty, guilty, guilty.* She wished she had had more self-control the night before. What had come over her?

"You know, Harry," Samantha said as she sat down at the table, "there's only one problem with your friend Ted."

Harry arched an eyebrow. "You mean he's not perfect, Sam?"

"Well, he is a bit shy," Samantha said.

"In my day we called it being polite," her father teased, taking his place next to Samantha.

Amanda helped her mother carry a freshly baked coffeecake, juice, and coffee to the table. She fought to keep the images of the previous night's secret meeting with Ted out of her mind. It was over, she told herself. It hadn't even happened.

"Well, I'm sure Ted will be back," Harry said.

Amanda tried to ignore the tingle that went through her. When Ted did come back, she was going to remember that she was very fond of Geoff. And that Samantha and Ted would make a perfect couple.

Amanda clutched the letter in her gloved hand. *T. Wakefield,* the return address read. With her free hand, Amanda closed the mailbox. Under her coat, Geoff's class ring, which she wore on a chain around her neck, was heavy on her blouse —or at least she imagined it was.

Ted Wakefield. The memories she had worked

154

to forget surged inside her—the sound of a jazz trumpet, the flood of moonlight through the living room window, Ted's tender, lingering kisses.

Amanda let herself into the house. She could hear Samantha upstairs, going over her lines for the school play. Amanda hung her coat up and quietly let herself into the downstairs bathroom. She locked the door. Then she tore open Ted's letter. *He's just your brother's roommate*, she told herself sternly as she began to read. *Just a friend.*

But as Ted wrote about jazz poetry and their midnight embrace, she felt the warmth and dizziness of their night together come rushing back over her. Then she had to keep herself from laughing out loud as he told her about the student who'd tried to set a record for flagpole sitting. Ted's words were so vivid, so clear, that it was almost like being with him. Every detail of his face was bright in her mind, and she could almost feel his arms around her. She tried to push the feeling away, but it was too strong.

I want to see you again, Ted ended his letter. *I miss you. Please write.*

Amanda thought about Samantha, who was upstairs practicing her lines. Her hand went to Geoff's ring, cool and sharp and very real to her touch. Struggling against the desire to read Ted's words over and over, she put the letter back in its envelope. She would write back to Ted. But once, and only once. And she would keep it purely friendly. Nothing more. She folded the letter and tucked it into the top of her stocking.

Up in their bedroom, Samantha looked over the top of her script. "Any mail?"

"No," Amanda said. Ted's letter pressed against her leg. She turned away from Samantha, shame welling up inside her. It was the first time in her whole life she had lied to her twin.

"Amanda, what happened to Geoff's ring?" Samantha demanded.

It was unusually warm for early March, and Amanda's coat was draped over one arm as she and her sister walked home from school. Her hand automatically went to the spot where Geoff's ring had been for the past several months. Her fingers found only the light wool of her dress. Not that she expected anything else.

Amanda sighed. "I know Geoffrey Aiken is one of the most decent fellows there is," she said. "Not to mention the best running back on the football team. But, well—I don't know. I suppose I realized that Geoff just isn't the boy for me."

"You mean you decided he's a flat tire," Samantha said.

Amanda shook her head. "No. That's not it. Some other girl will be lucky to be with him."

Poor Geoff. She thought about the sadness in his eyes when she had given back his ring. Then she thought about the growing pile of letters from Ted that she had hidden under her mattress. She thought about how she raced to the mailbox each morning to make sure no one in her family saw Ted's letters to her. How much longer could she deny what was going on between them? If she and Ted hadn't fallen in love on that moonlit night, then they certainly had done so through their letters. After that first one there had been one more—just one more. And then one more after that. She had not been able to stop writing. Her love was just too strong.

She knew she had done the right thing about Geoff. It wasn't fair to be thinking about someone else while she was with him. But it wasn't fair to Samantha to keep her in the dark, either. Amanda frowned. She hated having a secret from her twin. And Ted hated the deception as much as she did. In his letters he had urged Amanda to tell Samantha the truth. Amanda took a deep breath. She was going to tell her sister straight out.

Samantha mistook her frown. "Amanda, don't look so grim," she said. "There'll be a life after Geoff Aiken. You know, Harry and Ted have a spring vacation coming up, and maybe they have another friend for you. I'm sure Ted knows all kinds of interesting boys."

Amanda heard the breathy, excited note that came into her sister's voice as she talked about Ted. All her resolve to tell Samantha about the two of them fizzled away.

"Maybe we could even double-date,"

157

Samantha went on. "The Watson twins and their college men."

Amanda nodded weakly. At some point she was going to have to tell her twin the truth. And there was no way she could make it not hurt.

Samantha felt like a robber in her own house. "Mother?" she called. No answer. So far, so good. She checked downstairs, then up. The house was empty. She looked in the broom closet to make sure the big straw basket her mother took to market was gone. It was. Excellent. Her father was at work, and Samantha had just left Amanda at school, on her way to the office of the *Klaxon,* the school paper.

Samantha filled the kettle with water and set it down on the heavy iron stove. She took a match from the black-and-red tea tin they used as a matchbox and lit the burner under the kettle. Then she pulled her Latin text from under the pile of schoolbooks on the kitchen table and shook it until an envelope fell out from between its pages.

As she waited for the water to boil Samantha held the envelope up to the light. She had tried looking through the envelope a hundred times already, and she couldn't see any more than she had before: nothing. The only thing that was certain was that Ted Wakefield had written to Amanda. The letter was addressed to Amanda! Not Samantha!

The kettle whistled and a plume of steam rose from its spout. Samantha took the letter over to the stove and put the back of the envelope in the path of the steam. She held it by the edges, careful not to touch and smear the ink and not to let the steam burn her arm. Gently, she eased a finger under one corner of the envelope flap, but the paste was still holding tight. She steamed the letter for a few minutes longer. Working gently, a little at a time, she was able to peel the letter open without tearing the envelope.

Dear Amanda, she read. *Your letters are exquisite agony.*

"*Your letters*"? So Amanda had been writing to Ted? Samantha couldn't believe it. How lousy. How absolutely, positively lousy. And what in the world was "exquisite agony"?

Each time you write, I know you better—and miss you so much more.

What kind of hokum was this?

I remember how beautiful you looked in the moonlight, and I long to embrace you again.

Samantha gasped out loud. Embrace? Again? She read the sentence two more times, not believing she had gotten it right. No. It couldn't be possible. Not good-as-gold Amanda, not little Miss Perfect. But there was the proof, right on the page. Her goody-goody twin was carrying on a romance with Ted Wakefield—a secret romance! Amanda had let Samantha go on and on about Ted, listened to her private dreams about him, all the time never saying a word. Samantha felt like the world's biggest fool. Anger and hurt rushed through her veins. Amanda was the person she loved the most in the whole world. How could she have done this? Samantha read the rest of Ted's letter—some dumb, mushy love poem about the blues in his heart.

Red-hot fury and disbelief shot through her. She read the letter over and over. It came out the same every time: good, loving, caring Amanda had turned Benedict Arnold! She knew what Samantha wanted, and she had taken it for herself!

Well, Samantha was going to take it away from *her*. Samantha's hands shook as she slid the letter back into its envelope. Amanda was going to be sorry. Samantha rummaged in her pocketbook for the glue she had bought on the way home from school. She spread a thin coat on the inside of the envelope flap and resealed the letter. Early the next morning she would go out to the mailbox and put Ted's letter inside, as if it had never been opened.

Next time Ted came to visit, she was going to make him hers. Either that, or nobody was going to have him.

Nineteen

The sun filtered in through the bedroom curtains, spilling a soft pool of daylight on Amanda's covers. She stretched lazily in her bed. What a perfect Saturday morning. Especially for someone in love. *Ted. Ted Wakefield.* Amanda repeated his name silently, a thrill going through her.

Then she turned her head. Samantha was still asleep, a little scowl on her face. A dark cloud passed over Amanda's feeling of bliss. She had to tell her twin about her and Ted. And she had to do it soon. After all, she and Ted had been writing to each other for over two months. And she had let Ted believe she had already spoken to her parents about him, and that she had talked to Samantha, too. It was what Ted wanted. But it was so hard. If only Samantha would forget about Ted and find some other boy who made her head spin. Amanda kept waiting for it to happen. She'd never known her twin to stay stuck on any one boy for very long. But then, Ted Wakefield was not just any boy.

Amanda shut her eyes, as if she could shut out the unpleasant task ahead of her. Every day she vowed to level with her sister. Every day she managed to find a reason to put it off. Part of it was that Samantha seemed so cool and distant lately. It made Amanda miserable to feel so far away from her twin. And it made it even harder to come out and tell her the news. Things between them were strained already, and Amanda could imagine how it would be after Samantha knew.

But there was an even stronger reason Amanda couldn't bring herself to tell her sister. She hurt all over at the thought of causing Samantha so much pain. Amanda knew that love had a way of catching people unaware, and that all she had done was to fall under Ted's spell, the same as Samantha had. If Ted returned Amanda's feelings, she had every right to let their love blossom.

Amanda looked over at her sleeping sister again and let out a sigh. Samantha looked so unhappy already, her mouth turned down as though she was having a bad dream. Perhaps she sensed something without having been told. There had always been an unspoken communication between the two of them, a closeness and understanding only twins could share. Amanda had written a poem about it, which she had titled "Part Of Me."

As if hearing Amanda think about her, Samantha rolled over and opened one eye. "Ugh. Isn't having to wake up utterly lousy?" She dived under her pillow.

Amanda bit her lip. No, that morning was not the right time to tell Samantha about Ted. But she couldn't put it off forever. She had to reveal the truth before Ted's next visit.

Samantha watched Ted's words of love go up in smoke. She held his newest letter by a corner, part of it already eaten away by flames. Ted's feelings for Amanda were going to be devoured the same way. She let go of the remaining sliver of flaming paper just before it burned her fingers, letting it fall into the sink. All that was left of Ted's message was in Samantha's memory.

She allowed herself a slippery smile as she scooped up the ashes and threw them away. Amanda wouldn't know that Ted was planning on going home to Chicago for a few days, and that he was going to stop in Detroit the next weekend. Amanda wouldn't know that Earl was playing at the Café Car, and that Ted wanted to take her there—alone this time. Until she saw him in person, Amanda wouldn't even know Ted had written.

And by that time it would be too late. By that time, Ted was going to belong to Samantha. She closed her eyes and pictured Ted's handsome face—his deep brown eyes, his fine, straight nose, his full mouth—yes, his mouth, his face, coming closer to hers. Closer and closer, until their lips met. . . .

Samantha gave a little shiver of anticipation.

When Ted arrived in Detroit next Friday afternoon, Samantha was going to be ready. And poor Amanda was going to be left in the dust.

The coast was clear. The school corridor was empty. Samantha could hear no footsteps echoing in the stairwell, no voices carrying from around the hall corner. She jiggled the brass-plated doorknob of the *Klaxon* office. It turned easily, and she felt the door latch give way. Her eyes darted left and right as she made one more sweep of the hall. Quickly, she pushed the door open.

On a long table that ran the length of the room, articles for the upcoming issue of the *Klaxon* were arranged page by page, as they would appear when the paper went to print. The newspaper staff had taken a long time to lay the typed columns out carefully, piecing each page together like a jigsaw puzzle. Samantha swept her arm along the table. All the staff's time-consuming handiwork went fluttering to the ground haphazardly.

She glanced around the room. She had to work quickly, before someone found her in there. Along one wall were several bulky wooden filing cabinets. Samantha pulled several of the file drawers open and scattered their contents all over the floor. As a crowning touch, she went over to the big black typewriters and pulled the ribbons out of each and every one of them, flinging them about like inky streamers.

There. That ought to do it, Samantha thought. The *Klaxon* staff was going to have an awfully busy Friday afternoon ahead of them. And while Amanda was staying late at school, Samantha would be entertaining her twin's unexpected visitor.

Samantha put the finishing touches on her makeup. Her eyes shone a brilliant blue-green against the dark, dusky frame of kohl she'd drawn around them. Her lipstick was a perfect, bright red that said "kiss me." Her cheekbones were rouged lightly, and her golden bob was brushed to a shine. The beads of her dress caught the light. Actually, it was Amanda's dress, but Samantha had borrowed it out of the closet they shared. Her armful of bangles jingled delicately. She had rolled down her silk stockings and powdered her knees.

Samantha thought about the frumpy skirt and blouse Amanda had worn to school that morning. As far as Samantha was concerned, Amanda wasn't nearly spiffy enough on most days. But that day her outfit was particularly dull. Of course, that might have something to do with the fact that Samantha had purposely let her twin oversleep. Samantha had watched with satisfaction as Amanda had thrown on the first clothes she'd grabbed out of the closet, pulled on her

165

thick white stockings, and stuffed her feet into her oldest shoes. Hah! Ted was going to see his beloved pen pal looking like a real biddy. But by then it wouldn't matter.

Samantha pictured what Amanda was doing at that moment—refiling, realphabetizing, and reorganizing the tornado of paper on the *Klaxon* office floor. The softest note of guilt sounded in her head, but she silenced it immediately. Amanda had double-crossed her, pure and simple. And now Samantha was going to do some uncrossing.

As she dabbed perfume on the inside of her wrists, she heard a car pulling up and stopping in front of the house. She ran to the window. Ted's coupe! Her heart beat faster as she watched him hop out of the car. In his charcoal slacks and vanilla-colored coat he was even more handsome than last time. Samantha had a bird's-eye view from her bedroom window as Ted made his way up the front walk and announced himself with a rap of the brass door knocker.

Downstairs, the radio was turned off. There was a rustle of pages as Mrs. Watson closed her newspaper. A moment later, her heels sounded against the foyer floor. The front door creaked open.

"Ted! Ted Wakefield!" Samantha heard her mother say. "What a surprise! Come inside, come inside," she added.

Ted disappeared from Samantha's window

view, and she heard him stepping into the foyer. "Didn't Amanda tell you?" His words floated upstairs.

"Amanda?" Confusion rang in Mrs. Watson's voice.

"Yes, I wrote to her, telling her I was coming," Ted said.

"To *Amanda?*" Samantha could imagine the surprised arch of an eyebrow that went with her mother's words.

She felt the painful blade of betrayal sink deeper. Even her mother knew that Ted was supposed to be *her* young man. She had every right to take him away from Amanda. She glanced in the mirror above the vanity table, rehearsing her most sultry expression. No, not rehearsing, she reminded herself. This was the performance. Opening night. Her best movie-star manner in place, she began her descent down the stairs.

"I—I thought Amanda had explained. . . . I mean, I wonder if my letter arrived at all," Ted was saying, his face flushed. "Goodness, I'm so sorry to drop in on you when I wasn't expected."

"Nonsense, Ted," Samantha's mother said. "Harry's roommate is always welcome in our home. Come, take your coat off and have something cool to drink. You've had a long trip, I expect."

Ted seemed to regain his composure. He laughed and nodded. "Well, there *was* one swampy stretch where I got stuck in the mud

167

twice. One time a farmer had to hitch up his horses and pull me out. He told me to forget those newfangled vehicles and get a horse. Said cars would never last."

Mrs. Watson laughed. "Taylor thinks we just need to pave the roads faster and start putting in more of these new traffic-regulating lights we're seeing in the cities. He says that one day this whole nation will be united by these vehicles."

"That and motion pictures," Ted agreed.

"Motion pictures, here, here!" Samantha said, announcing her presence.

A huge smile blossomed on Ted's lips.

"Samantha," her mother said. "Well, don't you look lovely, dear. Do you see who's come to visit us?"

"Sam?" Ted asked. His smile drooped a touch. His mistake was written across his handsome face. "Oh. Well, hello," he said. As Samantha reached the bottom of the staircase his gaze swept the space behind her. The corners of his mouth turned down even further when he saw that nobody was behind her.

Samantha wasn't going to let that stop her. She favored Ted with her most dazzling smile. "Why, Ted Wakefield!" she said, making her voice rich with surprise. "What are you doing here?"

"I wrote," Ted explained. "But apparently my letter never arrived. I wanted to stop here on my way home."

"Oh?" Samantha said, the picture of innocence. "Well, it's wonderful to see you."

"Good to see you, too," Ted said politely. "You look very nice."

Very nice? Darn that Amanda! Samantha thought. She was dressed to stop the new fire trucks of the Detroit fire squad, and all Ted could come up with was "very nice."

"So," Ted said. "Where's your other half?"

Samantha inhaled sharply. *Stay calm,* she told herself. *You've barely begun to work on him. Getting angry is not part of the plan.* "Oh, Amanda's still at school," she answered. "I guess she had to work late on that dumb school paper."

"I'll bet it's not too dumb if they've got a writer like Amanda on the staff," Ted said.

Samantha shrugged. "Yes, well . . ." Then she allowed a glimmer to come into her eye, as if an idea had occurred to her that very second. "Say! What if we went and picked Amanda up right now, so that she doesn't have to walk home this afternoon? Wouldn't that be the right thing to do?"

"Samantha," her mother said, "Ted just got off the road. He might like to wash up and have something to drink."

But Ted played right into Samantha's hands. "Oh, that's swell of you, Mrs. Watson, but I don't mind going to get Amanda. In fact, I think it's an excellent idea."

Samantha felt a trill of hope. "Good. It's

settled. Why don't you leave your bag here for now? We wouldn't want to miss Amanda, would we?" She put a light hand on Ted's sleeve.

"No, we wouldn't," Ted agreed.

A few minutes later, they were seated in his coupe. Samantha shifted over so that she was as close to him as possible. "Go down to the end of this street and take a left," she said. She opened her window wide. "What a beautiful day. You brought spring with you."

"I guess so." Ted laughed.

Samantha directed him down one street and up another. She tingled at his nearness, looking up at his face. "So, have you seen the new Charlie Chaplin film?" she asked breathily.

The Gold Rush?" Ted's face lit up. "Isn't it wonderful? The man is a true genius."

Samantha smiled—and this time it was genuine. She and Ted had plenty in common, too. Amanda didn't have a corner on that. "I especially loved the part when he boiled his shoe for dinner. Oh, bear right here."

Ted followed a long dirt road that climbed slowly upward. "And how about when he makes his potatoes do that dance?" he said. "I don't know how he manages to be so funny and so sad at the same time." Ted followed the road as it curved up the side of a hill. "I think I could see that film over and over and never get tired of it."

The road narrowed into little more than a pitted path. Samantha held onto her seat as the car bumped over the rutted surface. "Boy, they sure chose an out-of-the-way spot to put a high school," Ted commented. He steered the car around a bend. The road came to an end at a bluff high above a scenic valley filled with deep green pines. A glimpse of Lake Erie shimmered in the distance. The breeze blowing in through Samantha's window was mild and sweet.

Ted stepped on the brakes. "Now where?" he asked in confusion.

Samantha leaned toward him. "Now, nowhere," she said in a throaty, low voice. "Welcome to Overlook Valley."

"I thought we were going to your school!"

"But this is so much nicer than school, don't you think? And it's such a lovely day."

Ted turned toward Samantha. A look of comprehension dawned in his eyes. "What about Amanda?"

"She'll get home," Samantha said. Without giving Ted time to protest any further, she leaned over and kissed him on the cheek.

Ted colored noticeably. "Samantha, I—"

"Don't talk, Ted," she commanded. She kissed him again, brushing her mouth softly across his face toward his mouth. His lips met hers and lingered there for a moment. Then he pulled back and shut off the car engine.

Victory! thought Samantha. She tilted her face up toward Ted's for more kisses.

But he turned and looked straight ahead, his

171

eyes on the far-off, cold glitter of Lake Erie. "Samantha, I thought you already knew," he said softly. "Amanda and I—" He took a deep breath. "We love each other. I'm in love with your sister."

Samantha felt as if Ted had slapped her. Not that his words were news to her, but it was so awful to hear Ted say it in person, right in front of her, when he could be kissing her.

"Sam, please don't be upset," Ted said gently. "You're a swell girl. There will be other boys."

Samantha felt anger mixing in with her hurt. Of course there would be other boys. Lots of them. She could probably have any boy she wanted. Except Ted.

"You know, Sam, Amanda loves you," Ted said. "She would never do anything to hurt you intentionally."

Not much, Samantha thought. *Only steal away the boy she knows I'm stuck on, and carry on a secret correspondence with him month after month.*

"It's just that the feelings between us are so strong," Ted went on. "I'm sorry."

Samantha felt the fury raging inside her. She had failed. Amanda had won. Suddenly Ted's little car felt too small. It was as if Samantha's anger was an enormous, unwieldy third party, taking up every pocket of space in the coupe. Her hand trembled on the door handle as she pushed open her door. Her legs were weak with frustration, but she got out of the car quickly. All she could think was that she had to get away from there. Away from the whole horrid situation, away from her failure, away from Ted.

"Sam, please don't run away," he called to her.

But her feet kept moving. The fancy shoes that she had put on for Ted's visit sank into the dirt. Stick around for a guy who couldn't warm up to her most heated kisses? A guy who preferred sugar-sweet Amanda to Samantha's spice and adventure? Ted Wakefield was nothing but a louse. Samantha hurried down the road. Ted and her twin were going to be sorry they had ever set eyes on each other. She was going to make sure of that.

Twenty

The narrow, dank stairwell stank of stale alcohol and stagnant air. Samantha felt as if she were descending into a worm-filled hole in the ground. Her beaded dress, already dusty from the long walk from Overlook Valley, brushed against the dingy walls. At the bottom of the stairs was a heavy, scarred wooden door. Samantha took a resolute breath and put her hand to it to push it open. It was slightly sticky. The Cellar Door. Ugh.

Samantha passed through the doorway into a hall lit by a single dim bulb. At the end was a second door, behind which she could hear the raucous, drunken voices of the Cellar Door's patrons. The entrance to the speakeasy was guarded by an extra-large man who would have looked right at home as a linebacker for the Detroit Panthers. His arms were crossed over a huge chest that strained his jacket.

Samantha's heels clicked against the grimy floor, her breath coming fast and nervous as she made her way toward him.

"Yeah?" he said, the single syllable ringing in the sour air like a challenge.

"I'm looking for Kevin Hughes," Samantha said.

"Kevin?" the big guy repeated. "This here is a private club, you know." Samantha gave a shiver of disgust as he looked her up and down. "But I bet Kevin wouldn't mind having a classy dame like you as his guest." He pulled a key from his jacket. Samantha forced a tight smile as the guard unlocked the second door and let her into Kevin's lair.

A few dozen men sat in the dingy booths and along the bar. Heads turned toward her. "We-ell, a dame!" announced a raspberry-nosed man slumped at the bar. "A gorgeous dame!"

Samantha ignored him, her eyes making a sweep of the room. It wasn't hard to spot Kevin Hughes immediately. Sitting at a back booth, he was surrounded by fellows—one bringing him a drink, another lighting his cigarette, several more hanging on his every word. His new cash and flash had clearly made him a celebrity around his old haunt. Celebrity in the Cellar Door—that was one kind of fame Samantha could live without.

She wanted to turn right around and race home. Instead, she set a course toward Kevin. *Remember, you're an actress,* she told herself. She held her head high, gliding gracefully as if making her way across the most elegant ballroom. She felt all eyes following her.

"Kevin, darling," Samantha sang out as she approached his booth, trying to make it sound as if he were a desirable leading man.

Kevin's face lit up. Then he seemed to reconsider. His smile curled into a wounded pout. "If you're looking for Rudolph Valentino, he just left."

"Aw, Kevin, don't be sore," Samantha said. She rolled her hips as she approached his table. One of his friends let out a low whistle through his teeth. Samantha felt a shudder of revulsion go through her, but she didn't let it show.

"Last time I saw you, you told me to grow up," Kevin said.

"Last time I was wrong. We all make mistakes. Remember? That's what *you* told *me*."

Kevin arched an eyebrow.

"You said you wanted to give me another chance. And, well, I've decided that all those other boys are just big bores. You live so much faster than they do." Samantha made her voice go breathy.

"You got it, sister," Kevin said.

"So? Aren't you going to invite me to sit down?" Samantha gave him her most bewitching look.

Kevin was still wary. "Why? So you can give me the high-hat routine again?"

"Kevin, do you think I'm going to snub you after searching half of Detroit to find you?"

"Well . . . OK, you guys, scram. Let the dame and me have some room to breathe." Kevin's boys moved to a different part of the speakeasy, and Samantha slid into the booth up close to Kevin.

"You look great today, Sam," he said.

At least her fancy outfit wasn't a total waste, Samantha thought. "Thanks," she said. "Swell ring." She touched the jewel-encrusted band around one of Kevin's fingers and let her hand graze his.

"Yeah, ain't it?" There was a swagger in Kevin's voice. He took a gulp of his drink. "Want one?"

Samantha forced herself to lean in toward Kevin so her arm was touching his. "A drink or a ring?" she asked with a throaty laugh.

"Let's start with the drink, doll." Kevin's cheeks flushed. Was he blushing or was it the liquor? No matter, Samantha thought; either one might soften him up enough for her purposes.

"Thanks, Kevin, but I think I'll just keep you company while you have yours," she replied. She watched him put it away as if it were soda pop. Then she offered to get up and get him another.

"That's what I like. A dame who waits on you," Kevin said, his words beginning to slur.

Samantha made her way to the bar, attracting attention from Kevin's fellow drinkers. Her skin crawled. What a low-down crowd. Still, the catcalls and unabashed stares would probably make Kevin feel like a big man for sharing his table with her.

177

She did her best to flatter him as he drained his new drink. When she came back with yet another one, Samantha let him sling his arm around her.

"I've missed you," he said drunkenly.

Samantha looked into his bloodshot eyes. "It has been a while, hasn't it? Maybe we can start making up for lost time."

Kevin pulled her more tightly against him. "Yeah? What'd ya have in mind?"

Samantha fought the temptation to move away. "You could take me out again. We could go see a motion picture at the Bijou."

"Yeah?" Kevin gave a leering grin. "Just like that?"

"Well . . . there is one little, tiny favor you can do for me," Samantha said.

"Oh." Kevin seemed to sober up immediately. "So this is why you came in here talking sweet." He took his arm away from her.

"It's almost nothing," Samantha said quickly. "In fact, it's as much a favor to yourself."

"Oh yeah?" Kevin gave her a sidelong glance.

"Yeah," she said. "See, the way I've been hearing it, a lot of people are talking about you."

Kevin seemed to puff up his chest like a blowfish. "Is that right?" he said proudly.

"Sure," Samantha said. "New clothes, new style . . . new man." She made her voice rich with admiration.

Kevin took a self-assured swig of liquor. "Of

course, there's a dangerous side to all the attention," Samantha added.

Kevin banged his glass down on the table. "There is?"

"Well, people are also talking about where all your cash is coming from," she said. "Word gets around fast."

Kevin gave a drunken grin. "Money talks."

"Kevin, did it ever occur to you that maybe it talks too much?" Samantha asked.

The grin stayed plastered to Kevin's alcohol-flushed face. He didn't seem to get the point.

"What you're doing is illegal," Samantha said.

"Hey, thanks for telling me." Kevin laughed noisily.

Samantha held in a sigh of exasperation. "Kevin, aren't you afraid that somebody's going to say something to the wrong person one day?"

The dumb grin slipped off Kevin's face. Samantha could see that she had finally gotten an idea through his thick skull. "Are you saying the Feds are on my tail?" Kevin asked. His voice was suddenly shaky.

"I've heard talk about it," Samantha lied. "That's why I thought you might like this idea I have."

Kevin took another long swig of his drink. "I'm all ears."

She told Kevin what she had in mind, step by sly step. Was he drunk enough to agree to it yet?

179

Each sip he took seemed to bring her closer to getting even with Amanda and Ted.

Kevin listened closely and nodded. "Smart dame," he said.

Samantha felt a spark of satisfaction.

"But I don't know if I want to part with a whole night's work," Kevin said.

The spark went out. "Kevin, it's as much for you as for me," Samantha said. She slid closer to Kevin, as close as she dared.

"You're talking about a lot of liquor," he said. "I hate to pour out all the profits. Even for you, pretty lady," he added, bringing his face only inches away from hers.

Samantha resisted the urge to pull back. She could see her plan melting away like the ice in Kevin's drink. She let her hand rest on his shoulder. "Not for me. For you," she whispered. "You don't want to go to jail, do you?"

Kevin rested a hand on top of hers and stroked her fingers.

"No fancy suits. No boys to run your errands. No me," Samantha added. She tried to sound sultry, but she knew there was a note of desperation in her voice.

"And if I say no?" Kevin asked. "I bet I can forget about seeing you around anymore."

Samantha played her riskiest card. "It's all right, Kevin. I don't want you to do anything you don't want to do. I'll still be here for you."

"Yeah?" Kevin asked. He put his arms around

her and pulled her toward him. Samantha steeled herself as Kevin's liquor-moistened lips pressed against hers.

"Yeah," Samantha whispered when he pulled away. Luckily, Kevin was too drunk to notice her shudder of disgust. She let him kiss her again. "I just think an ounce of prevention is worth a pound of cure. Think about it."

Kevin nodded slowly. "I suppose you're right."

Samantha felt a breeze of relief in the smoky speakeasy. "I knew I could count on you," she said.

"She hates me." Amanda's tears wet the front of Ted's shirt. "We've never had a secret from each other in our whole lives before. It's all my fault." The icy hatred in Samantha's eyes burned in her memory. Her twin had come home, glared at her wordlessly, and locked herself in the bathroom.

Her mother and father had traded looks that didn't need an explanation. *Poor Sam*, their faces said. It was clear Ted had made a different choice than they'd expected.

Amanda felt like the sneakiest, worst sister in the whole world. No amount of coaxing would bring Samantha out to talk.

"Just let her be," Ted advised. He stroked Amanda's hair and tried to soothe away her tears as they sat together on the living room sofa.

"There's no sense trying to reason with her when the anger is so fresh."

"I wanted to tell her about us before, but I couldn't stand to hurt her. I know you wanted the same thing, and I know I was wrong to let you think I'd explained everything to my family. But I didn't know you were coming back so soon and I thought I'd still have time. . . . Oh, Ted, I didn't want to hurt *anyone,* and that's exactly what I've done!"

"Shh, Amanda, shh," Ted whispered. "Don't blame yourself. It's partly my fault, too. Maybe I should have written to your parents. As for Sam, well, she needs time to calm down. Just let her be by herself for a while. And you need to relax, too. Maybe Earl's music at the Café Car will help."

Amanda shook her head, gulping back a fresh stream of tears. "How can I go out and have fun when Samantha's so unhappy?"

"Amanda, what good is it going to do to stay here and make yourself miserable? Samantha's not ready to talk, and you can't push her. Let her sleep on it. Things have a way of looking brighter in the morning."

Amanda shrugged out of Ted's warm arms. "Just let me try once more." She went down the hall and knocked on the bathroom door. "Sam?" she said timidly.

Sam's answer was like machine-gun fire. "Why don't you just leave me alone? Take your stupid boyfriend and get out of here."

Amanda swallowed hard. "Sam, please come out and talk to me. I never meant to hurt you."

"I'd rather talk to a python," Samantha said.

Tears stung Amanda's throat. She hung her head and stood helplessly outside the bathroom door for a few moments. Then she turned and went back to the living room, her steps heavy with sadness.

Ted's strong, caring hug helped a little. "She can't stay mad at you forever," he reassured her. "You just have to give her time." Amanda buried her face against Ted's chest. "Come on, Amanda. What do you say we go out, try to get your mind off this?"

Amanda sighed. "I think that's exactly what Sam wants—to get rid of us."

"Does that mean yes?" Ted asked gently. "We might even have some fun, you know."

Amanda looked up into Ted's loving face. She felt a flame of love and warmth inside, drying her tears. "You're right," she said. "Just let me do one thing before we go."

She ran upstairs to her roll-top desk, and took out her poetry notebook. She flipped through it until she came to the poem called "Part Of Me," which she'd written about her and Samantha. Carefully, she tore it loose from the sewn binding. In capital letters on the top of the page, she printed *I LOVE YOU, SAM.*

She left the poem on Samantha's bed.

Twenty-one

In the dark bedroom, Samantha listened to Amanda's slow, even breathing. Thank goodness her twin was asleep. She had come home just at the stroke of midnight, the twins' weekend curfew, but she and Ted had stayed down in the living room so late, Samantha had started to worry that her twin would never come to bed.

Finally, Samantha had heard her washing up, humming away, all lovey-dovey and dreamy. Samantha had opened one eye just long enough to see Amanda float into the bedroom, a look of bliss on her face.

Her happy expression had disappeared as her gaze had come to rest on Samantha. Samantha had shut her eyes and pretended to be asleep. But she had heard Amanda picking up that dumb, mushy poem Samantha had crumbled up and left in the middle of the floor, heard her smooth the paper out and begin to cry softly.

Good. Let Amanda feel horrible that she had deceived the person she was supposed to be closest to in the whole world. Let her feel miserable that she was a double-crossing fink. Maybe once she paid the price for it, Samantha would be more willing to forgive her.

Now Samantha peered over at her to make sure Amanda was asleep. She called her name softly to be extra certain. Once, twice. No response. Excellent. Samantha tiptoed out of bed and over to the chair where Amanda had draped the outfit she had worn for her night out with Ted. Silently, Samantha slithered into the peach silk dress and draped herself with the ropes of pearls. She pulled on one of Amanda's silk stockings, then slipped a foot into the other.

Darn! Double darn! She felt her finger go right through the second stocking, the hole spreading out into a long, obvious run. She took the stockings off and threw them back on the chair. Moving as silently as she could, she rummaged around in her drawer for another pair. She did her best to find the same color, but the closest she could come was several shades darker. She hoped Ted wouldn't notice.

In the closet, she found the shoes Amanda had been wearing. She carried them out of the room, giving a backward glance at her sister.

"Sweet dreams," she whispered. "They may have to last you for quite a while."

Holding Amanda's shoes, she padded down the hall in her stocking feet to the guest room. She pushed the door open quietly. Ted was asleep, a beam of moonlight bathing his face. Samantha went over and put a hand on his cheek. "Ted," she whispered.

As her fingers touched the warmth of his skin, she felt a tiny flicker of the old feelings inside her. Ted might be a fink, but he certainly was handsome.

"Ted. Ted, wake up," she said, letting her voice rise and fall in her sister's sweet, soft cadences.

Ted's eyes opened. "Amanda?" He looked up at Samantha with a sleepy smile. "You're still dressed. Haven't you gone to sleep yet?"

Samantha leaned down toward him without answering. Their lips met in a long, passionate kiss. Samantha could feel Ted's heart beating against her chest as he pulled her close. His breath was one with hers. She couldn't resist. She gave in to what she had wanted for so long.

"Mmm," Ted murmured drowsily. "I know it's not proper for you to be in here, but I love it. I love you."

Samantha drank in another kiss. *Just one more,* she told herself. *You can't forget what you're doing here.* But Ted's kisses felt so good, she couldn't bring herself to pull away.

"Amanda, Amanda," he whispered in her ear. That brought Samantha down to earth. She drew back.

"Ted, listen. Someone just came by from the Café Car," Samantha said.

"Came here?" Ted asked. He gave her a sleepy kiss on the forehead.

186

Samantha nodded. "Earl sent for you. Something's up."

Ted pulled back. Suddenly, he looked wide awake. "Earl? What's wrong?"

Samantha shrugged. "I don't know, but the boy he sent said to come right away."

Ted swung himself out of bed, his bare legs sticking out from underneath his long nightshirt. "Say, Amanda, how did they find me here?" he asked, his worry tinged with confusion.

Samantha gulped. She hadn't quite thought of everything. "I—ah, there must have been someone at the club tonight who saw us together and knew where I lived."

Ted knitted his brows. "I don't remember you saying hello to anyone."

"Um, uh, there was someone I recognized from school. We, ah, sort of nodded to each other," Samantha improvised.

Ted nodded. "Well, we'll find out soon enough. If Earl needs me, he can count on me."

"Of course he can. I'll come with you. Why don't you get dressed and I'll meet you downstairs?"

"All right. I'll be right down," Ted said.

As Samantha left the room, she allowed herself a satisfied smile. So far, so good.

"Whoa! What's going on here?" Ted asked as the coupe neared the club. The area around the entrance was barricaded off and the headlights of several cars flooded the scene with light. A noisy crowd was gathering.

"It's the Fe—the police!" Samantha said. Amanda would never use a word like *Feds*.

"I hope Earl's not in trouble," Ted said. He steered the car right up to the barricades. They were immediately approached by two burly men in dark suits.

"Miss Amanda Watson?" the heavyset, red-faced one asked.

"Yes, that's me," Samantha said. She could feel her heart beating nervously. This was her biggest role ever. She had to play it to the hilt.

"Agent Samson," the man said, flashing a badge. "Perhaps you'd like to step out of the auto."

Samantha could see Ted stiffen. "Is there a problem, sir?" he asked.

"Not for this young lady," Agent Samson replied. Samantha let him help her out of the car. "I'd just like to thank her for doing her duty and bringing you to us."

"Me? To you?" Ted's handsome face was a mask of confusion. "Amanda, I thought Earl sent for me."

Samantha let the G-man answer for her. "As for you, pal, we hear you've been financing your college tuition with some illegal money, if you know what I mean."

Ted's brow furrowed. "Excuse me?"

"I think you heard me the first time," Agent

188

Samson said. "You know what's in this car as well as we do."

Ted shook his head. "I do? I'm in this car, sir, is that what you mean?"

"Oh, a wise guy," the agent's partner said, swaggering over to the car. He was even bigger and more intimidating than Agent Samson. "OK. Get him outta there." He made a motion with his hand, and two more agents stepped forward and roughly pulled Ted from the coupe.

"I don't understand," Ted said helplessly. "What's going on?" He looked at Samantha. "What does this have to do with Miss Watson? If you do anything to hurt her . . ."

Samantha's big moment had arrived. She blinked fast and hard, calling up several fat tears. "The only person who's hurt me is you," she said in her shakiest voice.

Ted's face crinkled up with hurt and bewilderment. "Me? What are you talking about? Amanda, why are you crying? I don't understand what's going on here!" He looked from Samantha to the federal agents, then back to Samantha again.

"Maybe she's crying because her boyfriend turned out to be a crook," Agent Samson said.

Ted looked as if someone had slapped him. "A crook?"

"Yeah. Now, how's about you open up the trunk for us so we can take a look at what you got in there?"

Ted looked thoroughly bewildered, but he did as he was told. Samantha watched as the headlights from one of the agents' cars caught the sparkle of dozens upon dozens of glass bottles in the coupe's trunk. Ted let out a loud gasp.

"Right. An innocent. Sure, buster. Next you're going to be telling us you didn't know it was a crime to be transporting intoxicating drink." Agent Samson turned to Samantha. "Thanks for making us wise to this guy."

"What?" Ted looked at Samantha, his eyes wide with astonishment. "You knew what was in my trunk? You told them that I had . . ." His words trailed off in disbelief as he gestured at the contents of his car. "But what about Earl?"

Samantha made a show of bravely sniffing back her tears. "This isn't about Earl, Ted. It's about you running bootleg liquor."

Ted's face contorted with hurt. "Amanda, you don't think I really put this stuff in here, do you? Why didn't you say something to me? I would have told you I didn't know a thing about it."

"And you'd expect me to believe you? The same fellow who took my sister up to Overlook Valley and . . . oh, I can barely say it . . . tried to—to seduce her. Oh, Ted, I thought you loved me!"

Shock was written all over Ted's face. "No, Amanda, no! You've got it all wrong."

"I do?" Samantha let her tears flow fast and strong. "My twin has never lied to me, Ted Wakefield. Which is more than I can say for you. And to think how I felt about you!"

"Amanda, I didn't try to seduce Samantha. I swear to you." Ted reached out toward her. "This is madness."

One of the agents grabbed Ted's wrists and handcuffed them behind his back. "Sir, there's been a mistake. I'm not the man you want," Ted protested.

"Sure, pal. That's what they all say." He turned Ted over to Agent Samson, who dragged Ted toward a waiting car.

"Amanda!" Ted said. "Amanda, believe me. I never made a move for your sister. And I didn't put the bottles in my car."

Agent Samson pulled Ted forward. "Sure you didn't. They just walked in there by themselves."

"Please, sir," Ted said. "Somebody else must have planted those—" Suddenly Ted whipped around toward Samantha with such force that the agent momentarily lost his grasp on him. But Ted didn't break away. He stood rooted to the spot, staring at Samantha. "No, Amanda! It couldn't have been you . . . could it? Did you do this because you thought I had made a play for your sister?"

Samantha held his gaze in silence. She watched Ted's hurt and confusion turn to fury. His mouth set into a tight, tense line. His hands clenched up. There was ice in his eyes where not too long

191

before there had been fire. "I don't believe this! You can't be the girl I fell in love with," he said.

"Come on, big fellow," Agent Samson was saying. "We've been looking for the guy who's been supplying these parts for quite some time."

"Good heavens, Amanda! You can't just let them take me away like this," Ted said over his shoulder. "You know I'm innocent."

Agent Samson pushed Ted into one of the unmarked cars. Ted gave Samantha one last look full of astonishment and grief and fury. "I thought I loved you, but I was wrong. Maybe I should have gone for Samantha after all."

Samantha nodded solemnly and whispered under her breath, "Yes, Ted. Maybe you should have." She watched the FBI men drive away with Ted.

The score was settled. Amanda had taken Ted away from her. Now she had taken Ted away from Amanda. They were even. It was over. Ted Wakefield was out of their lives for good.

Twenty-two

Amanda waited.

She stood at the bedroom window, holding back the curtain and peering out at the empty street. The house was silent. Her parents were out visiting friends, and Samantha had left for her play rehearsal before Amanda had woken up. Amanda swallowed hard. It was as if her twin couldn't bear even to be in the same room with her. And Ted? His bag was still in the guest room, his bed slept in and unmade. But he was nowhere to be found. His car was gone, too.

At first Amanda told herself he had just gone out for a drive. It was a good day for it. The sun was shining and the air was sweet with spring. Or perhaps he had had an idea for a story and he was chasing down a lead. Writers got like that sometimes, didn't they? They had an idea and they just threw themselves into it. Amanda told herself that Ted would be back soon. But it was strange that he hadn't left so much as a note for her.

She tried to distract herself with various chores. She straightened up the room, putting away the clothing she had worn the night before.

Funny that she hadn't noticed the huge rip in one stocking when she was taking it off. She threw the stockings into the back of her drawer, making a mental note to bring them down to the ragbag later. Then she tackled her mathematics problems for school. Afterward, she tried to write some poetry, but by this time her words were frozen with worry. Where was Ted?

She put her poetry notebook away and stationed herself at the window again. She felt like Elsie DeCecco, waiting for her boyfriend to come home from the war. *How silly!* she told herself. *Ted's just out for a little while.* But the sky was now bright with the midday sun. Ted had been gone more than a little while.

It didn't make sense to Amanda. The night before, even sleep had been a painful separation for her and Ted. They had lingered over their goodnights with kiss after kiss, each one deeper and more passionate than the next.

"I almost can't bear to wait until morning," Ted had whispered in Amanda's ear.

What if something had happened to him? What if he'd gotten lost? Had an accident? Why had he even gone out in the first place, if he'd been so eager to see Amanda as soon as he woke up?

Amanda worried. And waited.

Amanda watched her parents come up the walk. From her bedroom window, she could just make out the grim looks on their faces. There was no mistaking their expressions. They had bad news.

Amanda felt a cold shiver go through her. Had her parents found out something about Ted? She raced downstairs, her heart beating out of control. She met them at the door.

"It's about Ted, isn't it?"

Her father nodded, his brow furrowed. "Maybe you'd better sit down, Amanda."

Amanda had visions of the coupe overturned by the side of some road, Ted's lifeless body covered with a sheet. "Tell me!" she yelled. "Please, just tell me right now!" It couldn't be any worse than what she was imagining.

"It's in the late edition of the paper. I think you'd better prepare yourself." Mr. Watson held out the folded newspaper. "Fourth page."

Amanda nearly ripped the paper from his hand. She shook as she riffled through the pages.

The headline blared out at her. *Chicago Youth Arrested for Transporting Bootleg Liquor,* it read.

"Ted!" Amanda gasped. "But that's impossible!"

"We're shocked, too, Amanda," her mother said. "I don't know what to think. According to the paper he was found with a trunk full of bottles in front of some club called the Café Car."

"The Café Car? That's where we went last night. I was with him. We went and heard his friend Earl play. Then we came home. There wasn't a bit of trouble." Quickly, Amanda skimmed the newspaper article for details. "Four A.M.? But we were asleep." She kept reading. Then she came to the biggest shock of all. " 'He was accompanied by a beautiful blonde in a pink dress!' Why, that almost sounds as if it could be me. The dress I had on was peach-colored. But I wasn't . . . I didn't . . . heavens, no! It can't be the right Ted Wakefield!" She heard her words coming out in a rush of disbelief.

"Amanda." Her father enveloped her in a strong hug. "Darling, I know how terrible this must be for you."

Amanda buried her head in the soft flannel of her father's jacket. It couldn't be! It mustn't be! Her beloved Ted a criminal? Her beloved Ted sneaking around in the dead of night with bottles of moonshine and another girl?

She remembered Harry's words the first night she had met Ted: "That's Ted for you. Polite, well-mannered, smart—and then you find out he knows every nightspot in town." She put that together with Ted's story about his Grandfather Wakefield and how the family money had begun to run out. Could Ted be desperate enough to try making it back in a way he hadn't told Amanda about? And what of this other girl?

Amanda thought about the kisses she and Ted had shared. She thought about his beautiful words and the deep openness in his eyes. Another girl? There had to be some explanation that wasn't in the newspaper.

"Father, Mother, I've got to go see him. I've got to hear Ted's story in person," she said.

"Amanda, he must be in a holding cell at some police station," Mr. Watson said. "Or in jail."

Amanda freed herself from his arms. "I don't care. I have to talk to him. Ted is a good person. The best person. There must be something we don't know."

He took the newspaper out of Amanda's hands. "Amanda, it's always hard to admit we've misjudged somebody, and I know how you feel about Ted—"

"Don't say it!" Amanda cried. "Don't say 'but.' I won't listen to you condemn Ted when he hasn't had a chance to tell his side of the story." She heard the loud, angry way her words came out, and suddenly she felt ashamed. She had never talked to her father this way before. "I'm sorry," she said more softly.

He cupped a hand under her chin. "Amanda, look at me. I know people make mistakes about other people. It's only human."

"Father, I haven't made a mistake," Amanda said.

Mrs. Watson put a hand on Amanda's shoulder. "Sometimes, dear, it's hard to know," she said. There was a faraway note in her voice. "I made a mistake once. A big mistake. I almost ended up with the wrong man."

"Mother, Ted's not the wrong man," Amanda said. "And even if you're right, don't you think I should be able to find out for myself?" she argued.

Her parents exchanged looks. "I can't say I approve of my daughter running around from police station to police station, chasing after someone who might be a bootlegger," her father said.

"Father, all that's going to happen is that I'll find out the truth," Amanda said. "Please," she added.

"Taylor, she's right. Goodness knows, I ran off a long way farther than the local police station when I was Amanda's age. And she needs to find out the truth. It's the only way." Amanda flashed her mother a grateful look.

Her father sighed. "Well . . . all right. Go if you must. I always thought your sister was more like your mother than you are. But now I see that you have an impetuous streak, too. Go on."

"Thank you, Father." Amanda stood on tiptoe and gave him a kiss on the cheek.

"Good luck, Amanda."

Amanda turned on her heel and headed for the door. She had told her parents she was going to find out the truth. Would it be something she really wanted to hear?

It was dark. Amanda's legs ached from walking from one neighborhood to the next, hopping one streetcar after another. She had cried herself out and now she felt numb. Numb and exhausted. She climbed the steps to another police station, pulled open the heavy metal door, and approached the high wooden front desk. Timidly, tiredly, she asked the officer on duty the same question she had been asking all afternoon.

"Wakefield?" the wiry, red-haired officer asked.

Amanda was getting to know this procedure by heart. Next she said, "Nineteen years old. Tall, dark-haired, handsome."

The police officer shrugged. "I don't know. We get all sorts in here. Let me look in the record. *W, w, w.*"

Amanda anticipated the shake of his head. Instead, the routine changed. "Ah, Wakefield, Theodore," the officer said.

"He's here?" Amanda felt herself become alert instantly.

The policeman ran his finger across the line of blue ink in his ledger. Amanda felt her spirits sink again as he shook his head. "Was here. The Feds told us to let him out. Couldn't make the charges stick. Left this morning."

Amanda felt a peculiar mix of relief and despair. They couldn't make the charges stick. That meant Ted was probably innocent. Oh, she knew he was! But it also meant she had no way of finding him.

"Hey, Joe," the policeman yelled to another officer seated at a desk in the room behind him.

"You were here when they released this Wakefield kid, weren't you?" He turned back to Amanda. "Maybe Officer Johnstone knows something."

Officer Johnstone lumbered over to the front desk. He was a big, older man with a long nose and a shock of white hair. "Yeah. We had him in the holding pen overnight. Kept insisting he was innocent—said some dame set him up." Officer Johnstone peered at Amanda. "You're not the gal he was talking about, are you, miss?"

Amanda thought about the newspaper reports of the girl in the pink dress. She shook her head miserably.

"The guy said his heart was broken," Officer Johnstone went on. "Said if he was wrong about the girl he loved, he was wrong about everything."

The girl he loved? Amanda felt like a tornado was whirling inside her. Did that mean her, or the mysterious blonde in pink? Ted had told her he loved her, but if he had lied about how he was paying for college, maybe he had lied about that, too. Less than twenty-four hours earlier Amanda had been so sure of Ted's feelings—and her own. Now she didn't know what to believe.

"So you don't know where I might be able to find him?" Amanda asked, feeling hopeless.

Both officers shook their heads. Officer Johnstone ran a hand through his white hair. "I'm sorry, Miss—"

"Watson," Amanda supplied. "Amanda Watson."

Officer Johnstone's bushy white eyebrows knitted together immediately. "I thought you said you weren't the girl he was talking about."

Amanda shook her head. "I'm not."

Officer Johnstone was giving her a funny look. "But that was her name. Amanda. I'm sure of it. He kept repeating it as if he couldn't believe what she had done . . . or what *you* had done," he said, more than a hint of suspicion in his voice.

"You know, dragging the law into a lovers' quarrel is a very serious matter, young lady," the front desk officer added gravely.

Amanda's head was spinning. "I—I'm not the girl he meant," she said weakly. Her legs felt so shaky, she thought she might fall down. "But I think I know who is."

"Miss, are you all right?" Officer Johnstone asked. "You're looking pale."

Amanda most decidedly did not feel all right. In fact, she felt thoroughly sick at the ugliness of the thought forming in her mind. But it would explain everything. Goodness knows it wouldn't have been the first time Samantha had pretended to be her. She had even gotten away with fooling their parents a few times.

The last time had been when Samantha had stayed out past curfew on a date and their father had punished her, saying no nights out for a week. The very next night, she had pretended to

201

be Amanda and had gone out with the same fellow again, that horrible Kevin Hughes, the one who was still so stuck on Samantha, the one they said was running bootlegged—heavens! Bootlegged liquor! Just like what Ted was arrested for!

The picture kept getting clearer and more monstrous. Amanda felt as if she were living a nightmare. Samantha, her identical twin, her best friend in the whole world, had framed the boy she loved. And she had somehow made him think Amanda was responsible.

It was war. Amanda stormed up the staircase and into the bedroom.

Samantha was seated at the vanity, trying on a new shade of lipstick. She eyed Amanda warily in the mirror.

Amanda slammed the bedroom door and marched across the room. She grabbed the lipstick right out of Samantha's hand. *S-N-A-K-E,* she wrote in thick, blood-red letters on the mirror.

"Amanda! What in the world are you doing?" Samantha yelled. "That's a brand-new tube of lipstick!"

Amanda took the lipstick and smashed it against the mirror. The finger of soft, waxy red squashed into a shapeless blob.

"That cost me five whole cents at F. W. Woolworth's!" Samantha said. "You owe me, Amanda."

"I owe you?" Amanda barely recognized her

own hard voice. "And what about what you owe me?"

Samantha spun around on the vanity bench. "Amanda, what are you talking about? I'm the one who's angry with you. You're the snake, not me."

Amanda took her twin by the shoulders and shook her. "Snake. Double snake. You know very well what I'm talking about."

Samantha shrugged out of her grasp. "Ow! You're hurting me. What in the world is going on?" She put on her most innocent voice.

"This is about Ted and you know it," Amanda said. As she pronounced his name, she felt a new surge of fury against her twin.

"Oh, him," Samantha said. "Mother and Father told me."

"Not that you didn't already know," Amanda said, her voice just barely under control.

Samantha scowled. "Amanda, I don't know what you're trying to say or what kind of game you're playing."

"Losing the boy I love is no game. At least to me it's not."

"Amanda, I'm sure finding out about Ted was a shock, but look at it this way: it's good riddance to bad rubbish."

Amanda felt her whole body trembling. "Ted Wakefield is not bad rubbish."

Samantha arched an eyebrow. "That's not what the newspapers said."

"And the girl in pink? What does the mysterious girl in pink say?" Amanda had never dreamed she could feel such hatred toward her own twin. How could Samantha have done this?

Samantha held her ground. "I don't know what you're talking about, Amanda."

Amanda yanked open her drawer and pulled out one pale silk stocking. "Sam, while I was up here waiting for Ted, I had lots of time to put away my clothing from last night. And guess what I discovered?"

"A stocking. I see," Samantha said. "But I don't understand what that has to do with Ted. Why are you acting so batty? Ruining my lipstick, talking about some girl in pink—"

"Samantha, this stocking has a run in it," Amanda said.

Samantha turned her face away from Amanda. "Gee, that's too bad," she said. "Those darned things run awfully easily, don't they?"

"It didn't have a run in it when I took it off," Amanda continued.

"Maybe you just didn't see it."

"I don't think so. But if someone else put it on after I took it off, it could have ripped then, right?" Amanda asked pointedly.

"Amanda, what is all this fuss about stockings? You're acting positively goofy."

"I think you know," Amanda said. "I think that the person who put on my stockings probably also put on my dress. Pink isn't too far from peach. It

204

would be easy to get the two colors mixed up, wouldn't it?"

Samantha was silent.

"Admit it," Amanda said. "You were so jealous of me and Ted that you planned this whole horrible thing."

Samantha got up. "Amanda, maybe you've forgotten, but as of yesterday I'm not even talking to you." She went over to the window and stared outside, her back to Amanda.

Amanda followed her. "Oh, no you don't. You're not going to get out of telling me the whole truth and nothing but the truth. I seem to remember you reminding me, not too long ago, that we didn't keep secrets from each other."

Samantha whirled around, her jaw set. "And who was the first to turn into a lying sneak?"

"I didn't lie," Amanda said. "I just couldn't find the right time to tell you. I couldn't bear to make you unhappy. Now I see that you have no trouble doing that to me. And my God, think about what you've done to Ted! You may have ruined his life!"

"Me?"

Amanda could feel her fury spiraling like a whirlwind. "I'm not as blind as you seem to think."

"Well, golly," Samantha said with fake surprise, "that's exactly how I felt when you were carrying on your lovesick letter writing with Ted. What do you think of that?"

205

Amanda gasped. "You knew about the letters?"

" 'Dear Amanda,' " Samantha quoted in an overly gooey voice. " 'Your letters are exquisite agony.' " She made a face. "Exquisite agony? Who does the fellow think he is? William Shakespeare?"

Amanda felt as if she'd been punched in the stomach. "You read them." Hearing Ted's words drove home the pain of what had happened.

"Every one of them. I found them under your mattress. And how do you think they made me feel?"

"I don't even have to guess," Amanda told her twin. Any sympathy she had had for Samantha was gone. "It made you feel like plotting the most miserable, evil revenge you could possibly dream up. Something that could ruin Ted's life, and tear apart two people who truly loved each other." Her throat stung as tears welled up inside her. "All Ted and I wanted was to be happy together. We had every right to be."

"Well, you don't have to get so dramatic about it," Samantha said. "I was only trying to even the score."

Amanda felt warm tears running down her face. "Sam, I wonder if you've ever known what it's like to really love somebody. Or if you'll ever know. I don't think you're capable of it."

Samantha's shoulders slumped. "You're wrong, Amanda. I loved someone. I *love* someone. And that person did something that hurt me very badly." She turned toward Amanda, and Amanda could see that her sister's lips were trembling. Was this another one of Samantha's poisonously good acting jobs? "The person was my own twin sister," Samantha said.

Amanda studied Samantha through a film of tears. She thought about Ted. No. She would never let Samantha twist her around her little finger again. She would harden herself to Samantha. No matter what her twin said, she would keep an icy distance.

"It's not the same," Amanda told her sister. "I did what I did for love. You did what you did for spite and hate."

"That's the way you see it," Samantha said. "The way I see it is that you hurt me and I hurt you. We're even. It's over. Now maybe we can go back to the way things were before."

"You must be mad to think things will ever be the same again," Amanda said.

Samantha's face crumbled into a look of anguish. "Amanda, listen, I know I said I wasn't talking to you, but how about if we call a truce? I'll forgive you if you forgive me."

"No," Amanda said. The word fell like a lead weight. "Not until Ted and I are together again."

"Amanda . . ." Samantha protested.

Amanda turned her back on her twin without another word.

Twenty-three

"Bye! Watch for me up on the screen!" Samantha said, giving her mother a huge hug and kiss. "Next time you see me, I'll be a star!"

Amanda watched from the bedroom window as her father loaded Samantha's bags and her trunk into the car to take her to the train station. Hollywood! It was so far away. And so different from staying at home in Detroit and beginning college in the fall, as Amanda was doing. She felt a twinge of regret as she watched Samantha climb into the open-top car. It seemed like a million years ago that her twin had been her best friend in the entire world. In fact, it had been only a couple of months. Two months of wordless, tension-filled days, a potent, silent war in the Watson house.

The early-June sunlight streamed in through the open bedroom window. The perfume of flowers scented the air. Amanda's friends from the *Klaxon* had invited her to picnic down by the lake but she'd declined. It was hard for her to join in the spirit of carefree vacation days. All she could think about was Ted. All she could feel was Ted.

It was better this way. Amanda could never forgive her sister. Not so much for herself, though she was sure her heart would never mend. But Ted had lost everything. He had never returned to school after the arrest. He had sent a brief note to Harry asking him to send his belongings home to Chicago, but when Amanda had written to him there, her letters had been returned unopened. Harry had been equally unsuccessful at getting any further word from Ted. All Amanda could assume was that Ted's world had been so shattered that he had moved as far away as he could go, wanting nothing to do with her or even her brother, severing all contact with the family that had caused him so much pain.

Down in the car, Samantha turned and looked up at Amanda. She gave a sad, tentative smile. Amanda stood motionless. She felt hard inside, a wall of hurt and anger separating her from her twin.

Samantha touched her fingers to her lips and blew her sister a kiss.

Amanda couldn't help feeling a lump in her throat, but she refused to cry. She spun on her heel and walked away from the window. She heard the car start. The two people she loved the most were gone from her life.

* * *

Amanda lay on her bed trying to read, the hot July sun beating through the open window. It seemed as if she'd read the same page over a half dozen times already. Her thoughts kept drifting away from the book as memories of Ted played in her mind.

Suddenly, she heard the telephone ring in the foyer below her room. She jumped up and raced downstairs, trying not to get her hopes up. There wasn't really any way it could be Ted. Even after all the months since she had seen him, she could hear the sound of his rich baritone voice in her mind. She grabbed the earpiece of the telephone.

"Hello?" she said hopefully, speaking into the box attached to the wall.

"Amanda!" Samantha's voice came through the bell-shaped receiver.

"Sam!" Amanda felt a confusing mix of emotions wash over her. There was a sizzle of disappointment at it not being Ted. But there was also an unchecked little shimmer of warmth at hearing from her twin. Amanda had to remind herself that their days of being friends had been buried in front of the Café Car nearly four months before.

But conveniently, Samantha seemed to have forgotten about that. "I've got the best news!" she announced. "I wanted to be the first to tell you."

"Oh?" Amanda asked coolly.

"Amanda, I'm going to be starring in a new movie!"

Amanda felt a thrill go through her. Samantha? In a Hollywood picture? Then she thought of Ted and willed away any excitement. "Oh," she said flatly. "That's nice."

On the other end of the line, Samantha drew in her breath. "You're still angry."

Silence was Amanda's answer.

"Please don't be," Samantha pleaded. "Amanda, you're my best friend, my other half. We can't spend the rest of our lives hating each other."

Amanda swallowed hard. She did feel awfully lonely without Samantha. But the person she missed was the old Samantha, the one she had trusted, the one she had loved. She gripped the earpiece wordlessly.

"Amanda, how long are you going to keep being so darned hard-boiled?" Samantha asked, her words colored with frustration.

Amanda measured her answer carefully. "As long as I keep thinking about Ted. Which means forever."

Over the wire, Samantha sighed. "Listen, Amanda, I know it feels like you'll never get over Ted, but there are other men in the world, and one day soon you're going to meet one of them."

"There aren't any other men. Not for me," Amanda said, her voice low but hard. All she had were her memories—memories that would stay alive forever, like the carved wooden rose her mother had given her. The flower had once belonged to her mother, Amanda's grandmother, Alice. For Grandma it had held memories of her first love, an Englishman she'd met on her voyage to America but had never seen again once their ship had landed. For Amanda's mother, the rose was a remembrance of *her* twin sister, Elisabeth, who had died in a riding accident at the age of seventeen. For Amanda, the wooden flower would always remind her of Ted. She knew no one else would ever take his place in her heart.

"You're wrong," Samantha said. "Believe me. I know. You think you're all alone and then—well, someone like Jack comes along."

"Jack?"

"Mmm," Samantha murmured dreamily. "Jack Lewis. Oh, Amanda, I wish you could meet him. He's the most wonderful man in the entire world. He's a journalist. He's covering the Hollywood scene and he's going to make me and my movie famous!"

Amanda bit her lip. Another journalist. It wasn't fair that Samantha should take Ted away from her and then find someone to make her forget the whole ugly episode.

Samantha continued to rave about Jack Lewis. "He's incredibly handsome, and he loves me so much. Listen, Amanda, Ted's in the past. I promise you, I'm completely over him, so you've got to forgive me. Say you will, please, Amanda?"

Samantha's words did exactly the opposite of what she was intending. Completely over Ted?

That easily? Amanda felt her blood boiling. She would never get over Ted. Ever.

"You did this to me over someone you've forgotten about less than half a year later?" Amanda shouted into the telephone. "Don't call me again, Samantha. I don't ever want to see or talk to you again." She slammed the earpiece into its cradle.

It's what you wanted, Amanda reminded herself for the hundredth time. *Sam invited you. She begged you to come. You refused.*

Amanda sat on the sofa in the Watsons' living room, a two-month-old newspaper clipping in her lap. A photo of Samantha stared up at her. *Starlet from Detroit Married in Hollywood,* the caption read. The paper usually favored the traditional hand-drawn sketches to illustrate their stories, but a budding star was clearly important enough for the most up-to-date technology. Accompanying the newspaper account was another photograph showing Amanda's parents and brother standing on either side of the bride and groom. Amanda studied the face, identical to her own, that radiated so much happiness. In the wedding picture, Samantha was gazing up at a tall, fair-haired man who looked as happy as she did. Amanda had to admit that he was awfully good-looking. Jack Lewis. Samantha's husband. *Husband.* She rolled the word around in her head. She couldn't get used to it. Not for Samantha.

Though Amanda would never have admitted it to her twin, over the past few months she had followed Samantha's career through newspaper articles. She had carefully clipped the stories about Samantha's movie, which had garnered rave reviews from all the critics, and about her meteoric rise to fame. Often she had sat on her bed poring over the photos she had collected— Samantha at the Brown Derby, Samantha and Jack getting out of a limousine. Samantha with the movie mogul Samuel Goldwyn.

Amanda looked at the wedding photo again and sighed.

It was as if Amanda's twin was playing another form of their favorite childhood make-believe games—make believe you're a movie star, make believe you're all grown up, make believe you're married. Maybe if Amanda had been closer to Samantha during the half-year she had been gone, it would have seemed more real to her. She would have heard about the first date, the courtship, the proposal. Had he sent her flowers and taken her out to the most romantic spot in Hollywood? What was he like? The grainy photos offered little clue.

Amanda sighed again. The only other sound was the ticking of the tall grandfather clock at the other end of the living room. She felt overcome by sadness at what might have been. If things had gone differently, she and Samantha might have giggled over wedding plans, dreamed up the perfect honeymoon spot, chosen the most beautiful wedding dress. A bitter thought formed in Amanda's mind. If things had gone differently, they might have been choosing Amanda's wedding dress—for her walk down the aisle with Ted.

Of course, Samantha had done just fine with the dress on her own. In the wedding photo she wore a sleeveless, straight-bodiced, embroidered gown that flared softly at the bottom into folds of gossamer silk. She had on a simple white cap with a fringe of gauzy veil and long white gloves; in her hand she carried a single white rose.

Amanda felt restless, so she got up and went into the kitchen, where she put the teakettle on and took down a canister of tea from the cupboard. Idly, she picked up that day's newspaper from the table and began to flip through it. About a third of the way through she spied another picture of Samantha, this time in a dazzling beaded sheath. The accompanying article described the outfit in detail, giving the dressmaker's name and even Samantha's dress and glove sizes. *But if the rumors going around Hollywood are right,* the article went on, *Miss Watson won't be fitting into her perfect size-six dress for much longer.*

Amanda let out a loud gasp. *Won't be fitting into her dress?* Did that mean that Samantha was going to be a mother? Just then the teakettle began to emit a piercing whistle, but Amanda ignored the boiling water. She reread the same sentence a half-dozen times. *If the rumors are right* . . . Samantha, her twin, with a child of her own? Was Amanda going to be an aunt? The photo in the newspaper smiled mutely.

Could it be true? Amanda tried to imagine her sister cradling a tiny newborn, its downy tuft of hair as pale as its mother's and aunt's. Even the wall of anger and sadness that separated Amanda from her twin couldn't keep out a wave of joyful amazement.

Twenty-four

1927. Somewhere in the western United States.

Amanda's throat was raw from crying. Her cheeks and lips were chapped. Her head was cloudy from lack of sleep, and her body ached from so many days and nights of traveling. *Hurry!* she willed the train. *Hurry, hurry!* Every minute of her trip seemed to stretch out into hours.

The words of the doctor from California echoed in her head with the chugging of the train. "The birth is going badly . . . your sister has lost a lot of blood . . . she keeps asking for you . . . she might not make it . . . might not make it . . . might not make it. . . ."

Couldn't the train go any faster? She had to get to Samantha. If only the Watsons had an airplane parked in front of their house instead of an automobile.

But would even the fastest airplane do any good if the best doctors in Hollywood couldn't pull her twin out of danger? What if Amanda got there too late? Her parents had been visiting Harry at school when the word came. The three of them had left the day after Amanda and were now on their way to join her at the hospital. But what if Samantha was already—

No! Amanda couldn't let herself think that way. She had to concentrate on positive thoughts. Samantha was going to get better. She was going to have a beautiful, healthy baby. She and Jack Lewis were going to be proud parents. She and Amanda were going to make peace and become as close as they had ever been. Amanda would take her niece or nephew to the zoo, read to the child, spoil him or her with presents. . . .

"Samantha," Amanda whispered. *I promise, I swear, that if you get better, we'll never fight with each other again. Please hear my thoughts, Sam.* Once upon a time, she and Samantha had been so close that they could almost read each other's minds. There was a kind of silent communication between them, a bond that people who weren't twins couldn't possibly understand. Since reading the news of Samantha's pregnancy, Amanda had had time to reassess her own part in the destruction of that special bond, and she had come to realize that she had been very wrong not to have told her sister about Ted right from the start. She was as guilty as Samantha in betraying their unique relationship. Now Amanda hoped with every nerve in her body that Samantha could feel the love she was sending to her.

I'm coming, Sam. I'm coming. We're going to be together once again.

* * *

She was the first one off the train. She raced through the bustling station, skirting travelers, edging through crowds, and working her way toward the street.

"Excuse me, miss," a young woman in a blue cloche hat said, putting her hand on Amanda's sleeve and stopping her dash out of the station. "Aren't you Samantha Watson?" Her voice was breathy with excitement.

Amanda pictured her twin lying in a hospital bed. She had to get to her. Fast. Now. She shook her head. "I'm sorry to disappoint you," she said to Samantha's fan, "but you're mistaken." She eased the girl's hand off her arm as gently as she could.

"Oh, but I know you are. I'd recognize you anywhere," the girl called after her.

Amanda bit her lip as she found her way out to the street and hailed a taxi. She climbed into the closed auto and gave the driver the name of the hospital.

"Say, aren't you—"

"No," Amanda said quickly. "But I've been told I look like her. Now, if you please, I'm in a terrible hurry." The driver took one more look at her, shrugged, and stepped on the gas.

Amanda could barely have said what Hollywood looked like, from that ride to the hospital. Never in her nineteen years had she been so far from home, yet the elegant mansions, the waving palm trees along the wide boulevards, the throngs of smartly dressed people all went by in a blur. The only thing Amanda could think about was Samantha. *Be alive, be alive,* she prayed silently, stuffing a large bill in the driver's hand as she ran toward the hospital entrance.

Amanda burst through the hospital doors. "Samantha Watson," she announced to the woman behind the reception desk. "I'm here to see Samantha Watson. I'm her twin sister."

"Yes, of course! You look exactly like her!" the woman said.

"Ma'am, it's an emergency," Amanda said, her voice rising frantically.

"An emergency? Why, everyone in Hollywood knows your sister is having a baby. My dear, women do it every day. Even starlets. Especially starlets." The receptionist chuckled as she consulted a list of names and room numbers. "Yes. Here she is. 'S. Watson.' Isn't that something? A movie star right here in this hospital. She's in maternity. Wing C, down the hall and to your right. Then take the stairs to the second floor, and go to room two-oh-two. Betty," she called to a nurse standing in the lobby, "did you know Samantha Watson has checked in here? That's her twin sister," Amanda heard her add as she hurried down the hall.

Poor Samantha! All the fame in the world wasn't helping her right now. Her heart beating wildly, Amanda half stumbled, half ran toward room 202.

Room 206, 204 . . . 202. A uniformed hospital guard stood outside her sister's room. He looked at Amanda and did a double-take.

"I'm her twin," Amanda explained.

The guard nodded. "Yes, they're expecting you." He put his hand on the doorknob.

Amanda took a deep breath. *Please, please, be all right!* she thought to herself. She stepped into the room.

"Amanda!" Samantha's voice was a shadow of a whisper.

"Oh, Sam!" Amanda breathed. Samantha's face was almost as white as the pillow on which it rested. Her lips were pale and her eyelids were heavy, half-closed. But a smile played at the corners of her mouth and in her arms was a tiny baby wrapped in a pink blanket. Sitting in a chair next to the bed, his arm outstretched and resting on Samantha's, was a man Amanda recognized from the wedding picture in the newspaper. On the other side of the bed were a doctor and a nurse, crisp in their hospital whites.

"Sam!" Amanda could feel her tears forming as she rushed toward the bed.

"Amanda," Sam whispered, "meet my daughter, Marjorie. Marjorie, your Aunt Amanda, my best friend in the whole world."

Warm, salty tears streamed freely as Amanda gave Samantha the most gentle kiss. She reached out her hand and touched the baby's cheek. Marjorie. Samantha's daughter, Marjorie! She was so teeny, so soft. Her eyes were closed and she breathed lightly and evenly.

"She's beautiful!" Amanda said, trying to gulp back her sobs. Her sister looked more frail and weak than she could have ever imagined, but the baby was the most wondrous creature she had ever seen.

"If you can stop crying for a second, I'll introduce you to my husband, too," Samantha managed to whisper. Amanda had to lean close to make out some of her words.

"Shh, Sam, don't wear yourself out talking," Amanda said. She turned to face Jack Lewis. "Pleased to meet you," she said. He had dark circles under his eyes and his face looked drawn.

"Pleased to meet you, Amanda. I've always looked forward to meeting the twin sister Samantha talks so much about." He gave a smile, but his eyes were red, and Amanda could see he had been crying for a while, just as she had been.

"Amanda," Samantha said, the syllables coming out in the faintest breaths. "I waited for you. I held on just for you."

Amanda fought back more tears. "Held on? Nonsense, Sam. You're going to be fine. We're going to take Marjorie to the zoo, teach her all the games we played when we were little . . ."

Samantha shook her head. It looked like even that tiny motion was an enormous effort. "No, Amanda. I'm tired. I'm so tired. . . ." Her eyes closed as she spoke.

"Shh, shh," murmured Jack Lewis, stroking Samantha's forehead.

The doctor stepped forward. "I think your visit has gotten Miss Watson a little too excited. She needs to rest quietly." He gestured to the nurse and she came over to take the sleeping baby from Samantha's arms. But as soon as she reached down for Marjorie, Samantha's eyes opened.

"No! Please! Let me hold her. Don't take her away from me," she said. The nurse looked at the doctor. He nodded his permission.

Samantha gave a ghost of a smile. "My Marjorie. My beautiful Marjorie," she cooed, her words growing weaker all the time. Then she looked up at Amanda. "Amanda, promise me."

"Anything," Amanda said. "I'll promise you anything."

"Help Jack. Help him look after Marjorie. You'll be a better mother than I could have been, anyway. . . ." Her voice drifted off.

"Oh, Sam, please don't talk like that," Jack pleaded, echoing Amanda's most fervent thoughts. "You heard your sister. You're going to take our daughter to the zoo and play games with her. We're going to be the happiest family in the world. You'll see." Amanda could hear her sister's husband battling the tears that were flooding inside him.

But if Samantha heard, she didn't answer. Her eyes closed. Her head rolled to the side. Her arms, holding baby Marjorie, began to go limp.

The nurse rushed forward and scooped up the newborn. Amanda felt a wave of panic swelling inside her as the doctor immediately took Samantha's wrist in his fingers. He looked at his watch, measuring her pulse. He shook his head.

"No!" Amanda's voice bounced off the walls of the hospital room. "Sam, no!" she cried. "She's sleeping. That's all. She's just sleeping. Sam, wake up. Please, Sam! Oh, wake up. I'll do anything. Just wake up, wake up!"

"I'm sorry," the doctor said. He put a hand on Amanda's shoulder. "Miss Watson, Mr. Lewis, I'm so sorry, but she's gone."

"No! No, it can't be true!" Amanda heard herself yell.

Her words collided with Jack Lewis's uncontrollable sobbing. "Samantha, Samantha! My love! Oh, Sam!"

And then a third mournful voice joined the grief, a high, heartbreaking wail. Baby Marjorie. The nurse held the tiny bundle out toward Jack. "Mr. Lewis," she said softly.

But he could only shake his head, gulping in huge mouthfuls of air and crying so that his whole body shook. He slammed his eyes shut, as if he couldn't even look at his new daughter—the tiny baby who had cost Samantha her life.

Through her own tears, Amanda reached out her shaking arms for the pink-swaddled infant. She felt the baby's warm, defenseless body through the blanket as the nurse placed her in her arms. "Shh," Amanda murmured. "Shh, sweet Marjorie. Don't cry. Let's neither of us cry. I'll love you enough for both Sam and me. I'll love you as much as Sam and I loved each other, deep down. . . ."

Twenty-five

1935. Sweet Valley, California.

"No, Jack, you can't take her away," Amanda said. Jack Lewis sat at Amanda's kitchen table, his face buried in his hands.

"Amanda, why do you have to make it so hard for me?"

Amanda got a bottle of milk out of the icebox, then closed the door quickly so the ice would keep as long as possible. She shook the bottle to mix the cream into the milk, removed the piece of cloth that covered the stopper, opened the bottle, and added a little milk to the two cups of coffee she had poured. "What did you expect me to do? Let you take Marjorie five thousand miles away without batting an eyelash?" She set the coffee down on the table.

"Amanda, you've done everything for Marjorie. Don't think I don't know that," Jack said. "Moving all the way from Detroit to finish school and take care of Marjorie at the same time, accepting a job here so we could all be near one another, being the parent whenever I had an assignment out of town. I know you're as much a mother to her as I am a father."

"Then how can you do it?" Amanda asked. "France is so far away."

Jack sighed. "Amanda, I've been offered a good job there. Foreign correspondent. It's a dream come true. Besides, do you know how long it's been since I've had steady work?"

Amanda bit her lip. Just the other day she'd seen a man she had gone to the university with selling apples on the street. Would the depression ever end? Would there ever be jobs for everyone again?

"And think what a wonderful experience it would be for Marjorie," Jack added.

"Yes, I suppose it would be," Amanda said reluctantly. She wanted the world to be Marjorie's, and living abroad would certainly open up new avenues for her. But how could Amanda bear to lose her?

"Amanda, what would you do if you were me?" Jack asked.

Amanda fumbled with her coffee cup, picking it up and putting it down nervously without taking a sip. "I'd like to tell you that I'd leave Marjorie here with me." She paused. "But I know how much you love her. And you're her father. I'm just—"

"—the most important woman in the world to her," Jack said. "And I know I couldn't have raised her without you. But I need the work. And I need Marjorie."

Amanda felt her chest tighten. What was the

use in arguing with Jack? She was going to lose her niece, Samantha's daughter. And yet she knew it was the right thing. Jack Lewis was a good man and a good father. And Marjorie adored him.

"Are you sure you won't reconsider coming with us?" Jack asked. "Can't I tempt you with fine perfumes and French fashions and charming little cafés?"

"Oh, Jack, it sounds wonderful," Amanda said. "But this is my home. What would my students in Sweet Valley do without an English teacher? Besides, I'm awfully fortunate to have a job right now." She thought again about the man selling apples. "You and I are the lucky ones."

"That's true," Jack said. "It seems that every day the bread lines are longer. But I'm going to worry about you all alone here. I wish I were leaving you with some tall, dark, and handsome friend to take care of you."

Tall, dark, and handsome. Amanda brushed away an image of Ted Wakefield. Even after all the years, it was still painful to think about him. "I'll be just fine on my own," she said. Amanda felt the tears rise to her eyes. "But promise me you won't keep Marjorie away too long."

The banner stretched across the ballroom of the ocean liner read *Bon Voyage!* A brass band belted out "I Got Rhythm." Men and women danced and sipped champagne. Amanda helped herself to a bite-size puff pastry from the long table covered with plates of elegant finger foods, but as soon as it was in her hand she realized she had no appetite.

"Where is my little rascal?" Jack asked, coming over with two glasses of sparkling water and handing one to Amanda.

Amanda pointed to the other end of the long banquet table. She hadn't let Marjorie out of her sight for a second. But holding Marjorie in her gaze was not going to do a bit of good when the ship set sail and Amanda was left behind on the docks of New York City.

Amanda had always wanted to see the impossibly tall buildings and visit the fine museums, to feel the nonstop energy of this great city—especially since their brother Harry had moved here. But how was she going to be able to take in any of the sights when her heart would be sailing away with Marjorie? Now Amanda watched Marjorie filling a large plate with food. She worked her way toward Amanda and Jack, taking two or three of everything.

"She certainly has an appetite," Jack said. Amanda watched Marjorie fill up every bit of space on her plate. Then she came over to where they stood.

"Marjorie, my little princess," Jack said, "they're going to feed us every day on this voyage."

"Oh, Daddy," the eight-year-old said, as if she

were the parent, "it's not for me. Didn't you see all those people living in those tar-paper shacks down near the docks?"

Amanda put a hand on Marjorie's shoulder. "Yes, that's one of the places called Hoovervilles. It's very sad, all those people living without proper homes, and you're a very wonderful girl for thinking about all the people suffering through these hard times. But Marjorie, you can't just steal the ship's food," she chided gently.

Marjorie opened her blue-green eyes extra wide. "Aunt Amanda, who do you think needs it more? Him?" She pointed to a very, very large man, his fancy suit bursting at the buttons, who was heaping his plate with as much food as Marjorie's.

Amanda swallowed a giggle. "Don't point, dear, it's not polite." She saw a smile pull at Jack's lips.

Marjorie must have seen it, too. She stubbornly moved her index finger toward a new victim. "Her?" she asked, indicating a tall, elegant lady with a fur stole wrapped around her shoulders.

Jack laughed. "Nah. She's probably on a diet."

Brashly, Marjorie helped herself to as many rolls as she could stuff into the pockets of her dress.

Amanda shook her head. "You two. Marjorie, you are every bit as nervy as your mother was."

"And as good-hearted as your aunt," Jack added.

"Don't try to sweeten me up," Amanda said, trying to keep a straight face. "It's not right to steal food."

"Aw, come on, Aunt Amanda. No one will miss it," Marjorie said. "And think how much those poor people out there will appreciate it. I'll bet they're hungry."

Amanda knew they were the same people who waited on those long, long lines at the soup kitchens every day for a single bowl of watery soup and a slice of dry bread. "Oh, all right, dear. I'll look the other way just this once. But you'd better deliver that food in a hurry. The ship is sailing in less than an hour."

And taking you far, far away, she added silently. She watched Marjorie scurry off, her pockets bulging. *My baby. Sam's baby. I'll miss you.*

Twenty-six

1939. Val-le-Doux, France.

Dear Aunt Amanda,

I wonder if you would recognize me. Daddy says I look and sound just like a French school-girl. I guess it's true, because no one at school knows I'm American until I tell them. But I still miss California, and hot dogs, and Coca-Cola, and you!—even though Mademoiselle Pinget takes good care of us. She's a wonderful cook, and she takes me shopping for all the latest French fashions.

How are your classes at Sweet Valley High? What are the latest fads in America? Did you ever get to San Francisco to see the World's Fair?

Lots and lots of kisses.

Love,
Marjorie

P.S. Don't be worried about me. Daddy says to tell you that the war is behind the border in Germany and that we are fine.

My darling Marjorie,

I have the photo you sent me in my pocketbook, so I can look at it whenever I like. Your father is right: you do look like a beautiful French girl, very grown up with your pierced ears.

One of my ninth graders, Walter Egbert, says he's going to duck into a telephone booth to put on his Superman costume and fly across the Atlantic to bring you back to Sweet Valley. Superman is the latest rage in the United States. He is a comic-strip hero who has special powers, and all the boys in my class dream of being like him. The girls dream of being Scarlett O'Hara. Perhaps Gone with the Wind hasn't come out yet in France. Well, Scarlett O'Hara is a beautiful and clever Southern belle—but not as beautiful and clever as my darling niece. I do wish Walter Egbert could really bring you back to me. I miss you so, and worry about you when I read the newspaper.

I did get to the San Francisco World's Fair, and it was wonderful. I also saw the new Golden Gate Bridge, which was for me just as miraculous as all the exhibits at the fair. It seems to sail across the sky like some heavenly highway. I hope you will come home soon so we can make a trip together to see it.

All my love,
Aunt Amanda

Please send my fondest regards to your father.

Dear Amanda,

You must try not to worry about us. I am not going to tell you that France at war is a pretty picture, but as American citizens, Marjorie and I are quite safe. Reporting firsthand from the very thick of the situation is the career opportunity of a lifetime for me, and I would be a fool to leave. Rest assured that at the first sign of danger I will send Marjorie home immediately. As long as we are safe, I can't bear to be separated from her. She reminds me so much of Sam, and she is all I have in this foreign land. I know you will understand.

> *All my best,*
> *Jack*

Twenty-seven

1940. Val-le-Doux, France.

"Sieg Heil!" the German soldiers shouted, raising their beer glasses. "To victory!" they laughed, translating their words into French as if to make their brutal point to anyone who might be listening.

Marjorie flinched at the sound of her beautiful, fluid second language being roughened by the harsh accents of the soldiers. She pressed close to her father as they walked quickly past the café where the soldiers held court at two of the outdoor tables. The rest of the café was deserted, except for Mme. Huppert, the owner. Her round, wrinkled face was lowered, her normally spry step slowed to a sad, humble shuffle as she carried frothy glasses of beer to the soldiers.

"Where is everybody?" Marjorie asked, a wave of sadness and anger washing over her as she watched the soldiers laugh and drink, loud and confident in their crisp gray uniforms. The guns they carried gave them power over every man, woman, and child in Val-le-Doux. "They've stolen our town from us."

"Yes, they have," her father said, hurrying

Marjorie away from the café. "But sweetheart, it's important to understand that the café is empty because the townspeople chose to leave. They didn't flee out of fear, but to show that they would not sit by and dine or drink with the enemy. It's their small way of fighting back. Do you see?"

Marjorie nodded solemnly, taking big strides to keep up with him as they made their way through the familiar streets of the town. "Michel Bourget's parents gave the wrong directions to two soldiers who were looking for the train station the other day. I guess it's the same idea." Not too long before, Marjorie could have seen herself giving the wrong directions to a rival town's soccer team as a practical joke. But the men in the gray uniforms had turned life in Val-le-Doux into a deadly serious business.

"Well, every effort helps. But the small things alone are not enough to win a war." Marjorie could hear the tight, fearful note in his voice. It made her cold all over.

"Dad, I'm frightened," she said softly. She couldn't remember ever feeling this way before. She thought about the time she had been pulled under a huge wave at the beach back in Sweet Valley. She had felt her heart drumming wildly as she fought to get air. For a nightmarish moment, she had been sure she would never make it. But then she had pushed to the surface, gulping in huge breaths. Soon she was smiling and playing again, building a sandcastle by the water's edge with Aunt Amanda.

Now, in the nearly deserted streets of Val-le-Doux, she felt a more subtle, lasting fear—one that seemed to grab icy hold of her deep inside, one that she could never shake free of. "Maybe Aunt Amanda is right. Maybe it *is* too dangerous here."

Her father stopped walking. He put his arms around Marjorie and wrapped her in a strong hug. "Do you want to go back to America? Do you want me to go?"

Marjorie shrugged, burying her head against her father's strong chest. Their home in Sweet Valley seemed like a faraway dream. Val-le-Doux was her home now. How could she leave it? How could she abandon her friends and classmates to the enemy soldiers? Besides, her father's job was here. He wanted to stay. Still, she missed her aunt terribly, and she knew how much her aunt worried about her. Back at Aunt Amanda's she would be safe. The balmy breezes of peaceful California would melt away her ice-cold fear.

"You just say the word, princess," her father said. "If you want to leave, you let me know. It's you and me. We're going to stick together, I promise. I'm not going to send my only little girl off on her own."

Marjorie looked her father in the eye. This was the perfect opportunity to bring up something that had been on her mind a lot lately. "What about Mlle. Pinget?" she asked. "Dad, you might think I'm your little girl, but I'm not so little anymore. I've noticed how much time you spend with her. Are you falling in love?"

Her father's laughter broke the tense stillness in the street. "With Mlle. Pinget?"

"Yes," Marjorie said. "She's awfully pretty. And the two of you are always whispering about stuff, like you've got all these secrets."

"Pumpkin, it's true that she is young and beautiful. And she is someone we can trust. That's important to know. We can trust her." Marjorie heard the weight he gave those words. "But as for me and Mlle. Pinget, she is my friend. That's all. It's just you and me."

"I don't want to leave yet, Dad," she said firmly. She tucked her hand into his, frowning as they passed more soldiers in gray.

Twenty-eight

1941. Val-le-Doux, France.

Through the living room window of their little
stone house, Marjorie could see them talking.
Her father's face was tense. Mlle. Pinget's ges-
tures were fraught with urgency. Marjorie tried
to listen through the door, but their words were
muffled. She rummaged around in her book bag
for her key. As soon as she put it in the lock, the
talking stopped. The two adults were waiting for
her, already looking in her direction as she poked
her head into the living room.

"Am I interrupting something?" she asked,
hesitating at the doorway of the small, cozy room.

"Marjorie. We were just talking about you,"
her father said.

"About me?" Marjorie put down her book bag
and took off her coat. Underneath it, she wore her
school uniform—a blue calf-length skirt and a
white middy blouse with a red bow tied around
the neckline.

"Princess, I've changed my mind," he said.
"Your aunt is right. You're going home."

Marjorie noticed he hadn't said "we." "And
what about you?" she asked him.

239

"I'll be staying here," he answered. His voice was gentle but firm. She knew his mind was made up.

"But you said it was you and me," Marjorie protested. "You said we would stick together." She heard her voice rise in the small room.

"I know, princess," he said. "But things have changed."

"Things? What things?" Marjorie felt a trickle of betrayal. He had promised. She saw him and Mlle. Pinget exchange a look.

"Pumpkin, you'll just have to trust me," he said. "One day you'll understand."

Marjorie felt her famous temper rising. "I think I understand right now. I think I understand that you two want to be alone, and that I'm in the way. Isn't that right?"

Mlle. Pinget shook her head, her neatly coiffed blond curls bobbing back and forth. "Chérie, your father is a good man, but please believe that there is nothing romantic between us." Her delicate face colored as she said this.

"Why do you both insist on treating me as if I were a baby?" Marjorie demanded. "I'm fifteen years old. I see the looks you give each other. I hear you whispering. I know you meet after I go to sleep, when you think no one knows. Why don't you tell me the truth?"

"Sweetheart, we *are* telling you the truth," her father insisted.

"Then why do you want me to leave?"

"Marjorie, it's just too dangerous for you here." He came over and put his arms around her. Marjorie shrugged them off.

"Then it's too dangerous for *you*," she told him.

He sighed. "You're right. It is. But I have to stay anyway. I want you to know how hard I'm going to find it to be here without you. Pumpkin, you mean more to me than anyone or anything in this world." Marjorie heard his voice crack. When he reached out again, she let him fold her into a hug.

"Then why don't you let me stay?" she asked. "I want to stay. I could be brave, just like you."

He hugged her even more tightly. "I know you could be brave. You *are* brave."

"Then I can stay?"

He let Marjorie go. "No, princess. You're going home. It's final." There was an expression in his eyes that Marjorie had never seen before. She knew she wasn't going to be able to change his mind.

Marjorie waited until Mlle. Pinget closed her front door. She stood outside and listened to her throw the catch from the inside, her shoes clicking against the clay tiles as she walked away from the door. Then Marjorie burst into tears, letting loose the flood she had been holding back all afternoon.

She had walked up and down every street in town, trying to memorize each building, paying

241

special attention to the feel of the smooth, worn cobblestones under her feet and the cozy narrowness of the streets, so different from California's spacious, tree-lined boulevards. She had paused in the main square, taking in each café, each restaurant, each shop. She had breathed in the faint but not unpleasant odor of old, moist building stones that rode on the air of Val-le-Doux. It was the scent of many, many centuries, a smell one would never find in the young towns back in America, and Marjorie wanted to remember it forever.

Then she had said goodbye to her friends, impulsively taking off her favorite butterfly earrings and giving them to her best friend, Marthe Giradoux. Back when Marjorie had first arrived in France, Marthe had convinced her to let her pierce her ears. She'd sat Marjorie down at her kitchen table, numbed her earlobes with ice, and used a sterilized needle and a piece of thread to make the hole, all the while telling jokes about different boys at school to keep her distracted. Marthe had been Marjorie's first friend in France, and she had stayed her best one. At school, it was always Marthe and Marjorie, Marjorie and Marthe.

Marjorie and Marthe had promised to write to each other and to visit as soon as the war was over. But Marjorie knew that a terrifying, silent question loomed in both their minds. When the war was over, would a visit be possible? Who knew what might happen between now and then? Who knew what might happen if Germany won the war? Would Marjorie ever really see Marthe again? She had swallowed back her fears and tried to stay brave.

Mlle. Pinget's house had been Marjorie's last stop, and her hardest. Not even saying goodbye to Marthe was as difficult. Mlle. Pinget had been the one to look after Marjorie when her father had to travel on assignment, the one to bring her soup when she was sick and read Marjorie her favorite stories out loud. If Marjorie knew every trick French women had for looking good, it was thanks to Mlle. Pinget. If she felt she belonged in Val-le-Doux, that was probably thanks to Mlle. Pinget, too.

As she moved away from the door of Mlle. Pinget's house, Marjorie couldn't contain her tears. She let them flow freely as she made her way along the familiar route home. Home. By this time the next day, she would have left it behind. Would it be swallowed up by the soldiers in gray? Would she ever see Val-le-Doux and the people she loved again? She didn't even dare to think too much about her father. He had promised to join her in California just as soon as he could. But would he be able to keep his promise? Marjorie felt scared and tired and old, as if she had lived many years in the past few weeks.

As she wiped at the seemingly never-ending stream of tears, Marjorie saw a short man in dark clothes and a black beret coming down the street. As he got closer, she saw it was Michel Bourget's father.

"Bonjour, Monsieur Bourget," she greeted him, sniffling back her sadness. This was the last day she would be saying bonjour to people in the street.

"Bonjour, mademoiselle," Michel's father replied. "Have you heard the news?" His words were quick with excitement.

"What news?" Marjorie asked.

"The United States has just entered the war! They are going to help us throw out the evil that has taken over France!"

"They are? We are?" Marjorie exclaimed. "That's wonderful!" She felt a swell of pride.

M. Bourget nodded eagerly. But suddenly the smile slipped off his face. "You're Jack Lewis's daughter, aren't you? You're a classmate of my son Michel's."

Marjorie nodded.

"Then, you are American."

"Yes." Wouldn't M. Bourget be glad about that? Her country was helping his. But he looked scared.

"You're now the official enemy of the Germans," he said. "It's not safe for you here any longer. We'd better get you out of the open right away!" He took Marjorie by the arm. "You live on

244

the rue de la Colline, don't you? We've got to get you home."

"Yes," Marjorie said. She felt her pride turning to fear as what M. Bourget was telling her sank in. All of a sudden her little Val-le-Doux was the enemy camp. If the German soldiers found her, she would be like a sheep among a pack of wolves. Had her father somehow sensed this was going to happen? Was that why he had decided so abruptly to send her back to America?

Her father! Marjorie shuddered at a new thought. If she was in danger, so was he. She had to get home to warn him. She pulled on M. Bourget's arm and began to run.

"Non, chérie," he said, holding her back. "If a soldier sees you running, he'll get suspicious. We must walk as if there is nothing wrong. If anyone stops us, you must pretend to be French."

Marjorie nodded, forcing herself to slow down to Michel's father's pace. She felt as if she were walking in molasses. She wanted to sprint home and make sure her father was all right, to throw her arms around him and feel his solid, comforting presence. Marjorie felt M. Bourget stiffen beside her as they rounded a corner.

"Soldiers," he said, jutting his chin toward the two men at the end of the street. "Greet them politely as we pass," he whispered.

Marjorie's pulse raced. If M. Bourget hadn't been holding her arm, she probably would have turned and run as fast as she could.

"Keep calm," M. Bourget murmured. "You are just a normal French girl on her way home. There's no reason they should suspect a thing. Bonjour, messieurs," he said as they passed the two gray-uniformed soldiers.

Marjorie pulled the corners of her mouth up, sure it looked more like a grimace than a smile. "Bonjour, messieurs," she echoed, her words coming out high and shaky in a voice she barely recognized.

"Guten Tag," the soldiers replied in their own language, nodding and passing by without incident.

Marjorie's relief lasted until she got to her front door. It was thrown wide open, and she knew instantly that something was wrong. She broke away from M. Bourget and ran inside.

It looked like a tornado had whipped through the house. The furniture was pushed out of place and turned over. The contents of drawers had been spilled out onto the floor, the curtains ripped off the windows. "Dad! Dad!" Marjorie yelled frantically.

She raced through every room. Each one looked the same—their belongings strewn all over the place. "Dad! Where are you? Dad!"

But there was no answer. M. Bourget followed Marjorie through the vandalized house. "Ma petite," he said, voicing the terrible truth she already knew inside. "Little one, your father is not here." He put a thick, work-roughened hand on her shoulder. "They must have come while you were out. Thank God they missed you. But I'm afraid your father was not so lucky. He could be a prisoner of the Germans."

Twenty-nine

The night descended, extinguishing the cold light of the most frightening day of Marjorie's life. She huddled in the attic of the Bourgets' house, her knees pulled up to her chest, her arms wrapped around her knees, rocking numbly, her tears frozen deep inside her by fear. The blue daylight filtering through loose slats in the attic walls darkened until Marjorie felt like a shadow.

The sound of footsteps coming up the narrow staircase shocked her out of her hollow stupor. Had her hiding place been discovered? Her pulse beat double time.

"Marjorie, ma chérie," a familiar voice said softly.

Mlle. Pinget! Marjorie's fright melted into relief. A moment later, she found herself in the woman's arms. "Tell me it isn't true," she said. "Tell me Dad is all right!"

Mlle. Pinget stroked her hair gently. "I wish I could. God, I wish I could. My poor Marjorie." They stayed locked in a sorrow-filled hug for a long time.

"I've got to find him. You've got to help me find him," Marjorie said.

"Non, chérie," she replied. "You would only find yourself behind prison walls or barbed wire. No. You are in grave danger. I am going to take you to a hiding place where you will be safe."

"And I'll have to stay there? While Dad needs my help?" A note of protest rose in Marjorie's voice.

"Shh, ma petite, shh," Mlle. Pinget said. "The best thing you can do for your father is to save yourself. He thought you would be home in America by now. Home and safe. But we'll have to do the best we can here. At least you'll have company."

"I will?" Marjorie asked. "Who?"

"A girl a few years younger than you," Mlle. Pinget said. "But come, you'll meet her soon enough. It's not a good idea for you to stay here any longer. M. Bourget says some soldiers saw you with him this afternoon and they may come looking for you. It's a small town. Word could get around. Now that it's dark out, we have to move quickly."

Marjorie knew she was right. There was nothing she could do for her father except hope with all her might that he would be all right. She let Mlle. Pinget take her hand and lead her out of the attic. Something her father had once said to her echoed in her mind. "Mlle. Pinget is someone we can trust. That's important to know."

Mlle. Pinget put a finger to her lips. "We have to move as silently and as quickly as possible, yes? M. Bourget wishes you luck," she whispered.

"May I thank him and say goodbye?" Marjorie whispered back.

She shook her head. "He's with his wife and son in the kitchen. It's best if his family doesn't know you were here—in case anyone comes asking questions."

Marjorie breathed in sharply. It was like being in some kind of spy movie, except that this was perilously real. She followed Mlle. Pinget outside and around the back of the house. Every twig that snapped under their feet sounded to Marjorie like a gunshot. Every branch that waved in the evening breeze cast dangerous shadows on the ground. She almost didn't dare to breathe as she followed Mlle. Pinget through narrow back streets. A man's voice floated toward them from somewhere down the street.

"Quick," Mlle. Pinget whispered, gathering up her skirt and pressing herself into the shadows of a doorway. Marjorie did the same and crouched down next to her. She could hear the voice coming closer, talking about war rationing and how long it had been since he had had a nice, juicy steak for dinner. Another man's voice answered him.

"I know where you can get black market meat, Jean-Louis, conveniently borrowed from the supply the Germans keep for themselves." His voice grew louder, then faded as the men passed by.

Mlle. Pinget remained motionless until there was silence again. Then she poked her head out and motioned to Marjorie that the coast was clear. They continued their wordless walk, the evening air growing chilly as they left town and wound down a path that led them through the woods and eventually alongside a large, moonlit expanse of fields. Row upon row of jewel-like grapes grew in clusters on high trellises. They walked down a path through the vineyard. In the distance, Marjorie could see an old stone farmhouse. Closer by was some kind of outbuilding with several chimneys poking out of the roof. This was the building toward which they were headed.

The air around the building was sharp with a funny odor. Marjorie breathed deeply, trying to place it. It smelled a bit like some of the old bars in town. Mlle. Pinget fitted a huge old skeleton key into the lock. The heavy wooden door opened onto a room full of large oak barrels and vats adorned with strange pipes and spigots. Marjorie could see them silhouetted in the silver-gray moonlight that stole in through the small, high windows. Of course! The wine from the vineyards was made here—no wonder the room smelled funny!

Mlle. Pinget closed the door behind them and led Marjorie toward the rear of the room, darting between casks and wine presses. Another door, unlocked by another key, led down a damp, narrow staircase. As Mlle. Pinget closed the cellar door behind them, what little light there had been was blotted out. Marjorie felt her way down the stairs, sliding her hands along the cold stone wall.

"Sophy!" Mlle. Pinget called softly.

A spark accompanied the sound of a match being struck. A flame flared up, casting its flickery light on a young, blond girl lighting a candle. It also illuminated rack upon rack of wine bottles against the walls. Marjorie was able to see her way down the rest of the stairs to where the blond girl stood. She looked familiar. Marjorie thought she was a couple of grades below her, though it had been quite some time since she'd seen the girl around school.

"Sophy, this is Marjorie Lewis," Mlle. Pinget said. "Marjorie, Sophy Berg."

They smiled shyly at each other. As Marjorie studied her in the dim candlelight, she thought back to the last time she had seen Sophy in school, and she suddenly realized why Sophy was in hiding. She was a Jew. When the Germans had invaded France in 1940, they made all the Jews wear a yellow six-pointed star on their clothes; Sophy had had to sew the star on her school uniform. That had been the first step in the enemy's murderous plan—to order anyone who was Jewish to wear a star of David, as if branding a herd of cattle that had been rounded up. But Marjorie knew that it had gone way beyond a humiliating gesture. Jews were being sent off to labor camps, where they worked like slaves. Other, more horrible stories were beginning to filter back into France from camps with names like Dachau and Birkenau. No one knew what would become of the Jews who were shipped off. No wonder Sophy was in hiding.

And as of tonight, this damp, musky room was Marjorie's home, too.

Sophy lit another candle and stretched out on her thin straw mattress. Marjorie did the same, pulling her blanket up to her chin, as if it might ease the chill of fear in her.

"My parents were taken away while I was having a flute lesson at my teacher's," Sophy said, her voice wavering ever so slightly. "My mother never came to pick me up."

Marjorie stretched her hand out to Sophy, and their fingers met. "So what did you do?" Marjorie asked gently.

"I was very, very lucky," Sophy responded. "Although I didn't feel lucky at the time. My flute teacher turned out to be a member of the Resistance. He arranged for me to be hidden."

"The Resistance?" Marjorie asked.

"The people who are fighting for France," Sophy explained, pride coloring her words. "They're fighting in secret—right under the nose of the enemy. My brother has joined up with them."

"You have a brother?" Marjorie was glad Sophy wasn't all alone now that her parents were gone.

"Jacques. He's seventeen, and he's the bravest boy in the whole world," Sophy said. "What he's doing is terribly dangerous. He should be in hiding, too, but he's fighting for our country. He, my flute teacher, Mlle. Pinget—they're our real heroes."

"Mlle. Pinget?" Marjorie asked. "She's part of this—this Resistance, too?"

In the soft flicker of candlelight, Sophy nodded. "Yes, of course. Just bringing you here could have gotten her arrested."

Arrested. Like Dad, Marjorie thought. Suddenly all the whispering between Mlle. Pinget and her father made sense. It wasn't about romance; it was about something even more important. It was about justice and triumph over the enemy. Marjorie remembered her father saying that winning back France would take more than leaving a restaurant when the German soldiers came in or giving them wrong directions to the train station. Why, he must be part of the Resistance, too.

Marjorie felt a tremor of pride. Her father was so brave. But she felt dreadfully frightened for him. What if the Germans found out he was not only an American, but also a part of the secret battle against them? Marjorie closed her eyes, blocking out the sight of the green wine bottles gleaming in the candlelight. The tears that had been trapped inside her all day welled up, stinging her eyes and nose. Lying in her secret bed, Marjorie wept.

She heard Sophy get up, then felt her warm, thin arms go around her. "It's OK. Go ahead and cry all you want," she said softly. "I know how you feel."

Marjorie let the younger girl hug away her sobs, as if they'd switched places and Sophy was the older one. Was it grief that had made Sophy grow up so quickly? How could a twelve-year-old stay so steady when both her parents were gone? Marjorie swallowed the last of her tears and vowed to be as brave as Sophy.

Thirty

1942. Sweet Valley, California.

It had become a bedtime ritual. Amanda opened the top drawer of her night table and took out the last photo Marjorie had sent her. It was worn around the edges from so much handling, and the shiny surface had cracked just above Marjorie's head. It was as if the sky was falling on her, Amanda thought, as if her universe had been split open—which wasn't, after all, that far from the truth.

Amanda clutched her niece's picture to her heart, thinking about the last news she had received. A few months back, she had been correcting exams at her desk after school when a silver-haired gentleman had knocked on her classroom door.

"Miss Amanda Watson?" he had said with a slight French accent.

Amanda had stood up. "Come in. What may I do for you?"

The gentleman had drawn close to Amanda and said, very softly, "Miss Watson, I have news of your niece."

Amanda's heart had skipped a beat.

"She is fine, and is being safely hidden," the man said. "She wishes you to know this, and not to worry."

"Hidden? By whom?" Amanda asked. "Where? How do you know this? And what about her father, Jack?" She searched the man's lightly lined face. "Who are you?"

"I am a friend of France," the man had said, "as are the people who are helping your niece. I cannot tell you any more, and if anyone asks, I was never here." He turned on his heel and headed toward the door.

"No! Wait!" Amanda had called, stretching out her arm as if the mysterious Frenchman's presence in her classroom could magically bring Marjorie back to Sweet Valley. "Don't go! Please! Tell me more!"

The man had shaken his head. "I cannot. You must be brave. We all must be," he had said, vanishing through the wooden door. Amanda had never seen him again.

Now, as she held Marjorie's picture, the visit seemed as strange and distant as a dream. Amanda prayed that the man's words were true and that Marjorie was safe. But even if his information was correct, how safe could she be, hidden deep within the boundaries of occupied France?

Amanda thought about her students at Sweet Valley High, where Marjorie would have been in school if she'd been in California. In spite of several invasion panics that had hit the area in the past year, to most of her students, the war was far away, a faceless, shadowy evil, only barely more real to them than the villains in their comic books. Of course, they were patriotic. They collected scrap metal for the war effort—cans and broken machine parts. They collected war stamps and made posters in art class encouraging people to buy war bonds. They wrote letters to the troops to keep up their morale. The boys in Amanda's class talked bravely of enlisting as soon as they turned eighteen. She knew some students in other classes had lost family members— soldiers not much older than they were who'd been killed overseas in battle.

But the war hadn't touched most of her students. They did their best for their country, but life went on. The girls kept up with the latest styles and trends, wearing their carefully casual bobby socks, giggling about boys, and dreaming of being movie stars like Rita Hayworth. The boys traded baseball cards and practiced pitching curve balls and talked about Joe "the Yankee Clipper" DiMaggio's latest home run and their favorite girls at school.

And Marjorie? Amanda ran her finger over the photo, pretending she was actually touching her niece's face. At best, Marjorie was hidden in some dank cellar or attic, never going to the movies, never having a Saturday-night date, never walking on the beach and listening to the crash of waves on the sand. It was a jail sentence—one filled with uncertainty and fear, one that stole Marjorie's adolescence and plunged her into a bitter, grim world.

Amanda kissed Marjorie's picture and prayed she would see her again.

Thirty-one

1942. Val-le-Doux, France.

Marjorie awoke in the dead of night. Quietly, so she wouldn't wake Sophy, she slipped off her straw pallet and splashed her face with not-so-fresh water from a large basin. Shivering a little, she put on her skirt and sweater. Mlle. Pinget had recently washed them, bringing them back to the cellar with the most recent food supply. Marjorie's shiver dissolved in a tickle of pleasure at the luxury of fresh-smelling, clean clothes.

She padded up the staircase, unlocked the door to the wine cellar, and peered out into the main room to make sure it was empty. She was always afraid that one day one of the workers was going to sample too much of the product on the job, fall asleep amid the funnels and barrels and vats, and wake up to find her or Sophy coming up out of the cellar. Marjorie made a stealthy tour of the room, tiptoeing around the winemaking equipment. She was alone.

She relaxed a bit, clambering onto a barrel under one of the high windows. She balanced on top of it, looking up and out at the night sky. It was clear, the heavens full of stars. Marjorie focused on the brightest one and made the wish that filled her every moment. *May peace come quickly, and may Sophy and I be free, and may Dad be safe,* she whispered to the night.

She remained perched on her lookout for a while longer, savoring the open sky. How she longed to walk beneath the stars, to feel the wind on her face, the soft ground beneath her feet.

When she had first arrived, she and Sophy had often taken nighttime walks around the winery, staying close by the building, protected by its shadow. But one night they had come around the side of the building and found themselves face to face with a man they didn't recognize. They had said hello and continued around the winery again, pressing against the side of the building to watch and wait, their hearts pounding in their ears. Marjorie had peered around the corner of the building and seen the man go inside. A few minutes later he had emerged holding a straw basket that he hadn't had when he'd gone in. A worker who'd forgotten something?

Marjorie and Sophy had watched the man cross the vineyard toward the farmhouse. Not until he was a distant speck in the night did they dare to go back inside and down to the cellar. After that they hadn't ventured out again. They had spent night after night in terror, afraid the worker might say something to the wrong person.

Even after days and weeks had passed, they were frightened. They no longer spent their nights running around in the big winemaking room upstairs, or telling each other stories by the light of the moon that came in through the high windows. Sometimes they allowed themselves a few minutes upstairs to stretch their legs or to look briefly out at the night, but they always returned quickly to the cellar. There, they dared only to imagine they were outside the single room that had become the limit of their world.

Marjorie climbed down off the barrel and went back downstairs. She could hear Sophy stirring under her blanket. "Marjorie?" Sophy's voice floated in the dark.

"Good morning," Marjorie said, even though it was the middle of the night. They had learned to sleep to the sounds of the winery in operation, waking up to begin their day when everyone else's day was coming to an end. It was much safer that way.

Marjorie felt around on the floor near her sleeping pallet for the matchbox. She lit a candle and the bottle-lined room flickered into view. "Shall we have the last of the rolls M. DuClos brought for breakfast?"

M. DuClos owned the winery and the farmhouse. He was the only person besides Mlle. Pinget who knew about the girls. Since their arrival, only M. DuClos brought bottles up or down the stairs. The rest of the time, their door was locked to any worker who might want to investigate the vintage wines aging in the cellar.

Sophy sat up and stretched her arms. "I'm going to pretend my roll is a fresh croissant with blackberry jam, and that I'm having it with a huge cup of hot chocolate made with steamed milk at a little café overlooking a long beach."

Marjorie took two hard, stale rolls from a box that served as their pantry, putting them on the plank of wood that was their table. She set out a small piece of cheese and a jug of water, too. "One croissant and hot chocolate, mademoiselle."

Sophy got out of bed. "Mmm. That chocolate smells so good. And can you hear the waves down on the beach, Marjorie? I love that sound."

Marjorie shut her eyes and tried to hear the waves breaking rhythmically on the shore. All that filled her ears was the silence of the cellar. She opened her eyes and sighed. "I just can't do it today," she said. "How can we keep making up our silly fantasies day after day when the whole world is coming to an end?"

Sophy took a swig of water from the jug. "Marjorie, we have to do these things, or the enemy will have claimed two more victims."

Marjorie broke off a piece of her stale roll. "But I want to do something real for once. Something that makes a difference. Like my father was doing. Like Jacques is doing." She felt a little tingle as she mentioned Sophy's brother. Sophy talked so often of him, Marjorie felt almost as if she knew him, as if he were a special friend. "Tell me about him again, Sophy," she said. "Tell me all about what Jacques is doing for France, and what he is like. . . ."

"Jacques!" Sophy threw her arms around the young man standing in the middle of their cellar. "Jacques, you're alive! You're safe!" Tears streamed down her cheeks. In the whole year they had spent together, Marjorie had never seen Sophy cry before. "It's so wonderful to see you," she sobbed.

"You, too, *mon petit chou,*" Jacques replied tenderly. In the soft candlelight, Marjorie saw he had Sophy's delicate features and big blue eyes, but his hair was full and dark, and he was tall and broad-shouldered.

Marjorie watched Sophy's reunion with him shyly. It had been a year since she and Sophy had seen anyone besides Mlle. Pinget and M. DuClos. And now here was Jacques in their secret home— Jacques, a hero of the Resistance, a hero of France! What's more, he was by far the most handsome boy she had ever seen.

Jacques finally unwrapped his arms from around his sister's shoulders and turned to Marjorie. His smile made her warm all over. "Sophy," he said, not taking his eyes off Marjorie, "I know you don't get many visitors down here, but you haven't forgotten your manners, have you?"

"Oh, I'm sorry," Sophy said. "Jacques, Marjorie. Marjorie, Jacques."

"Hello," Jacques said, holding Marjorie's gaze.

"Hi," she said softly.

"Thank you for taking such good care of my little sister for me," he said.

"She's taken just as good care of me," Marjorie said, pulling away from the spell of Jacques's gaze to flash Sophy a smile. "I feel as if we've become almost . . . well, this is how I imagine it would be if I had a sister."

Sophy grinned. "Mlle. Pinget says we even look alike. What do you think, Jacques?"

"I think you're the two most beautiful hideaways I've ever seen," he said. Marjorie blushed, feeling his eyes still on her. "But I long to see the day when you don't have to hide," he added, his voice growing serious and sad. "Which is why I'm here. Marjorie, I hear you want to help us—help the Resistance."

"Oh, I've wanted to help more than anything," Marjorie said. "But how did you know?"

"I told Mlle. Pinget," Sophy explained.

"And she told me," Jacques said. "You see, we need someone to help transmit radio messages to our allies—to Britain and the United States— someone who speaks fluent English and French."

"Like me," Marjorie said, feeling a flutter of nerves and excitement. "And I know a lot about radio. I used to listen to it all the time back in California."

"Well, this is a different kind of radio," Jacques

said. "You'd be transmitting in code. It's extremely dangerous."

"When do I begin?" Marjorie said without hesitating.

Jacques took a step toward her. "Marjorie," he said softly, "the last radio operator was captured. That's why we need somebody new. I want you to understand that fully before you make a decision."

Marjorie nodded solemnly, her excitement tempered by a shrill note of fear. But her mind was made up. "I do understand," she told Jacques. "And I want you to understand that my other choice is to do nothing. Nothing to win my own freedom. Nothing to win Sophy's. Nothing to help your country or mine. I've been dreaming of this chance, Jacques, and there's no question about what I want to do."

"Marjorie, you are a brave woman," said Jacques.

Marjorie tingled at the sound of her name on his lips. No one had ever called her a woman before. She looked into Jacques's deep blue eyes, and in the candlelight she saw her own reflection —Marjorie Lewis: a woman of the French Resistance!

Two short taps. Three long ones. Marjorie worked the key on her radio transmitter, trying to remember everything she had been taught. Her head swam with all the new information. She

266

prayed she had gotten the secret code right. There had been no study sheets, no books or manuals. Crib notes, hidden under her sleeve the way some of the girls at school used to do, were out of the question. Writing down the code was far too dangerous. What if it fell into the wrong hands? Everything Marjorie learned had to be committed to memory—with no room for mistakes. It was a cram course on which lives depended.

Carefully, she translated her message into coded taps, sending it over the airwaves to a fellow Resistance fighter. *Dynamite received*, she transmitted. *Bridge sabotage planned for 0300 hours.* Marjorie glanced at her wristwatch. She couldn't allow herself more than a few minutes to send her message or the enemy might be able to trace her transmission.

She thought about the last radio operator, the one Jacques had told her had been captured. A chill ran through her. Quickly, she signed off, tapping out her code name: North Star. She had chosen it because back in Sweet Valley she had learned about the slaves on the underground railroad who had used the North Star to guide them to freedom. And the Resistance was a kind of underground railroad for her own time, wasn't it?

Marjorie waited for the return tapping that meant her message had been received. Then she closed the channel on her radio immediately.

Around her were large baskets full of juicy plums and ripening tomatoes and tender green heads of lettuce. The grocer who owned this little shop was a friend of the Resistance, and he had agreed to let Marjorie make this evening's transmission from his stockroom after the store had closed for the evening. Sitting at a rickety old table the grocer had set up, she began to take apart the radio. Piece by piece she packed it into her schoolgirl's book bag. As soon as she was finished, she slung her bag onto her back and left the shop by the back door.

The night was frigid, the sharp, tangy smell of winter riding a light breeze. There was no moon, and Marjorie had to strain to see her way down the street that led away from the shop. Sometimes she felt as if she had lived her whole life in darkness, as if daylight were a dream she had had long before, or something she and Sophy had made up in one of their games of Imagine.

Poor Sophy. Marjorie hated to think of her all alone in the wine cellar, no one to talk to day after day, no one she could tell her dreams or fears to. But Sophy had been so brave when Marjorie left.

"Don't worry about me for a second," she had said. "I want you to do this as much as you want to do it. I just wish I could be part of it myself."

"Sophy, it's too dangerous and you're too young," Jacques had said firmly.

"It's too dangerous for you, too," Sophy had retorted. "And when do I stop being too young?"

Jacques had taken Sophy's hands. "By that time, I hope there will be no need for a secret war. By that time, I hope we'll all be living in safety and peace."

Safety. Peace. Those things seemed as distant as daylight, Marjorie thought as she followed the road toward the spot where she and Jacques had arranged to meet. Her step picked up. Jacques! He was her shelter from the darkness and danger. Seeing him always seemed to make her fears temporarily vanish. Marjorie slipped into the daydream that kept her going as she lived in hiding, moving from one secret spot to another and facing danger every time she turned her radio on.

In her daydream, the war was over. The Allies had won. She and Jacques were happily married and had a little house in Val-le-Doux. Sophy lived next door.

Stop! Marjorie scolded herself. This was just another game of Imagine. She didn't know if Jacques felt the same way she did. And she didn't even know how to tell. In all the books Mlle. Pinget had brought them in the wine cellar, girls and boys were constantly falling in love. But so far, Marjorie's experience with romance had been all in her imagination.

Maybe what she and Jacques shared went no further than their work with the Resistance. He was her control—the person in her cell who knew her real identity, who gave her assignments, and to whom she passed along any information she received over her radio. No one else in her cell knew who North Star really was. It was safer this way. The enemy had its nightmarish ways of getting prisoners to talk, and it was dangerous for anyone to know too much. Like all Resistance members, Marjorie had a special relationship with her control; Jacques was the only person who could be trusted with her life. But maybe when Marjorie's work with the Resistance was over, it would be the end of her relationship with Jacques, too.

Or maybe he thought of her as a little sister. Maybe he had some beautiful secret-agent girl-friend somewhere—

"Your papers, Fraülein!" a deep voice said in Marjorie's ear.

German soldiers! Two of them! Marjorie had been so lost in thought, she hadn't seen them in the shadows of the road. She made a silent note to herself: Never, ever daydream when danger could be lurking up ahead. Her heart pounded so loudly, it was a miracle the soldiers couldn't hear it. *Act calm*, Marjorie reminded herself. *You are an innocent schoolgirl. There's absolutely nothing wrong. . . .*

"Good evening, messieurs," she managed to say. She dug into the pocket of her coat and produced the false identification papers that the Resistance had issued her.

One of the soldiers, flashlight in hand, took the papers and studied them carefully. "Marie Saint-Sault," he read. He glanced at the picture on the papers and then at her face. His eyes traveled over her schoolgirl's uniform. "When is your birthday, Mlle. Saint-Sault?"

Marjorie recited the date she knew was printed on the documents.

The soldier nodded. He was tall and had a round, pink baby face, but his expression was hard. He couldn't have been any older than Jacques. "Well, Mlle. Saint-Sault, it's almost curfew time. School has been over for hours," he said.

Marjorie felt the weight of the radio in the book bag strapped to her back. "I went to meet my boyfriend after school." She looked right into the soldier's chubby-cheeked face and forced herself to give him her most charming smile. "My parents don't approve," she said, lowering her voice as if confiding a huge secret, "so please don't tell anyone."

Baby Face exchanged a glance with the other soldier. Marjorie felt a beat of indecision pass between them. Keeping the smile plastered on her face, she reached out and actually touched the young soldier's sleeve. A shudder ran through her as her fingers made contact with the gray cloth of the hated uniform. But Marjorie made herself laugh. "You know how it is," she said. "Parents."

271

Baby Face's tight expression began to soften. He chuckled, raising an eyebrow at the other soldier. His partner cracked a smile, too.

Baby Face handed Marjorie's papers back to her and waved her on. She was safe—at least for the moment.

"I saw the whole thing," Jacques said. "From my hiding place, I saw them patrolling the road. I came to warn you, but they found you before I did. I saw them stop you. I was terrified." Jacques held Marjorie's hands in his, whispering under the shadow of a large tree. "But you were as cool as could be."

Marjorie trembled at Jacques's touch. This near to him, she didn't feel the least bit cool. Her face was flushed and she felt warm all over, especially where his hand rested on top of hers.

"You were a real professional back there on the road, Marjorie," Jacques said. "You were wonderful." He drew even closer to her. "You *are* wonderful."

Marjorie turned her face up to his. She could see a sparkle in his eyes. She could feel the warmth of his skin. *Kiss me,* she thought. *Please kiss me. Let's share one bit of joy in all this madness and horror.*

Jacques's lips met hers. He kissed her tentatively, softly. Marjorie kissed him back with all the passion that had fueled her deepest daydreams. Their kisses deepened. The world seemed to stop. All the terror and loss dissolved in the sweetness of their embrace. And for those lingering moments, Marjorie and Jacques were just two people falling in love, the horror of war forgotten.

Thirty-two

Marjorie's radio hummed and clicked as she received a message. Five short taps, one long one. *C, H.* Two more long ones. *A. Charles,* she spelled out, decoding as the message came in. *Charles Robertson and Marvin Feld arrived safely Barcelona,* the complete message said.

From her secret nest of straw in a farm silo, Marjorie smiled. Every message like this was a victory. Charles Robertson and Marvin Feld were two young American pilots who had been shot down over Marjorie's sector and had bailed out of their burning plane by parachute. They had landed near Val-le-Doux, where they had been picked up by members of Marjorie's cell. The Resistance had arranged for them to be smuggled to Spain. From there they were free to return to America.

Guiding the beam of her flashlight to her radio, Marjorie tapped out the code for "message received." As she worked she remembered Charles Robertson's strong-boned, handsome face, ripped open by flying metal as his plane had been hit. She remembered the hollow terror in his deep-set eyes. She wished as hard as she could that his wound was healing and that his terror had softened with the passing weeks. Did he have a girlfriend to take care of him back in the United States? Marjorie hoped so.

She pictured a happy Charles Robertson knocking on the door of her Aunt Amanda's house in Sweet Valley, as he had promised he'd do. She pictured her aunt's face lighting up as she heard that Marjorie was safe. But as she thought about her aunt, Marjorie's game of Imagine took a sad turn. When would she see Aunt Amanda again? When would she hear her voice?

Marjorie began taking apart her radio and packing it into her school bag. Sometimes it was best not to wish or imagine. Sometimes it hurt too much, as it did when Marjorie thought about her father or her aunt. She hadn't heard anything about her father since the day he had disappeared. She didn't even know if he was dead or alive. Marjorie played Imagine less and less these days. She had a new, real happiness to fill her days now. Thank goodness for Jacques, she thought, pulling on her coat, grabbing the bag that held her radio, and making sure she left no trace of her visit in the silo. She hurried across a grassy field illuminated by a crescent moon and followed a stone wall to her rendezvous with Jacques.

Her quick step became a run when she saw him waiting in the trickle of moonlight. She threw her arms around him, and as always, the world around her fell away in the space of a kiss.

"Marjorie," Jacques murmured, drawing her close, "Marjorie, I love you."

"Jacques, oh, I love you, too." Marjorie melted into the tender strength of his hug. "But how can this be happening to us? How can we be falling in love in the middle of all the hate, the fear, the death?"

"Because," Jacques said, punctuating his words with kisses, "we are human. We must see the hope. That's how we will win."

Tears streamed down Marjorie's face as she sat in the back room of a village pharmacy decoding the incoming message. "No," she sobbed. "Oh, no!"

Sophy Berg arrested. Enemy searching for Hélène Pinget. Marjorie's body shook with sobs as she struggled to break down the coded message letter by letter. *Also searching for . . . M . . . A . . .* came the taps.

Good heavens! *Marjorie!* The transmission spelled out Marjorie! The enemy knew about her, knew she had been hiding with Sophy until recently. They were looking for her! Marjorie wiped at her tears as the message kept coming in. *Lewis girl sought as vital link to getting information from American agent Jack Lewis.*

The news split through her storm of unhappiness. Her father was alive! But the slim ray of joy

276

could not evaporate her tears for Sophy. Conflicting feelings thundered inside her as she decoded the rest of the message.

Agent Lewis suspected of planning his own arrest to work within the walls of prisoner-of-war camp. Arrested on purpose! Marjorie's head spun. Her father was every inch a hero!

Suddenly, Marjorie had an idea for securing Sophy's freedom!

"Turn you over to the enemy?" Jacques asked. He held Marjorie close. "Never!" His voice echoed in the empty chapel where they were being hidden for the night.

"But Jacques, it's the only way to get Sophy back," Marjorie insisted. "If they want the information from my father badly enough—and it sounds like they do—it will be worth the trade. Me, and the power they'll have over my father once they have me, for your sister's freedom."

Jacques tightened his hug, as if Marjorie might vanish at any second. "And then what? What do you think happens once they realize you know nothing about your father's work?"

Marjorie was silent. The little stone chapel was cold and damp.

"No," Jacques said. "I won't allow it."

Marjorie let go of him. "And if I decide to do it anyway?"

Jacques gave a bitter laugh. "How will you do that? Will you turn yourself in to one of those swinish Germans and tell him you want to be swapped for one of the other prisoners? A lot of good it will do Sophy once you're in enemy hands." He shook his head. "No, it would require all the help and skill and delicate planning of our entire cell. And I am your only link to them."

"Then you have to help me," Marjorie said. "Or are you just going to accept that you may never see your little sister again?"

Jacques's face was a mask of misery and pain. "I'll figure something out," he said.

"What? There's no other way."

But Jacques was unmovable. "I'll never let you go," he said.

"But what about Sophy?" Marjorie said miserably. "If only there was some way we could trick them. Make them *think* they were going to get me in exchange for her, and then . . . then . . . I don't know." Her sigh of frustration rose up toward the vaulted chapel ceiling.

"Wait!" Jacques's voice took on a ripple of hope. "Marjorie, that's it! What if we pretended we were willing to make the trade, but once Sophy was safe, there was a little change in plan?"

Marjorie kept her optimism in check. "And how would you work a scheme like that? The Germans will be much too careful to let me slip through their fingers. Besides, you can't go to the enemy, either. You're in as much danger as I am."

"That's true," Jacques said. "But I know someone in Val-le-Doux who collaborates with the

Germans. Pierre Trichet—he used to be a class-mate of mine."

Marjorie nodded. Many French men and women were collaborationists. That was one of the things that made occupied France so danger-ous for her and Jacques.

"Well," Jacques continued, "perhaps we could take Pierre's twisted loyalty and turn it to our advantage. I could contact him and arrange for a secret meeting. . . ."

"I convinced Pierre that he would be a hero!" Jacques said triumphantly. He and Marjorie hud-dled inside an old shed that smelled of wood and damp earth. Rain beat on the roof. " 'One Jewish girl,' I said to him. 'A Jew means nothing. You know that. Our lives are worthless to the Ger-mans. Certainly they would be willing to let one worthless soul go free in exchange for someone who will unlock the secrets of the United States of America.' "

"And what did he say to that?" Marjorie asked.

"Well, he seemed embarrassed. I think he looked up to me when we were in school. Always picked me to be on his soccer team, things like that. Now here I was saying that I was worth nothing to the people he had sided with."

Marjorie rested her head on Jacques's shoul-der. "It must have been terrible to have to talk to a traitor like that."

Jacques sighed. "I don't know. I don't think it's

as easy as that. You might think Pierre is some kind of a monster, but he's really just a simple person. He takes orders from the people who are giving them. Right now, that means the Germans."

"And people die. People are murdered."

"Yes. People die," Jacques said. "But not this time. Pierre doesn't know it, but he's going to help save a girl's life."

"Tell me how," Marjorie said. "Tell me everything."

Jacques nodded. "Well, as I said, first I made Pierre see that Sophy was worth nothing to the Germans and that they'd be glad to trade her for you. Collaborationist though he is, he's still the impressionable boy I once knew. We talked over old times, and he is quite willing, I think, to have an excuse to reunite me with my sister. Maybe it makes him feel less like he is betraying our country," Jacques said.

"And then?" Marjorie prompted.

"Then I explained how we would make the trade at the train station. I told him he would have to get the Germans to provide all the proper false papers to assure Sophy safe passage to Spain. Pierre agreed to talk to one of the German higher-ups in Val-le-Doux, and we arranged to meet the next day."

"Which was yesterday, right?" Marjorie asked. Jacques nodded again. "And did you meet him?"

Jacques nodded and reached into a secret

pocket that had been sewn into the lining of his coat. "Voilà! Papers for Sophy!"

Marjorie took the papers from him. A photo of Sophy seemed to jump out at her from the documents. Sophy! She looked so drawn and frightened, her big eyes even bigger with fear. Marjorie stiffled a cry of alarm.

"I know. She looks awful. I wonder what they have done to her." Jacques let out a long breath. "But you have to keep thinking that soon she will be free. Free!"

"When?" Marjorie asked. Looking at her friend's picture, no time seemed soon enough.

"The day after tomorrow," Jacques said. "Pierre is to bring Sophy to the train station and I am to bring you. We'll give Sophy her papers and put her on the train that will be waiting. Then Pierre thinks I will hand you over and he will deliver his prize to his German superiors. That is where our people who work for the railroad come in."

"But surely the Germans will follow Pierre to the station now that they know of his plans. Surely that is why they agreed to issue Sophy papers at all. They'll try to stop the train. They'll try to take all three of us."

Jacques nodded. "I'm sure that's so. And our people will be ready."

Thirty-three

Marjorie saw Sophy at the front of the train platform, and her heart filled with joy. She was really there: Sophy, who had been Marjorie's sole companion for a year of her life; Sophy, whom she loved like a sister.

The younger girl looked thin. Her fair hair framed a pale, gaunt face. A chubby young man about Jacques's age held her tightly by the arm. Pierre Trichet! He looked as though he was clutching her tightly enough to raise a bruise.

Marjorie wanted to shout Sophy's name out loud and run up the platform with her arms outstretched. But she couldn't call attention to herself until Sophy was safely on the train that now sat on the tracks. Besides, if everything went according to plan, they would be having a reunion soon enough.

Jacques and Marjorie emerged from the shadows of the station house and walked up the platform toward Pierre and Jacques's sister. Marjorie's legs felt weak from nervousness, but she willed herself forward, keeping her back straight, her head up. Jacques held her arm as though she had to be prevented from escaping, but his grip was gentle and gave her courage as she walked toward Pierre and Sophy. When they reached them, Jacques nodded to Pierre and took Sophy from him gently. He and Sophy embraced, and Sophy cast a quick but loving glance at Marjorie, averting her gaze a split second later. Marjorie felt the tears welling in her eyes.

But their tender moment didn't last long. There was very little time. Jacques handed his sister her papers and helped her onto the train.

Around Marjorie, several passengers said their farewells to their families, handing suitcases up to a train conductor and climbing onto the train. An older couple who had just gotten off gave their suitcases to a uniformed baggage clerk, who loaded them onto his wheeled cart.

Pierre Trichet was reaching out for her, eager to secure his conquest. Marjorie felt herself recoil. Her legs didn't want to carry her any further. But Jacques encouraged her with a loving look, the silent strength and caring in his eyes helping Marjorie take the final steps into Pierre's rough grasp.

"Let's go, mademoiselle," Pierre said, pulling her from the solid warmth of Jacques's gaze.

As soon as he began to drag her away, Marjorie heard the sound of squeaky, rumbling wheels. Pierre heard it, too. He tried to jump out of the path of the baggage cart, yanking Marjorie along with him. But he wasn't fast enough. The baggage boy threw his whole weight behind the

283

loaded cart, aiming right for Pierre. Pierre cried out, his grip on Marjorie breaking as he was knocked to the ground.

Marjorie had rehearsed the next step over and over in her mind. She ran as hard as she could toward the head of the train and jumped on board. In her mental rehearsal, Jacques was always right behind her. But it was not his footfall on the metal step of the train that she heard. As she turned for a view of the platform, an explosion of gunfire rang out from several directions at once. Jacques was running toward her, the sound of his steps swallowed by the chilling thunder-crack of rifle shots. This was not in the plan.

German soldiers were flooding onto the train platform from both ends. Immediately, a smaller number of armed men in street clothes materialized around them, jumping from the roof of the station and from between train cars—French Resistance fighters. Both sides unleashed a torrent of bullets. The station filled with the acrid smell of gunpowder. Jacques disappeared from Marjorie's view amid the chaos of people running and shouting and screaming.

"Jacques!" she cried. But his name was lost in a shrill blast from the locomotive whistle. Marjorie could feel the train moving. "No! Not yet! Oh, no! Not without Jacques! Jacques, hurry!" She grabbed onto the rail with one hand, leaning out of the train, ready to help pull Jacques up with the other hand.

But the train kept moving. Marjorie looked back. The confusion was beginning to die down. Casualties from both sides were slumped on the station platform. Marjorie felt the scream boiling up from deep within her. Jacques was lying in a pool of blood. "No! God, no!" It couldn't be.

Jacques's motionless body grew smaller and smaller as the train pulled away.

Marjorie and Sophy sobbed. Behind the closed door of their train compartment, they held each other, their bodies shaking with shock and sorrow. Marjorie's blouse was wet from both their tears.

"It was . . . never . . . supposed to be . . . this way," she cried, forcing her words out between heaving sobs. "You . . . you were supposed to . . . live next door . . . to Jacques and me." Her voice rose in a wail of grief as she pronounced Jacques's name. Oh, how could it be true? How could Jacques be dead? She had kissed his warm lips just that morning, felt the love in his eyes only minutes earlier.

Sophy's silent flood of tears gave way to a heartbreaking lament of grief. "They're gone!" she cried, her face twisted in the most intense anguish. "My whole family. Gone. Dead." She rocked in Marjorie's arms. "I don't know what I would do if I didn't have you. Oh, Marjorie, at least I have you."

Sophy's words hit Marjorie hard. "Sophy,

Sophy, you know I'll be your family. You know I'll be your friend always. But you're going to have to be brave by yourself for a while." She swallowed back her own tears as she spoke.

Sophy's cries seemed to freeze in her throat. "By myself?"

Marjorie nodded. "I can't do anything about it. We have a person working on this train who's helped us. We'll be slowing down soon. That's where my ride ends. That's the place where Jacques and I were supposed to jump off together."

Sophy grabbed Marjorie's hands. "But why can't we both travel to freedom? Don't leave me. You're the only person I have now."

"Sophy, I don't have papers to travel," Marjorie explained. "I'll be taken off the train at the border. No, I have to do what was planned. Even without Jacques." She felt herself choke up. "I wanted to stay and fight with him, but . . . but I don't know how I will have the courage without him."

"Where do you get off?" Sophy asked quickly. "Where will the train slow down?"

"About twenty kilometers outside Val-le-Doux. We should be there soon. The train whistle will blow. Why?"

In the blink of an eye, Sophy pulled her hands away from Marjorie's, yanked open the door to the train compartment, and bolted out.

"Sophy?" Marjorie said, getting to her feet.

The door slammed shut, separating the two girls. As Marjorie reached for the door handle, she heard a faint metal-on-metal sound coming from the lock. She tried to pull the door open, but the latch would not give way.

"Don't bother." Sophy's voice came from the other side of the door. "I jammed it with a hairpin."

"Have you gone mad?" Marjorie shrieked through the door. Was her friend cracking under her load of grief?

Marjorie heard something being slid under the door a fraction of a second before she saw it. The hollow-eyed photo of Sophy stared up at her from the set of false identification papers.

"Take them," Sophy told her. "We look enough alike. Take them and find freedom. You've been enough of a heroine already. The enemy wants you too much. Go back to your country. Go back to your aunt whom you miss so much. Go where it's safe."

"Sophy, you can't do this!" Marjorie cried. "Your brother wanted *you* to use those papers. Do it for him. Let me keep on with my work."

"No. They're looking for you. It's too dangerous. You've done everything you can. Save yourself. Now it's my turn to fight."

"But it's dangerous for you, too," Marjorie protested. "Let me out. Come on. Open the door."

"Marjorie, France is my country, and I want to do something for her—just as you did. Jacques said I was too young, but he's gone and it's time for me to try to carry on for him. Please. Let me."

Marjorie jiggled the door handle. Then she leaned on it with all her weight. The door wouldn't open. "I don't think I have much choice," she said.

"No, you don't." The train whistle punctuated Sophy's sentence. "Goodbye, Marjorie. I love you," she said. Her footsteps sounded down the train corridor, growing fainter and fainter.

Marjorie could feel the train slowing down. She looked out her window just in time to see Sophy hit the ground, tuck into a somersault, and roll into the cover of the bushes that grew along the tracks. It was as if she had been jumping off trains all her life—as if she were already a seasoned Resistance fighter. Marjorie blew Sophy a kiss, even though she knew her friend couldn't see her. Sophy would be met by other members of the Resistance. They would be her only family now.

Marjorie picked up the false identification papers and put them in her coat pocket. She was going to Spain. And from there, home—to Sweet Valley. To her aunt. To liberty. The lush green countryside of France rolled by her window. She was going home, but her heart would stay here. Buried with Jacques. Forever.

Thirty-four

1949. Sweet Valley, California.

The strains of "Here Comes the Bride" floated to the back of the chapel. Marjorie's heart soared.

"Ready?" her father asked. His tuxedo was decorated with a pink-and-white orchid on one lapel. On the other, he proudly wore his medal for bravery during the war.

"Ready," Marjorie said, taking a deep breath to calm her nervous excitement.

"You look so beautiful, sweetheart." He moved her lacy veil to one side and kissed her cheek. Then he patted it back in place and took her arm.

The California sun streamed into the chapel through stained-glass windows, warming the aisle with softly colored light. Marjorie and her father stepped forward and the billowy satin folds of Marjorie's white gown took on a pale rose hue. A few more steps down the aisle and the rose changed to blue. Marjorie felt as if she were sliding down a rainbow. And at the end was a pot of gold—the man she loved! She could see him waiting for her, his face radiant with happiness.

The chapel was filled with everyone Marjorie cared for. Her father escorted her past Mlle.

Pinget and Sophy, who had come all the way from France for the wedding. Mlle. Pinget beamed proudly, and Sophy gave her a feisty thumbs-up sign. This was no game of Imagine. This was true happiness.

Across the aisle from them, at the front of the chapel, Marjorie's Aunt Amanda dabbed at happy tears with the edge of a handkerchief. She had told Marjorie that she knew what it was like to nurse a broken heart for many, many long years, and that she had always prayed fate would not have the same thing in store for her niece. Well, it didn't. Of course, Marjorie would always love Jacques, but she had found a new love. Now Marjorie could only wish that her aunt would somehow find the same happiness.

Next to her Aunt Amanda sat her Grandpa Taylor and her Grandma Jessamyn. Grandma was as stylish as ever in a wide-brimmed forest-green velvet hat that made her look far younger than her years. Behind them were Marjorie's Uncle Harry and his wife, Aunt Stephanie, along with their children, Peter and Stevie. They had gotten in from New York the night before.

Marjorie felt a tremendous amount of love around her. She floated on the special feeling all the way to the altar of the chapel, her eyes meeting the eyes of her husband-to-be. Her father let go of her elbow. He gave Marjorie one more kiss and slid into his seat next to Aunt Amanda.

The handsome groom reached out toward

Marjorie. The very tips of their fingers touched, and electric happiness flowed between them. Marjorie took her place next to him at the altar.

"Dearly beloved," the minister began. "We are gathered here together to join this woman, Marjorie Lewis, and this man, Charles Robertson, in holy matrimony."

Marjorie sneaked a sideways look at Charles. His face shone with joy. The faint scar that ran down one side of it would always remind Marjorie of how he had fallen from the sky, but the war wound was only a trace now. Marjorie felt as if it was the same way inside her. She would always carry a trace of the war, and of Jacques, carved in her memory like the everlasting petals of the wooden rose Aunt Amanda had given her. But time had healed her wounds and brought her happiness.

Thirty-five

1962. Sweet Valley.

"Wow! The first American to orbit the Earth!" Alice said. "Isn't it incredible?"

"Well, it would have been even better if we could have seen what John Glenn was seeing instead of that dumb drawing of a space capsule they kept putting on the TV," Alice's older sister, Nancy, said.

"Nancy, you were supposed to use your imagination," Alice said. "I mean, imagine what the Earth must look like from space! It must be so beautiful."

Nancy made a face. "So why couldn't they have shown a drawing of the Earth instead of that stupid space capsule?"

Their mother switched off the TV set and sighed. "Girls, I let you stay home to watch history taking place, not to fight with each other."

"Yeah," echoed Laura, the girls' younger sister. "We got to stay home because something like this doesn't happen every day. We can listen to you guys fighting any time we want. Right, Mom?"

Alice caught Nancy's eye. There was an unspoken truce between them—in order to team up against the common enemy. They both glared at their little sister.

But their mother took Laura's side. "That's right, dear. Putting a man in orbit is the beginning of the exploration of a whole new world. Space!" she marveled. "When I was a girl in France, it was a place you could get to only in your wildest dreams. Now there's even talk of putting a man on the moon."

"I'm going to be an astronaut when I grow up," Laura announced.

Alice and Nancy looked at each other and rolled their eyes. The day before, Laura was going to be a nurse. The week before, a ballerina.

"I think that's very exciting, dear," their mother told Laura encouragingly. "Space is the new frontier."

"Frontier?" Laura asked. "What's that?"

"A place to explore," Alice explained. "For instance, a hundred years ago the new frontier meant packing up all your possessions and moving west across the country."

"The way my great-grandmother, Alice Larson, did," their mother added.

"The one who I was named for?" Alice asked.

"Right," her mother said.

"Alice Larson was the one who had those twin girls," Nancy put in.

"You mean Great-Aunt Amanda and her sister?" Laura asked.

"No, dummy," Nancy said. "The first Alice was

the mother of Jessamyn and Elisabeth, the ones who lived in Minnesota. Jessamyn was the mother of Great-Aunt Amanda and her twin sister, Samantha."

"Right," their mother said. "And your real grandmother, my mother, was Samantha. She died when I was born, so Amanda, my aunt, became like a mother to me."

"Oh, yeah. I knew that," Nancy said. "Great-Aunt Amanda told us the whole story once, remember?"

"I don't remember it," Alice said. "I must have been too young. Anyway, it's kind of confusing." She tried to get all the grandparents and great-grandparents straight in her head. "I know! Why don't we make a family tree?"

"Good idea," their mother said.

They got out some construction paper and colored pencils and spread them out on the kitchen table.

"I'm going to put a ship next to Alice Larson's name, to show how she came over from Sweden," Alice said. As she drew, she tried to imagine what it had been like for her great-great-grandmother to leave her country forever, to cross the ocean on a huge ship and not know what she would find on the other side. "Was her whole family on the voyage with her?" Alice asked.

Her mother shook her head. "She was only sixteen, but she was alone on her trip. Her parents had died back in Sweden. So she started out by herself. Your Great-Aunt Amanda—Alice's grand-daughter—once told me that Alice had met a young man on the ship. But something happened and it didn't work out between them."

"But she met someone else, right?" asked Alice as she finished coloring the ship. "The father of the first set of twins?"

"Yes. Her husband's name was George," her mother said. "George Johnson."

Alice wrote that down next to Alice Larson's name and made a little heart between the two names to show they were married. Then she drew two lines under the heart, each one a branch of the family tree. "And the first twins' names were Elisabeth and Jessamyn?"

Her mother nodded, and Alice printed the twins' names under the lines she had drawn. Laura looked over at Alice's tree and printed the same information on her own paper, struggling with the letters she was just beginning to master.

"I wish you girls had known my grandmother, Jessamyn. She died just before Nancy was born," the girls' mother said. "She was really something, lots of fun, even a little wild. Sometimes she seemed more like a kid than a grandparent. When she was only sixteen, she ran away and joined the circus as a bareback rider."

"Wow, neat," Alice said. "And what about Elisabeth?"

Her mother frowned. "Elisabeth died in a riding accident. I don't know many of the details because my grandmother didn't like to talk about it."

Alice felt a wave of sadness wash over her. She might fight sometimes with Nancy and Laura, but if anything happened to them, she didn't know how she would be able to bear it.

Still, she wouldn't mind if Nancy were a little less bossy. Her older sister wasn't making a family tree, but that didn't stop her from telling Alice what to do. "You left out the brother," Nancy said. "Jessamyn and Elisabeth had an older brother. He died of some awful disease that people got a lot back then."

"His name was Steven," their mother confirmed. "He died when he was just a baby, of scarlet fever, I think."

"Like Beth in *Little Women*," Alice said, remembering how hard she had cried when Beth had died. It was even more tragic to find out that one of her own ancestors had died of the same thing. She wrote down Steven's name and drew a little angel over it.

"What picture are you going to put for Jessamyn and Elisabeth?" Laura asked, trying to copy the angel.

Alice thought for a moment, then sketched a picture of a horse. At first, it looked too much like her puppy, Pounce. She erased and redrew until she was satisfied. Then she colored it in with a maple-colored crayon and added a black mane.

Her mother looked over at her handiwork.

"That's beautiful, Alice. I think you have a real artist's eye." Alice smiled and blushed. It was her secret wish to grow up to be an artist or designer.

"Yeah, it's not bad," Nancy agreed. "But you forgot to put Mom's grandfather, Jessamyn's husband."

"I was just about to ask about him," Alice said, shooting Nancy a dirty look. "Mom, what was his name?"

"Taylor. Taylor Watson."

"And they had Grandma Samantha, Great-Aunt Amanda, and Great-Uncle Harry?" Alice asked.

"That's right."

Alice added the next generation to the family tree, linking Samantha to Jack Lewis with a heart. Next to Samantha's name she drew a movie screen surrounded by red curtains dotted with silver stars. She decorated Great-Aunt Amanda's name with a book. She knew her great-aunt had at one time taught English at Sweet Valley High.

The next generation was simple. From Grandma Samantha and Grandpa Jack's names she drew a branch for her mother. *Marjorie Lewis*, she printed. She made a heart, and added her father's name: Charles Robertson.

Her mother gave a little laugh. "I'm curious to see what you're going to draw for us, Alice."

"That's easy," Alice said. "I'm going to make a plane, to show how you and Dad met when he had to bail out near your town in France." She drew slowly and carefully. Then she added the final three branches of the family tree for her, Nancy, and Laura. But she was careful to leave space at the bottom of the page. One day, she would be able to fill in the spot where her own family would go.

Thirty-six

Late 1960s. Campus of the College of Southern California.

The electric wail of Jimi Hendrix's guitar rattled the windows of the frat building. Multicolored strobes painted the partygoers with flashing rainbows of light.

"Wow!" Alice exclaimed. "Even Pi Iota Gamma's going psychedelic! Can you believe it?" She and Jenny Jenkins looked around the party in amazement. Alice had met Jenny at a campus meeting of Women for Peace, and they had been friends ever since.

"The times, they are a-changing!" Jenny said, quoting the Bob Dylan song. "I never thought I'd see the day when these squares joined the revolution." Her dangling silver earrings jangled as she shook her head. "But maybe it's just skin-deep."

Alice laughed. "Jen, we're supposed to be here to make peace with these guys. Can't you give them the benefit of the doubt?" But she wasn't sure Jenny was so wrong. Pi Iota Gamma was the most conservative frat on campus.

"Well, if I've got to give anyone the benefit of the doubt, I know who it's going to be," Jenny said. She pointed to a tall redhead disappearing into the crowd. "He might be totally off base about politics, but he sure looks cute in that tie-dyed T-shirt. Mind if I go talk to him?"

"Of course not," Alice said, running a hand through her long white-blond hair. Her slender body swayed to the music as she watched Jenny go off after Mr. Tie-dye.

"Well, the lovely lady painter," said a voice behind her.

Alice whirled around to find herself face to face with Hank Patman. His dark brown hair was cropped as short as always around his face, but he'd donned a string of beads to be more in tune with the feeling on campus. The first time Alice had seen Hank, back during freshman orientation week, she had thought he was impossibly handsome. But as she'd gotten to know more about him, he seemed less and less her type.

"Hi, Hank," she said, politely but distantly.

"Welcome to my party," Hank said, as if he were single-handedly throwing the entire Pi Iota Gamma bash. "Haven't seen you around campus much lately. Are you spending a lot of time in your painting studio?"

"Enough," Alice said guardedly. Since when did Hank Patman talk about anyone but himself?

"Well, it's a great hobby," Hank said.

Alice felt a surge of annoyance. "Hank, my painting is not just a hobby. Women have professions, too, you know."

Hank chuckled. "A girl like you? You're too pretty to work."

"Hank," Alice said through clenched teeth, "get serious."

Hank leaned forward and put a hand on Alice's shoulder. "I am serious," he said. "In fact, you're more than pretty. You're beautiful."

Alice shook off Hank's hand. He might be handsome, but he was a real loser. "Hank, why don't you go greet some of your other party guests?" she suggested. She turned on her heel and walked away from him.

Alice watched the Frisbee sail up into the blue, cloudless sky. Stretched out on the grass, her long Indian-print skirt spread out around her, she tried to capture the Frisbee's spinning orbit on her sketch pad. No, that wasn't right. It looked like the boys she had drawn were playing catch with a flying hamburger. She erased her pencil work and tried again. That was more like it.

"Nice drawing," a familiar voice said. "Very nice." Hank Patman was standing over her, watching her sketch.

"Thanks," Alice said, a note of suspicion in her voice.

"I mean it," Hank said. "There's something about the way you work your lines that reminds me of some of Degas's sketches."

"Degas?" Alice was surprised to find out Hank knew something about art. Surprised and, she

301

had to admit it, a touch flattered. The French Impressionist was one of her favorite painters.

"Sure. You know how he liked to draw dancers and horses, and capture the feeling of movement and motion? That's what you're doing by sketching these guys tossing around the Frisbee."

"Thanks," Alice repeated. This time she was less suspicious. Hank clearly noticed the change in her voice and took it as a sign to sit down next to her. Alice was immediately sorry she had let down her guard. Hank drew so close that their arms touched.

"You should come over to my family's home sometime," he said. "We have several Degases. And the work of many other great painters, of course."

Alice rolled her eyes. "Of course," she echoed. What a braggart this guy was. "But then, Los Angeles isn't very far away, and it has an excellent museum where I can see all the great paintings I want."

"Yes, I know the museum's collection well," Hank said. "Father is on their board of directors."

Oh, brother, Alice thought. Didn't Hank ever give it a rest? She closed her sketch book and put it away in her fringed shoulder bag. "It's been nice chatting with you, Hank," she said as she got up, "but I have a lot of schoolwork to do. Excuse me."

Hank got up, too. "Yes, I suppose you would have quite a bit of work, staying on the dean's list every semester. That's one of the things I admire about you. Some of these other students are too busy playing revolution to bother with school. It's really just laziness."

"There's nothing wrong with trying to make the world a better place, Hank. You should try it sometime. See you later."

"I'm starved," Jenny moaned. She and Alice sat cross-legged on the floor of one of the offices in the administration building. Students were everywhere. A couple in faded bell-bottom jeans and bare feet were reading nearby. Other kids sat talking in small groups. Over by the windows, a boy with a long ponytail was strumming his guitar, and people were singing the chorus of "We Shall Overcome."

"I'm starved, too," Alice said. She could feel her stomach growling. She hadn't eaten anything since the chocolate-covered marshmallow Moon Pie she had bought from a vending machine in her dorm the previous afternoon.

"Do you think it would be awful if we sneaked out of here for a pizza?" Jenny whispered.

Alice's mouth started watering at the thought of a bacon-and-onion pizza smothered with spicy tomato sauce and cheese. She groaned. "Don't even say that, Jen."

"Well, look, Alice. How many people do you think are in this building?" Jenny asked. "There are twenty or thirty of us here in this room, right?

And this is only one of dozens of offices full of students. Do you really think anyone would miss us if we left?"

"Jen, we can't!" Alice said, wishing her stomach would stop making noise. "It's the principle of the thing. I mean, what if everyone started sneaking out? The administration would win. And you know how unfair it was of them to fire Professor Yarovitch. If he hadn't been such a vocal civil-rights activist, he'd still be teaching."

Jenny sighed. "You're right. I just don't know how much longer I can hold out. I mean, I thought a sit-in was going to be sort of like a big slumber party, you know? It never occurred to me that the administration would get dirty enough to cut off all the deliveries to the building and try to starve us out of here."

"That's all the more reason to stick it out," Alice said. But she knew that sooner or later she was going to have to give in. The students couldn't win this battle without food to keep them going. "Maybe we should try memorizing some more French verbs," she suggested. "That should take our minds off how hungry we are." She dug around in her fringed bag for her French text.

"Je mange, tu manges, il et elle mange," Jenny said, conjugating the verb *to eat*. "Alice, French verbs are just no substitute for a turkey pot pie. Or two or three."

"Jen, would you please shut up about pizza and

pot pies and just conjugate the verb *devoir*," Alice said, choosing a difficult verb to keep Jenny busy.

Jenny's conjugation and the singing across the room were suddenly drowned out by the sound of the air above the building being beaten by steel wings. "A helicopter!" the boy with the guitar yelled.

Alice felt her blood pumping fiercely. A helicopter? She jumped to her feet. What was the administration up to now? She felt as if she were on a battlefield. Should she take cover under a desk? Race for the nearest exit? Her breath came short and fast.

A few moments later, she heard the sound of cheering coming from out in the hall. A girl with a red bandanna wrapped pirate-style around her head paused in the doorway just long enough to pronounce the magic word. "Food!" she said. "Someone's dropping food onto the roof by helicopter!"

"Right on!" Jenny yelled, holding out her hand for Alice to slap her five. They joined the mass migration up the stairs of the administration building and out onto the roof.

Alice thought it looked like something from Woodstock—or at least what she imagined the music festival to have looked like. Up on the roof were hundreds of students in patched jeans and vests, shirts decorated with tiny mirrors or bright beads—a sea of flower children, arms stretched to the sky.

Overhead, a chopper hovered, its propellers spinning out the sound of victory. From its open door, dozens of bags were being dropped, each attached to a tiny parachute. The chutes were painted with bold peace signs and bright flower-power daisies.

"It's like manna from heaven!" yelled a tall, frizzy-haired blond girl. She caught one of the bags and ripped it open. Oranges and apples rolled out onto the roof. There were boxes of cookies, sandwiches, and containers of coleslaw and potato salad. There were even plastic forks and paper plates.

Someone handed Alice a sandwich. She ripped open the plastic wrapping and bit into it. Plain old egg salad had never tasted so good. The roof was filled with sighs of pleasure, cheers, and laughter as the picnic began. It looked like some kind of race to see who could wolf down the most food in the shortest time. Some people ate with one hand and held the other one up with fingers in a *V*, flashing peace signs to the helicopter still hovering above them. As Alice started on the second half of her sandwich, a voice from the copter spoke through a bullhorn, filling the air.

"Attention! Attention!" a man's voice said. Alice thought he sounded familiar.

"A voice from heaven!" said Jenny, talking with her mouth full.

The voice from the air continued. "I will keep feeding the people until their demands are met!"

As the students around her clapped and cheered, Alice was rocked by a huge wave of surprise. "Jenny," she yelled in her friend's ear, barely able to believe what she was hearing, "I know that voice. You're going to freak out when you hear this, but the guy up in the helicopter is —get this—it's Hank Patman!"

The crowd was going wild. "Right on! Power to the people!" they shouted. Hank Patman was a hero!

"I heard his father threatened to cut off his inheritance if he made that food drop," Jenny said. She sat across from Alice in the C.S.C. snack bar.

Alice took a sip of coffee. "Yeah, I heard that, too. The word sure gets around fast."

"Almost as fast as Hank Patman changes stripes," Jenny commented. "I wonder what made him switch to our side all of a sudden."

Alice shrugged. "Do you think it's for real or do you think he's up to something sneaky?"

Jenny sipped her tea. "Look, the way I figure it, the Patmans are worth millions, right?"

"I guess," Alice agreed. She had heard that Hank's house was an estate with dozens upon dozens of rooms, surrounded by sculptured gardens and fountains and acres of woods. It was said

307

that his father had business and political connections that stretched to every corner of the globe.

"Well, I don't think Hank would risk losing his entire inheritance if he weren't serious about what he was doing," Jenny said.

"I guess you're right," Alice said. "It's just that it seems like he's done a total about-face."

"Yeah, well, from what I know about Hank Patman, he's a pretty stubborn guy," Jenny said. "Maybe it just took him longer to see the light."

"But now that he has, he's just as stubborn about being on our side." Alice finished Jenny's thought. "Maybe you're right. Maybe Hank's stubbornness is turning out to be as much of a good quality as a bad one."

"He did help us get Professor Yarovitch reinstated," Jenny said.

Alice drank the last few sips of her coffee in silence, thinking about the change in Hank Patman. "Jen," she finally said, "Hank's been asking me out."

"Still?" Jenny asked. "Boy, that guy's persistent, isn't he?"

Alice nodded. "I keep waiting for him to give up, keep trying to discourage him. But now . . ." She felt herself blushing.

"Well, he *is* cute," Jenny said. "Really cute."

"Yeah, he is," Alice agreed. "And he knows a lot about art, too."

Jenny grinned, and the flower she'd painted on her cheek with body paint dimpled up. "Go for it,

Alice! You're the one who's always telling me to give people the benefit of the doubt, right?"

Alice nodded slowly. "OK. Maybe I will give Hank a chance." A giggle bubbled up in her throat. If anyone had told her a few weeks earlier that she'd be thinking about going on a date with Hank Patman, she wouldn't have believed it. But then again, the first time she had set eyes on him, he had been just what Alice had been dreaming about.

Thirty-seven

They were perched high above the ocean. Soft candlelight graced their corner table, glinting off the cut-crystal vase filled with fresh flowers. Below them, the waves broke rhythmically on the shore. The lulling sound rose up through the darkness to the restaurant up on the cliff. Out on the water, the lights of a ship sparkled like faraway Christmas decorations.

"To peace!" Hank toasted, holding up a glass of sparkling cider.

"To peace," Alice seconded.

"And to Russian caviar," Hank added.

"Mmm," Alice agreed, setting down her glass to help herself to another triangle of toast thick with tiny black pearls of caviar. They were silky on her tongue, exploding into rich bursts of the flavor of the sea.

"It's the best caviar in the world," Hank said.

Alice rolled her eyes and laughed. "Hank, isn't second-best ever good enough for you?"

Hank shook his head. "Absolutely not. I know you think I'm a show-off, Alice, but I wish you would see that you've got it wrong. It's just that I appreciate the finest things in life. As an artist, you should understand that."

Alice took a sip of cider. "I'm not sure I know what you mean, Hank."

"Well, say you're in a museum. The Louvre, maybe."

"The Louvre? In Paris?"

Hank nodded. "Say I've taken you there for the weekend."

Alice laughed. "Hank, it's only our first date and you've already got me going to Paris with you!"

"Does it sound so terrible?" Hank asked.

Alice grinned and shook her head. "No. I've always dreamed of going to Paris."

"OK, then. We're in Paris. We go to the Louvre. In one room there are several canvases by da Vinci."

"By Leonardo da Vinci? You mean we're in the same room with the *Mona Lisa?*" Alice said. She felt a tingle of excitement.

"Exactly," Hank said. "There are also several works by less well known artists. Which paintings do you look at?"

"Maybe I take a good look at everything," Alice said. "I might never get another chance to go to the Louvre, and some of those other artists might turn out to be awfully good, too."

Hank grinned. "Stick with me, Alice, and you can go to the Louvre anytime you want. But all right. I can see I have to be careful about the examples I use with you. Let's say you decide you *do* like the da Vincis best of everything in the room. That could happen, couldn't it?"

Alice laughed. "I guess I'm just playing devil's advocate. The truth is, I think da Vinci was a genius. But what does that have to do with your taste for the world's best caviar?"

"Well, listen. Wouldn't you spend more time looking at da Vinci's work than anyone else's?"

"Well, sure," Alice admitted. "I guess I would."

"That's what I thought. You look at the best paintings—the ones you like best. Same thing as ordering the best caviar or driving the coolest red Mustang. It's just a matter of good taste."

Alice laughed. "Hank, don't you think that's stretching the comparison a little?"

Hank laughed along with her. "Maybe. But I do know one thing." His voice grew serious. "If I were used to settling for second-best, I never would have gotten up the courage to keep asking you out."

Alice felt her face grow pink.

"I'm glad you finally said yes," Hank whispered, leaning across the table and taking Alice's hand. His touch was soft and gentle, and Alice found herself surprised by how nice it felt. Hank looked more handsome than ever, his deep blue eyes, high cheekbones, and chiseled features warmed by the candlelight.

"You are the best. The most beautiful," Hank said. "Thanks for giving me a chance."

Alice felt her heart flutter. "I'm happy I did. I think I was wrong about you, Hank. I was really impressed at the way you came through during the sit-in. You were a real hero."

Hank shook his head. "No, Alice. You were the hero."

"Me? But I was just one of the crowd. You were the one who saved us all from having to back down in defeat."

"Because you told me to do it," Hank said.

Alice wrinkled her forehead in confusion. "How could I tell you anything? I was inside the administration building all day, dreaming about my next meal."

"Don't you remember that day you were sketching those two guys playing Frisbee?" Hank asked.

Alice nodded, feeling a little ashamed about how rude she had been to Hank that day.

"Well, you told me I should try doing something good for the world," Hank said. "It got me thinking. So I'd say most of the credit for that food drop at the sit-in goes to you."

"Really?" Alice said. She felt extremely flattered.

"Really," Hank said.

Alice looked into his eyes, feeling his hand on hers. Maybe she had misjudged Hank Patman.

"Far out!" Alice said. The live sound of the Electric Blues Band filled the campus. C.S.C.'s

South Bowl had been transformed into a moving patchwork of people. Many kids were dancing. Others had spread out blankets on the grass and were lying in the sun. Music poured out of the huge loudspeakers that had been set up on either side of the makeshift stage.

Alice and Hank spread their woven Mexican blanket out at the edge of the crowd under the shade of a thick-trunked, leafy tree. Alice kicked off her sandals and grabbed Hank's hand. "Let's dance!" she said, half singing her words to the beat of the music.

Hand in hand, they zigzagged through the throng of people, making their way closer to the stage, where the wildest, most free-spirited dancing was going on.

"Patman!" called a heavyset boy with a leather headband. He flashed a peace sign.

"Hi, Hank!" a short girl in an embroidered peasant dress said.

"Hey, Hank Patman," a deep voice yelled out.

"Patman! Haven't seen you around the frat enough lately," said a boy Alice recognized from Pi Iota Gamma.

Alice held tight to Hank's hand. "You're a real big man on campus since the sit-in," she said with a laugh.

"And before the sit-in?" Hank said. "People have always known who I was."

Alice groaned. Hank certainly had his impossible side. But she had to admit that he was very

314

smart and quite sophisticated. And he liked her an awful lot.

After nearly a semester of dating him, Alice's pulse still raced at Hank's good looks. His straight dark hair had grown longer since they had started seeing each other, and he'd traded in his establishment clothes for a pair of patched bell-bottoms and a groovy vest.

He was a good dancer, too. He and Alice joined the crowd near the stage, the motions of the dancers riding the electricity of the music.

"Great song!" Hank yelled as the band went into a cover of "Good Lovin'."

Alice let the music sing through her body, following the rhythms of the band and the crowd. Up on stage, Jim Barton, the lead guitarist, went right from the last chords of "Good Lovin'" into a tune the band had written called "Turn It On."

Alice spun around and around to the wavering, vibrating notes until she grew dizzy. The sun was warm on her face. The grass and ground were soft under her shoeless feet. She sang out the chorus of "Turn It On," her voice blending with the band and the voices of the people around her.

As the band wailed out the final notes of the song, Jim Barton stepped up to the mike. "We'd like to dedicate the next song to someone in the audience," he announced, running a hand through his long, wavy blond hair.

The bass guitarist went into the lead riff of the band's best song, "Will You Love Me Forever?"

Whistles and cheers met the notes. The drummer added a pulsing beat. Jim Barton positioned his fingers on his guitar. "To Alice," he said, strumming his first chord of the song.

Alice's attention was riveted to the stage as Jim Barton spoke her name. But he had to mean some other Alice. She had never even met the Electric Blues' lead guitarist.

"From Hank," he added.

He *did* mean her! Alice turned and held Hank's gaze. "For me?" She felt her heart pounding along with the drummer's rhythm. "Oh, Hank," she said as he drew her close.

"Will you love me forever?" the band sang. "Share my life forever . . ."

"Will you?" Hank whispered in Alice's ear. He reached into his jeans pocket and pulled out a tiny enameled jewel box.

Alice felt as if she were in a dream. She took the jewel box from Hank and held it unopened, feeling the promise inside and feeling the joy of the moment. She couldn't believe this was happening to her.

"Go ahead," Hank said, giving her a light kiss on her forehead.

Alice flipped open the box. A diamond ring winked in the sunlight in its nest of black velvet. It took her breath away.

"Will you, Alice?" Hank asked. "Will you marry me? Please say you will."

Alice was overwhelmed by music and love.

"Yes! Yes, I will!" she said. "I'll share my life with you, Hank Patman."

"I love you, Alice," Hank said. He slipped the ring on her finger.

Thirty-eight

Alice wished with every nerve in her body that she was seeing a mirage rising out of the wavy-hot air above the sand. But she knew this was for real. Hank—her fiancé, the boy who had promised to love her forever—was walking along the water with his arm around a tall, striking brunette in a tiny polka-dot bikini.

Alice's first thought was to turn and run in the other direction. She could hear the happy voices and the music on the beach behind her. She could go back to the party, try to forget what she had seen. How awful it would be to run right into Hank with another girl. What would she say? What would she do?

Wait! she told herself. Why was she worrying about what she would say to Hank? What about what Hank had to say to her? She felt the weight of the oversized diamond on her finger. How could he do this to her?

She willed herself forward. Her feet sank deeply into the soft, wet shore. Her steps were heavy. Hank and a beautiful brunette. Hank and another woman. She squinted into the sun at them. Her eyes hurt.

Hank was looking at the girl and laughing. The sound rippled along the edge of the water, breaking over Alice in a wave of anger. How dare he? How dare Hank Patman? Hank took his eyes off the girl for a moment. Alice felt his glance come to rest on her. She held her breath. Then casually, the smile still on his face, Hank took his arm from around the brunette's shoulder and waved it over his head at Alice.

Alice could not believe it. "Hey, hello!" Hank called.

As Alice met up with them, a powerful wave crashed onto the shore. The brunette gave a little jump, squealing and giggling as they were hit with a spray of salt water.

"Alice, do you know Brenda? Brenda, Alice."

"Hi!" Brenda said sunnily.

"Hello." Alice heard her voice come out as cold as the ocean's depths. She knew it was really Hank she was angry with, but she couldn't help feeling icy toward Brenda in her little bikini.

"Hey, Brend, why don't you go enjoy the party?" Hank said.

"Groovy!" Brenda said. "Sounds happening back there. See you, Hank. See you, Alice." Alice watched Brenda skip down the beach in her bikini.

"Having fun, Alice?" Hank asked, slinging his

arm around her—the same arm that had been around Brenda just a moment before.

Alice shrugged away from Hank's touch. "You know, Hank, you've barely talked to me all afternoon. My most loyal companion at this party is the refreshment table you set up on the sand. And then I come looking for you and I find you with—with—" She stumbled over her words and felt her lower lip tremble.

"With Brenda?" Hank was the picture of innocence. "Alice, she's my friend. You don't mind if I spend some of my spring-break bash with my friends, do you?"

Alice gave a tight shrug. "Maybe if you hadn't looked quite *so* friendly . . ."

"Whoa, Alice! What happened to the idea of peace and love—everyone loving one another? You're the one who turned me on to that, babe."

"Did you call Brenda 'babe,' too?" Alice asked.

Hank let out a long breath. "Jeez, Alice. Why are you starting all this? Don't you want to have any fun at my party?"

"What do you care, Hank Patman? The only person you care about having fun is *you!*" Alice yelled.

"Fine, Alice. Be that way," Hank yelled back. "It's your own fault for coming after me and spying on me."

"Spying?" Alice was outraged. "The fact is, I was looking for you because I missed you. But right now I can't imagine why!"

320

"Look, Alice, if you're going to yell at me, I'm going to go back to the party and groove on some mellower people," Hank said. He started walking.

"Fine!" Alice called after him. Her blood was boiling. The sheer nerve of him. The sheer, selfish, pig-headed nerve. She felt like screaming. Instead, she picked up a rock from the water's edge and flung it out over the ocean with all her might. "Take that, Hank Patman!" she said, channeling all her angry energy into her throw. The rock dropped with a splash, disappearing forever to the ocean floor. She picked up another rock and threw again. She watched it sink. The bull's-eye ripples spreading out around where the rock had pierced the water's surface were twisted by the strong current.

There was something satisfying about seeing the water swallow up the stones. The ocean was so vast, so inhumanly powerful. One little lovers' quarrel was dwarfed to invisibility by its scale and scope. Against the largeness of nature, Alice's problems seemed tiny. Alice had the sudden urge to plunge herself into the ocean like one of those stones, to feel her hot anger cooled by the water, rocked away by the waves.

She waded in up to her thighs, waited for the next big swell, and dived into the curl. She surfaced for a breath of air and swam out to meet the next wave. She pulled against the current with her arms, ducking waves and swimming out further. With each stroke, she felt calmer. Her body surrendered its tension to the movement of the water.

She swam out past where the waves were breaking. The sounds of the party grew fainter and were replaced by the rush of wind over the water's surface. She kept swimming. And swimming. Her arms stroked through the water. Her legs fluttered in rhythmic, lulling kicks. Farther and farther out she swam. She flipped over on her back and floated, resting. The wispy clouds overhead seemed to sway as the water rocked her one way, then another. She floated for a long time, her mind emptying itself of anger.

She turned back over, treading water as she looked toward shore. The partygoers were like tiny dolls. She headed in. She didn't want to get any farther out.

She swam with the sure, strong stroke she had learned from years on the Sweet Valley swim team, surging forward smoothly. The kids at the party came into clearer focus. She could hear the laughter and music once again. She found herself scanning the beach for Hank. Should she try to make peace with him? Or should she let him come to her? There he was, getting in on a volleyball game with some of the guys from his frat.

As Alice's thoughts returned to the problem of Hank, she felt herself being pulled away from shore by a strong undertow. She worked against the current, using all her strength to power herself forward. But the shoreline continued to recede. She pumped her arms through the water and kicked furiously, grabbed by a surge of panic.

Suddenly, there was a stab of pain in her side. Her whole body contracted involuntarily around the cramp. Her knees jerked in toward her chest. She doubled over, somersaulting under the water's surface. She battled against the cramp, battled to come up for air. But the strong current tugged her down.

She wrestled against its pull. She beat at it, desperate to surface for a breath. *Oh, no! I can't get up to the surface*, she thought in a panic. She was no match for the violent sea. It toppled her dizzily, so that she didn't know which way was up. She felt it squeezing out her final seconds. *A breath. I must breathe.*

And then she could resist no longer. Alice inhaled the salty, furious ocean. It was the last memory she had.

She stared into the depths of his brown eyes. He brushed a tendril of wet hair off of her forehead with strong, gentle fingers. His face was etched with concern and caring.

Alice managed a weak smile. The young man smiled back, and she couldn't help noticing how handsome he was—the high cheekbones, the strong, straight line of his nose, the cleft of his chin. She tried to sit up, but she felt drenched to her very core, too heavy with water to move.

"Shh," the young man whispered. "Don't try to move yet. You have to rest."

Alice tried to figure out what had happened. There had been the strong current pulling her out to sea, that stab of pain in her side, and then . . . blackness. There was nothing. No memory, no feeling, until now, looking into the eyes of this young man. As Alice studied him more carefully, she noticed that he was as soaked as she was. His dark hair dripped salt water onto his handsome face. Around them, a small crowd of partygoers was gathering.

"What happened?" asked a strawberry blonde in a hot-pink two-piece suit. Concern filled her voice.

"She'll be OK," the dark-haired young man said. "She got into a little trouble in the water. I pulled her out."

Pulled her out? That meant the young man had saved her life! Alice looked into his eyes again. And again he smiled that wonderful smile, full of caring and tenderness. There was something so familiar about it, so comfortable about the way he held her gaze. Did they know each other? Alice tried to call up a name, or a place where she might have seen him, but all she got was a vague but comforting sense that he wasn't a stranger. Perhaps it was the special bond of looking into the eyes of the person who had saved her life. He had saved her! Maybe that was why Alice felt this instant intimacy, as if she had known him forever.

"Alice! Good heavens!" said a voice that was familiar in a much more immediate way. *Hank!* Alice sat up. "Alice, are you all right?"

Alice took in the worry etched on Hank's face. She nodded weakly. "I almost drowned out there, but this boy saved me."

The boy stood up and offered Hank his hand. "Ned Wakefield," he said.

Ned Wakefield. Ned Wakefield. It did sound familiar, but Alice had no idea why.

Hank clasped Ned's hand. "I'm Hank Patman. I owe you my deepest thanks."

"You don't owe me a thing," Ned said. He leaned down and looked at Alice. "How are you feeling?"

"All right," Alice said. She could feel her strength starting to return. "By the way, I'm Alice Robertson, and I . . ." Alice's sentence trailed off. What did you say to someone who had saved your life? She felt a hint of dizziness again as she looked at Ned Wakefield. "I've never had anyone save my life before."

Ned laughed. "I've never saved anyone's life before. I'm just incredibly glad that I was coming down the beach at the right time." Even Ned's voice was rich with that feeling of comfort and familiarity, Alice thought.

But there was no time to ponder it. Hank was squatting down next to Alice. "Maybe I'd better take you home," he said. He put his arm around her shoulder.

Alice's attention shifted. She remembered the girl in the polka-dot bikini. "I wouldn't want to spoil your spring-break bash," she told Hank frostily.

Hank looked as if he had been slapped. "Alice, please, let's not fight. When I saw you lying here I knew that if anything happened to you, I could never live with myself. There will be other parties. The important thing is that you're going to be fine. I'm going to take you back to the dorm and make sure of it."

Alice could hear the sincerity in Hank's voice. She knew this was his way of apologizing. Maybe she was being too hard on him. She managed a small smile and let him help her to her feet. Her legs felt shaky, but Hank slipped a strong, supporting arm around her waist.

"Are you OK?" Hank asked.

"I think so."

"We'll take it slow," Hank said. He offered Ned his free hand. "Thank you again. If there's anything I can do for you . . ."

"Just take good care of her." Alice caught Ned Wakefield's familiar smile again.

"I will. Bye. See you around campus," Hank said.

"See you," Ned said. He turned to Alice. "Bye."

"Bye," Alice echoed. "And thank you. Thank you a million times."

"You're welcome a million times," Ned said.

As they left him standing on the beach Alice had a deep and unexplainably sad feeling. It, too, seemed strangely familiar.

Thirty-nine

There he was again. In the cozy, crowded dimness of the coffeehouse, Alice spotted him almost immediately. Maybe Ned Wakefield sensed her presence, too. As Alice and Jenny sat down at a tiny, round wooden table at the back of the room, Ned swiveled around in his seat near the front, caught sight of Alice, and waved. She waved back. Up on stage, a moon-faced, curly-haired girl strummed her guitar and sang a sweet, simple version of "Because All Men are Brothers."

"Boy, that guy is everywhere," Jenny whispered.

Alice laughed softly. "I know. I can't believe I never saw him before the day of Hank's party. I mean, now every rally I go to, I see him. Half the time I'm in the library, he's studying next to me. Lunch at South Hall—he's there. Cynthia Grant told me he was at the sit-in, too, down in the dean's office giving legal advice to the people who were organizing the whole thing."

"Prelaw, huh?" Jenny said. "Well, I guess it's good to have some of those on our side. Plus he's pretty cute. Boy, I wouldn't have minded having his arms around me, rescuing me from the ocean like some hero in the movies."

Alice was glad it was smoky and dark in the coffeehouse and that Jenny couldn't see her blushing. "Jen, I was unconscious while Ned was pulling me out. I wasn't aware of anything." As she spoke his name, Alice could feel her face growing even warmer. She busied herself by rummaging around in her fringed bag for her wallet. "I'll go get us some coffee," she said, changing the subject. "You want to split a cookie?"

"Do you even have to ask?" Jenny said. The coffeehouse was known for their homemade giant chocolate-chip cookies, served hot from the oven.

Alice wove her way through the tables of students toward the small counter where refreshments were sold.

"Hi," said a voice behind her.

Alice knew who it was even before she turned and looked into those eyes. "Hi, Ned."

"We meet again," Ned said lightly, but Alice could see an intensity in his eyes that gave him away. "Would you and your friend like to join me?" Alice hesitated, and Ned added, "I've got a good table up front where you can see and hear really well. And the next singer who's performing is fantastic."

"Rob Morris?" Alice said. "Yeah, he's great. That's why my friend and I came tonight. He does a really amazing version of 'Blowin' In the Wind.' "

"Yeah, I love that song," Ned said.

Alice felt a flush of warmth go through her body. It seemed the more she ran into Ned, the more it turned out they had in common. But she couldn't let herself fall under his spell, she reminded herself. She was engaged to Hank. She loved Hank. In the weeks since the beach party, he had been extra attentive and sweet, as if making up for their fight.

The tall boy in front of Alice moved away from the counter with a cup of tea. Alice ordered two coffees and a cookie. "Can I get you something, Ned?" she asked.

"Thanks, I'm set," Ned said. "I just came over to see if you'd join me. It seems like we keep running into each other, but then all of a sudden you have to rush off someplace. I was hoping I could convince you to sit down for a while."

Alice lowered her eyes and studied the plain, dark tiles on the floor. She felt torn. "Ned, I, ah, I'd like to say yes, but . . ."

Ned sighed. "It's Hank Patman, isn't it?"

Alice nodded.

"Alice?" Ned said.

Alice couldn't fight the thrill that went through her as she heard Ned say her name. But she wouldn't let herself look at him again. There was something about his eyes that was too familiar and intimate, too appealing—too dangerous.

"Alice, I know you hang out with Patman a lot," Ned said. "But don't you think you could give me a chance? If you don't want to sit with me now, then let me take you out one night."

Several months earlier, Alice would have said yes. But several months earlier, she hadn't been engaged to Hank Patman. "It's not just hanging out," she explained to Ned. She held up her left hand. Her diamond ring sparkled even in the low light of the coffeehouse. "I'm going to marry Hank Patman," she said.

Ned's whole face melted into an expression of deep disappointment. "Oh."

In the uncomfortable space between them, Alice fumbled in her wallet for change for the girl behind the counter.

"Oh, I, uh, I just didn't realize . . ." Ned stammered.

The girl set two steaming cups of coffee with milk on a tray with a cookie. Alice paid her and picked up the tray. "It's OK," she said. She felt embarrassed, too.

"Well, Hank Patman is a lucky guy," Ned said politely. "I wish you the best."

"Thanks," Alice said.

Later in the evening, as the first chords of "Blowin' in the Wind" filled the coffeehouse, Alice noticed Ned looking back at her, smiling sadly.

* * *

"Alice, dear, hold still," her mother said as the seamstress pinned the bottom of her hem. "You don't want to be walking up the aisle with one side of your dress longer than the other, do you?"

Alice giggled, imagining one side of her frothy white gown as a miniskirt while the other side billowed gracefully to the floor. It would be interesting, all right. But she didn't think the Patmans would be too happy about it. Nothing short of the most traditional elegance would do for Alice's future in-laws. When they had first started planning the wedding, Alice had imagined a casual celebration—perhaps a clambake on the beach or a simple outdoor brunch. But Hank's parents had insisted on a more formal affair, right down to Alice's wedding clothes.

Alice stared at her reflection in the mirror on the back of her closet. A pearl-studded gown fell in voluminous folds around her ankles, lengthening into a small train at the back. Her headpiece was sewn with matching pearls and tiny flowers. She tried to get used to balancing on the tall, narrow heels of her white satin shoes. For a moment Alice had the funny feeling that she was looking at some stranger in a bride's magazine who'd gotten into her bedroom. She was about to get married! Alice Robertson would soon be Alice Patman. She wouldn't really believe it until she was actually walking down the aisle on her father's arm to meet Hank.

Out in the hallway, the phone rang. Then her

sister Laura's voice called from downstairs. "Alice! It's for you!"

"Excuse me," Alice said to her mother and the seamstress. "I'll be right back." She went out into the hall to pick up the upstairs extension, feeling her full skirt swirl around her. "Hello?" she said into the receiver.

"Alice." She knew the voice. It was Ned Wakefield. Alice felt herself growing hot under all the layers of material.

"Ned?"

"Yeah, it's me. I hope it's OK to call you at home like this."

"Sure," said Alice. "It's fine. I—I haven't seen you around much lately."

There was a brief silence on the other end. "Well, I . . . you know, it wasn't just fate that we kept running into each other on campus," Ned finally said. "I mean, sometimes it was, but I helped it a little, too. Looked for you, got to know where you'd be and stuff. After I found out you were getting married, well, I thought it might be better if I lay low."

"Uh-huh," Alice said. She wondered if Ned knew she was getting married that weekend.

"Anyway, maybe this is corny, but I just wanted to call you before the wedding and tell you that I'll never forget you," Ned said.

She felt a shiver of pleasure. "I don't think it's corny at all," she said. "It's very sweet of you."

"Alice, you're a special person," Ned said, his voice husky with emotion.

"So are you," Alice said. And then, to cover her embarrassment, she quickly added, "I mean, how often does someone save your life?"

"Well, I'll always be here for you if you need me," Ned said. "I mean it. And I hope you and Hank will make each other's lives very special."

"Thank you, Ned," Alice said. "I hope you'll find someone to make you happy, too." There was a long silence. "Well, I guess I'd better go," she said finally.

"Goodbye, Alice," Ned whispered.

"Bye," Alice answered. She heard the click of his receiver. She hung up her own phone, but she didn't go back to the bedroom right away. She thought about Ned's words. *I hope you and Hank will make each other's lives very special.* How different from what Hank had said when he had toasted her at their engagement party. "To the woman who will be by my side as I make my way in life." What a different way Ned Wakefield had of looking at marriage.

A picture flashed through Alice's head like a bolt of lightning, strong and unstoppable. She was in her pearl-trimmed dress, walking down the aisle on her father's arm. But the man waiting for her was not Hank. It was Ned.

Stop! she told herself. *You're not marrying Ned. You're marrying Hank. You're going to be Mrs.*

Hank Patman. She turned and went back to her bedroom, her skirts swishing around her ankles.

There would always be interesting men in the world, but she knew she could choose only one to share her life with. And Alice had chosen Hank.

Alice felt as if a family of fluttering bats had moved into her stomach. She couldn't sit still. She paced the small room in the Patmans' guest cottage over and over, making frequent checks in the full-length mirror from every conceivable angle.

"Are you sure my headpiece is on straight?" she asked. "Is my hair sticking up under my veil? Are my steps too big for these high-heeled shoes? What about my lipstick?"

"Alice, you look absolutely beautiful!" Jenny reassured her.

"Your hair's perfect," Nancy said.

"You're perfect," Laura said. "It's your day. The happiest day of your life."

"I know. But I'm so nervous," Alice said. "It's hot in here. When do you think they're going to start?" Part of her wanted the ceremony to begin as soon as possible, putting an end to her anxious waiting. Another part of her was so scared that all she could think was: *not yet.* It was a funny feeling for the happiest day of her life.

"Here, let's open a window," Jenny said. "You'd better try to relax. Hank's still out there milling around with the guests." She pushed the window up and a gentle late-afternoon breeze ruffled the curtains. "Ooh, he's coming this way. Don't look, Alice."

Alice did exactly what Jenny told her not to do. "Oh, come on. Hank won't even see me. I'll just peek out from behind the curtain."

"Alice!" protested Laura, "the bride and groom aren't supposed to see each other before the wedding!"

Alice laughed nervously. "Laura, I'm going to spend my whole entire life with Hank. What's one little two-second look going to do? I just want to see him once more before he becomes my husband. Husband!" She shook her head. "Wow, can you believe it?" She pushed the curtain aside just enough to see out.

The Patmans' lawn looked like the set for a movie about the perfect country garden party. Men in tuxedos strolled with elegant women in long, pale summer dresses. Waiters in equally fancy dress circulated among the guests, serving champagne and hors d'oeuvres from silver trays. A huge screened-in tent had been set up; inside it, many small tables were set with linen and crystal and fine china. Large bouquets of flowers graced every table. In the shade of the main house, a string quartet was playing. A few of Alice's friends stood out in their fluorescent miniskirts or patchwork vests, looking as though they had gotten lost on the way to a happening.

Alice spotted her parents chatting with Hank's

parents, elegant and proper in their formal dress. Her Great-Aunt Amanda stood near the musicians, listening to them play. Alice could hear the sweet notes of the violin coming in off the breeze.

And there was Hank! His long hair curled over the collar of his tux. He wore a white rose in his lapel. Alice felt her heart skip a beat. Hank was so handsome. He was coming toward two frat buddies standing near the guest-house window, his arms stretched out to them.

"Joe! Seth!" Alice could hear him say. He clapped each of them on the back. "Glad you could make it!"

"Hey, glad you thought to invite us Pi Iota Gammas," said Seth. Or was it Joe? "We haven't seen much of you since you became a hippie radical."

"Me, a hippie radical?" Hank snorted. "Cut out the nonsense."

"Doesn't seem like nonsense. Look at all these flower children planted on your lawn."

Hank shrugged. "Alice's friends."

Alice felt a shiver of annoyance go through her. Weren't her friends Hank's friends now?

"Patman, people say that you were the hero of the sit-in at the administration building, back at the beginning of the fall semester," the other frat brother said. "Sounds fairly radical to me."

"Joe, you know you're just jealous because it turned me into the biggest celebrity on campus,"

Hank said. "Bet you wish you'd come up with a scheme like that."

A scheme! Alice felt her annoyance boiling into anger. Was it possible that all Hank's talk about doing good for the world was no more than a kind of publicity scheme? And what about that story that had spread around campus—the one that had Hank risking his inheritance to help the student cause? Suddenly, Alice had a terrible thought. What if Hank himself had started the rumor? It wouldn't be unlike him.

Her sisters and Jenny were all looking at her with a mixture of sympathy and horror. "Wow!" Jenny murmured. "That's pretty heavy."

Alice felt as if the veil she was wearing had been over her eyes for far, far longer than she'd realized, and that it was just being lifted so she could see clearly. "Jen," she said. "Could you go out there and tell Hank I'd like to talk to him?" She turned to her sisters. "Why don't you spend some time with Great-Aunt Amanda?"

The three other girls suddenly all seemed to remember why they were there. "Alice, maybe this isn't the right time to start a fight with Hank," Jenny said.

Nancy nodded. "Yeah. Don't let this spoil your special day, Al. Besides, it's bad luck for him to see you in your dress before the ceremony."

Alice lifted the soft, gauzy veil. "Just go get him," she said. Her tone left no room for argument.

A few minutes later, she could hear Hank's sure-footed step on the ceramic tile floor of the guest cottage. He pushed open the door to her room without knocking. "Alice, you know we're not supposed to see each other before the ceremony." Alice caught his tight expression in the reflection in the mirror. Then she saw it soften. "But you look so beautiful. God, Alice, you're a vision of the perfect bride." In the mirror, she saw Hank coming over to her, leaning toward her to kiss her.

She took a giant step out of his reach. "Hank, don't," she said quietly.

"What? You let me see you before the wedding, but you draw the line at kissing me?" Hank said. He followed her step and bent his face toward hers.

Alice turned her head and Hank's lips grazed her cheek. "Hank, I can't," she said.

"Can't kiss me?"

Alice shook her head. "I can't go through with this. I—I can't marry you, Hank." Her words hung on Hank's stunned silence. She saw his handsome face crinkle into a grimace of pain. Alice felt a stab of pity. Hank might have many faults, but she didn't doubt that he loved her. What she was beginning to doubt was how much she could truly love *him*.

"What?" Hank's disbelief reverberated off the walls of the small room.

"Hank, I'm really sorry," Alice said. She knew

how flimsy her apology was. She thought of all the guests waiting expectantly as she and Hank stood there facing off, but she knew it wouldn't be fair to either of them to go through with the wedding.

"Alice, how can you do this to me?" Hank yelled. "The plans have been made for weeks! The celebration's already begun!"

"Hank, this isn't about one party. It's about you and me spending our lives together," Alice said. As she spoke she felt more and more firm in her decision. This wasn't about how she looked or whether her hair was properly coiffed or what her friends were wearing to the Patmans' perfectly elegant gathering. This was about the rest of her life.

Hank paid no attention to Alice's words. "Alice, what will my parents think? What will our guests think? You're going to make me a laughingstock." His words shook with anger.

"Please, Hank, I can't tell you how bad I feel about this. I just—well, maybe on some level I knew it all along, but I was afraid to admit it. I just wish I'd realized sooner so I could have spared your feelings. Hank, forgive me."

But Hank seemed less interested in feelings than he was in appearances. "And what about Mother and Father? Mother has planned this entire affair. Father is already greeting our guests. How will it look for them?"

Alice told herself that this was Hank's way of avoiding the terrible hurt that was burrowing deep inside him. Still, it only made her more convinced that Hank was not the man for her. "I'll try to explain to your parents, if it would make it any easier," she said gently.

"You'll do no such thing!" Hank commanded. "I don't want you near my parents." His glowering anger twisted his features into an ugly mask. "In fact, I order you to leave the premises immediately."

"You order me?" Alice looked at the man who could have been her husband. She was filled with disdain and anger, but she also felt deeply sorry for him. *Just do as he says,* she told herself. *Walk away from him. It will be the best thing for both of you. You should have done it long ago.*

Without another word, she turned and left the room, teetering on her pencil-thin heels. As she stepped out the guest house door, one heel sank deep in the soft earth.

"Alice! What are you doing?" she heard Laura's voice call out. Heads turned. Guests stared.

Alice slipped her feet out of her uncomfortable shoes and left them, one heel piercing the Patmans' flawlessly manicured lawn. Suddenly, she was running. She gathered up her full skirt in one hand, feeling the tender carpet of grass underfoot through her sheer pantyhose. The breeze was sweet on her face.

"Alice!" came the chorus of many different voices. "Alice!"

Alice ran and ran. She was free!

341

Forty

"U-V-W," Alice muttered to herself. "Wade, Wagner, Waitz, Wakefield." She knew she looked strange, standing in an open telephone booth in her wedding gown and stocking feet. She knew passersby were staring, but she didn't care. "Ned Wakefield. Thirty-three Northview Drive." She committed the address to memory.

It was a long, long walk, but every step felt like a step of liberation. The darkening sky seemed to be quietly singing the last act of Alice's relationship with Hank Patman. Twilight muted the tree-lined streets.

By the time Alice reached Ned's neighborhood, darkness had set in. But the stars were bright and clear and a full moon lit the sky. Alice's gown shone pale and shimmery. An elderly man walking a wire-haired terrier gawked openly at her. Alice was getting used to the stares of curiosity. She tried a smile on the man and asked the way to Ned's street. She knew Northview was nearby, but she wasn't sure precisely where.

The man gave her directions, then seemed to be considering saying something else. He looked down at Alice's feet, then at her dress again. "Dear, are you all right?" he finally asked.

Alice laughed. "Yes, I'm fine. In fact, I'm the finest I've been in months." She patted his dog's back and thanked him for directions. She ran the last few blocks to Ned's.

She found herself in front of a rambling white house with a big front porch. In the light of the street lamps she could see that the house needed a paint job, but there was something comfortable-looking about it. Once when Alice had run into Ned on campus, he had told her that he shared it with several other students from C.S.C.

Suddenly, she felt a shiver of nervousness. What if Ned didn't want to see her? What if she was disturbing him? What if he had somebody else over? Another girl, maybe. Then she noticed there were no lights on in the house. What if he wasn't home at all?

She raced up the front walk and took the porch steps two at a time, her wedding dress rustling loudly. She rang the doorbell and heard it sound inside the house. Nobody came to the door. She rang again and again. Her spirits sank. She left the porch and walked around to the side of the well-worn house, peering in through the ground-floor windows, but it was hard to see anything in the dark rooms.

Then Alice heard music coming from the rear of the house. Music! Someone was there! As she raced around to the backyard, she could make out the final verse of "Blowin' In the Wind." The song ended and there were a few seconds of silence. Then the same song began to play again from the beginning.

Alice's heart soared. Ned was playing their song! She shaped her hands into a megaphone around her mouth. "Ned!" she yelled. "Ned Wakefield! It's me! Alice! Ned, let me in! Ned! Ned!"

The lights in one of the upstairs rooms snapped on. And then Ned was bounding out the back door of the house, his arms already reaching toward Alice.

She ran to meet him, and they melted into each other's embrace. Alice felt her feet leave the ground as Ned lifted her toward the clear, perfect night sky. She felt her heart's pounding against his chest. She breathed in his nearness, the perfume of his skin. His fingers traced her face, his caress soft and gentle. Alice returned his touch. Their lips met, and Alice felt the heavens come closer. And then they kissed again . . . and again and again. . . .

Forty-one

A number of years later. Sweet Valley.

"Jess-ca?" Steven Wakefield asked. He touched a chubby little toddler hand to the newborn in Alice's arms. She slept peacefully in a cocoon of a pink blanket. Then he touched the infant in Ned's arms, wrapped in a yellow blanket. "Izzy-beth?" The baby's tiny face squinched up and she looked as if she might begin to cry, but the cry turned into a yawn, and her eyelids closed.

Alice cradled the baby in one arm and pulled Steven toward her on the bed with the other. "No, sweetheart. This one's Elizabeth. See, she has a tiny mole on her shoulder. Do you know what that means?" She pushed the pink blanket down just enough to show her son.

"And Jessica here doesn't," Ned said.

"Oh," Steven said. "Dent-cal twins?"

Alice laughed. "That's right, Steven. Your sisters are identical twins. That means they look exactly alike. But you know what? Once you get to know them, I'll bet you'll discover all kinds of differences in your sisters, especially as they get a little older."

She glanced over at the mantel above the

345

fireplace, where an antique carved wooden rose was protected in a glass case. It had been a silent witness to the character of Alice's family for many, many generations. It was a miracle that Alice had given birth to twins—the third set in six generations. Now Alice wondered whether her daughters would inherit the bravery and independence of their great-great-great-grandmother Alice Larson, who had come to this country all by herself. Would they have their Great-Great-Grandmother Jessamyn's spirit of adventure, or Great-Aunt Amanda's big heart? Would either of them inherit their grandmother Marjorie's courage in the face of danger? Maybe her daughters would even be a little like her.

The weathered old wood of the delicate flower, full of secret memories, held the past in its petals. Alice smiled at the infant in her arms, then leaned over and kissed the one in Ned's. In their perfect, identical faces, Jessica and Elizabeth Wakefield held the secrets of the future.